THE MIND'S EYE

'Van Veeteren is a terrific character, and the courtroom
scenes that begin this novel are cracking'
Daily Telegraph

'Håkan Nesser's Chief Inspector Van Veeteren has
earned his place among the great Swedish detectives
with a series of intriguing investigations . . . This is
Van Veeteren at his quirkiest and most engaging'
Seven magazine, *Sunday Telegraph*

'A psychological thriller in a class of its own . . .
This stunning novel by one of Sweden's foremost
crime writers might have been written as a
script for Alfred Hitchcock'
Sunday Times

THE RETURN

'Nesser made a strong impression with *Borkmann's Point*,
the first of his novels published into English.
The Return is just as tense and clever'
Marcel Berlins, *The Times*

'Nesser's insight into his main characters and gently
humorous narrative raise his otherwise conventional
police procedural to a higher level'
Sunday Telegraph

'This is splendid stuff: Scandinavian crime writing that
is so rivetingly written it makes most contemporary
crime fare – Nordic or otherwise – seem
rather thin gruel'
Barry Forshaw, *Waterstone's Books Quarterly*

BORKMANN'S POINT

BORKMANN'S POINT

Håkan Nesser is one of Sweden's most popular
crime writers, receiving numerous awards for his novels
featuring Inspector Van Veeteren, including the European
Crime Fiction Star Award (Ripper Award) 2010/11, the
Swedish Crime Writers' Academy Prize (three times)
and Scandinavia's Glass Key Award. The Van Veeteren
series is published in over 25 countries and has sold
over 10 million copies worldwide. Håkan Nesser
lives in Gotland with his wife, and spends part
of each year in the UK.

Also by Håkan Nesser

HÅKAN NESSER

BORKMANN'S POINT

AN INSPECTOR VAN VEETEREN MYSTERY

Translated from the Swedish by
Laurie Thompson

PAN BOOKS

First published in Sweden 1994 as *Borkmann's Punkt*
by Albert Bonniers Forlag, Stockholm

First published in English 2006 by Pantheon books,
a division of Random House, Inc., New York

First published in Great Britain 2006 by Macmillan

This paperback edition published 2012 by Pan Books
an imprint of Pan Macmillan
20 New Wharf Road, London N1 9RR
Associated companies throughout the world
www.panmacmillan.com

ISBN 978-0-330-49276-8

15 17 19 18 16 14

A CIP catalogue record for this book is available from
the British Library.

Typeset by Intype Libra Ltd
Printed and bound by CPI Group (UK) Ltd, Croydon, CR0 4YY

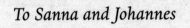

To Sanna and Johannes

But of course, necessity can never be a reason
nor an excuse. Only a cause.

C. W. Wundermaas, former detective chief inspector

ONE

31 AUGUST TO 10 SEPTEMBER

1

Had Ernst Simmel known he was to be the Axeman's second victim, he would no doubt have downed a few more drinks at The Blue Ship.

As it was, he settled for a brandy with his coffee and a whiskey on the rocks in the bar, while trying unsuccessfully to make eye contact with the bleached-blonde woman in the far corner; but anyway, his heart wasn't in it. Presumably, she was one of the new employees at the canning factory. He had never seen her before, and he had a fair idea about the available talent.

To his right was Herman Schalke, a reporter on *de Journaal*, trying to interest him in a cheap weekend trip to Kaliningrad or somewhere of the sort, and when they eventually got around to pinning down his last evening, it seemed probable that Schalke must have been the last person in this life to speak to Simmel.

Always assuming that the Axeman didn't have some message to impart before finishing him off, that is. Which wasn't all that likely since the blow, as in the previous case, had come diagonally from behind and from slightly below, so a little chat seemed improbable.

'Ah, well!' Simmel had said after draining the last drops from his glass. 'I'd better be getting back to the old lady.'

If Schalke remembered rightly, that is. In any case, he'd tried to talk him out of it. Pointed out that it was barely eleven and the night was yet young. But Simmel had been adamant.

That was the right word. Adamant. Just eased himself off his bar stool. Adjusted his glasses and stroked that pathetic wisp of hair over his bald head like he always did – as if that would fool anybody – muttered a few words, then left. The last Schalke had seen of him was the white outline of his back as he paused in the doorway and seemed to be hesitating about which direction to take.

Looking back, that was distinctly odd. For Christ's sake, surely Simmel knew his way home?

But maybe he just stood there for a few seconds to fill his lungs with the fresh night air. It had been a hot day; summer was not over yet and the evenings had started to exude a mellowness enriched by many months of summer sun. Enriched and refined.

As if made for drinking in deep draughts, somebody had said. These nights.

In fact, it wasn't a bad night for a journey to the other

side, if one might be allowed such a thought. Schalke's section of *de Journaal* was mainly concerned with matters sporting and a dash of folklore, but in his capacity as the last person to have seen Simmel alive, he had presumed to write an obituary of the property developer who had been so suddenly plucked from our midst . . . a pillar of our society, one might say, who had just returned to his native town after a sojourn of several years abroad (on the Costa del Sol along with other like-minded citizens with a bent for effective tax planning, but perhaps this was not the occasion to refer to that), survived by a wife and two grown-up children, having reached the age of fifty but still in the prime of his life, no doubt about that.

The scent of evening seemed full of promise; he paused in the doorway, hesitating.

Would it be a good idea to take a stroll over to Fisherman's Square and down by the harbour?

What was the point of going home as early as this? The sweetish smell of the bedroom and Grete's overweight body shot through his mind, and he decided to take a little walk. Only a short one. Even if there was nothing to pick up, the warm night air would make it worth the effort.

He crossed over Langvej and turned off towards Bungeskirke. At the same time, the murderer emerged from the shadows under the lime trees in Leisner Park and started following him. Quietly and carefully, a safe distance behind, not a sound from his rubber soles. Tonight was his third attempt, but even so, there was no trace of impatience. He knew what he had to do, and the last thing on his mind was to rush things.

Simmel continued along Hoistraat and took the steps down towards the harbour. He slowed down when he came to Fisherman's Square and sauntered across the deserted cobbles to the covered market. Two women were busy talking at the corner of Dooms Alley, but he didn't appear to pay them any attention. Perhaps he wasn't sure about their status, or perhaps he had something else in mind.

Or maybe he just didn't feel like it. When he came to the quay he paused for a few minutes to smoke a cigarette, watching the boats bobbing in the marina. The murderer took the opportunity of enjoying a cigarette himself in the shadow of the warehouse on the other side of the Esplanade. Held it well hidden inside his cupped hand so that the glow wouldn't give him away, and didn't take his eyes off his victim for a single second.

When Simmel flicked his cigarette end into the water and set off in the direction of the municipal woods, the murderer knew that tonight was the night.

True, there were only about three hundred yards of trees here between the Esplanade and Rikken, the yuppie part of the town where Simmel lived, and there were plenty of lights along the paths; but not all were working and three hundred yards could prove to be rather a long way. In any case, when Simmel heard a faint footstep behind him, he was barely fifty yards into the woods and the darkness was dense on all sides.

Warm and full of promise, as already noted, but dense.

He probably didn't have time to feel scared. If so, it could only have been in the last fraction of a second. The razor-sharp edge entered from behind, between the second and fourth vertebrae, slicing diagonally through the third, straight through the spinal column, the oesophagus and the carotid artery. Half an inch deeper and in all probability his head would have been separated completely from his body.

Which would have been spectacular, but was of minor significance for the outcome.

In accordance with all imaginable criteria, Ernst Simmel must have been dead even before he hit the ground. His face landed on the well-trodden gravel path with full force, smashing his glasses and causing any number of secondary injuries. Blood was pouring out of his throat, from above and below, and when the murderer carefully dragged him into the bushes, he could still hear a faint bubbling sound. He squatted there in silence while a group of four or five youths passed by, then wiped his weapon clean in the grass and set off back in the direction of the harbour.

Twenty minutes later he was sitting at his kitchen table with a steaming cup of tea, listening to the bath slowly filling up. If his wife had still been with him, she would doubtless have asked if he'd had a hard day, and if he was very tired.

Not especially, he might have replied. It's taking a bit of time, but everything is going according to plan.

Glad to hear it, darling, she might have said, putting a hand on his shoulder. Glad to hear it . . .

He nodded, and raised his cup to his mouth.

2

The sands went on forever.

Went on forever, the same as ever. A calm, grey sea under a pale sky. A strip of firm, damp sand next to the water where he could maintain a reasonable pace. Alongside a drier, greyish-white expanse where beach grass and windswept bushes took over. Deep inside the salt marshes birds were wheeling in broad, lazy circles, filling the air with their melancholy cries.

Van Veeteren checked his watch and paused. Hesitated for a moment. In the hazy distance he could just make out the church steeple in s'Greijvin, but it was a long way away. If he kept on walking, it would certainly be another hour before he could sit down with a beer in the café on the square.

It might have been worth the effort, but now that he had paused, it was hard to convince himself of that. It was three o'clock. He had set out after lunch – or brunch, depending on how you looked at it. In any case, at about one o'clock, after yet another night when he had gone to bed early but failed to drop off to sleep until well into the small hours. It was hard to tell what was the root cause of his worries and restlessness as he lay there, tossing and turning in the sagging double bed, as the grey light of dawn crept ever closer . . . hard to tell.

He had been on vacation for three weeks now, quite a long time by his standards, but not exceptional, and as the days passed, during the last week at least, his daily routine had been delayed just a little. Four more days and it would be time for him to return to his office, and he had the distinct impression that when he did so, there would not be much of a spring in his stride. Even though he hadn't really done much apart from resting. Lain back on the beach, reading. Sat in the café at s'Greijvin, or nearer at hand in Hellensraut. Strolled up and down these never-ending sands.

The first week out here with Erich had been a mistake. They had both realized that after the first day, but the arrangement couldn't easily be changed. Erich had been allowed out on parole on condition that he stay with his father on this remote stretch of coast. He still had ten months of his sentence left to serve, and the last time he had been out on parole the outcome had left much to be desired.

He gazed out to sea. It was just as calm and unfathomable as it had been for the whole of this last week. As if nothing could really make an impression, not even the wind. The waves dying a natural death on the beach seemed to have travelled vast distances bearing neither life nor hope.

This is not my sea, Van Veeteren thought to himself.

In July, as his vacation had approached, he had been looking forward to these days with Erich. When they finally arrived, he could hardly wait for them to end, so that he could be left in peace; and now, after a dozen days and nights of solitude, he wanted nothing more than to get back to work again.

Or was it quite as straightforward as that? Was that perhaps just a convenient way of describing what it was really all about – did there come a point, he had started to wonder, beyond which we no longer look forward to something coming, but only to getting away from what has passed? Getting away. Closing down and moving on, but not looking forward to starting again. Like a journey whose delights decrease in direct proportion to the distance travelled from the starting point, whose sweetness becomes more and more bitter as the goal comes closer . . .

Get away, he thought. Put an end to it. Bury it.

This is what they call going downhill. There's always another sea ahead.

He sighed and removed his sweater. Tied it around his

shoulders and started retracing his steps. He was walking into the wind now, and he realized that it would take him longer to get back home . . . just as well to have a few extra hours this evening, come to that. The house needed tidying up, the fridge emptying, the telephone unplugging. He wanted to set off early tomorrow. No point in hanging around unnecessarily.

He kicked an abandoned plastic bottle over the sands.

It will be autumn tomorrow, he thought.

He could hear the telephone ringing when he came to the gate. Automatically he started moving more slowly, shortening his strides, fiddling with his keys, in the hope that it would stop ringing by the time he entered the house. In vain. The sound was still carving stubbornly through the gloomy silence. He picked up the receiver.

'Hello?'

'Van Veeteren?'

'That depends.'

'Ha ha . . . Hiller here. How are things?'

Van Veeteren suppressed an urge to slam the receiver down.

'Splendid, thank you. It's just that I was under the impression that my vacation wasn't over until Monday.'

'Precisely! I thought you maybe fancied a few more days?'

Van Veeteren said nothing.

'I'll bet you'd love to stay a bit longer by the coast if you had the chance, wouldn't you?'

'. . .'

'Another week, perhaps? Hello?'

'I'd be grateful if you would come to the point, sir,' said Van Veeteren.

The chief of police seemed to have a coughing fit, and Van Veeteren sighed.

'Yes, well, a little something has turned up in Kaal-bringen. That's only about twenty or thirty miles away from the cottage you're staying in; I don't know if you're familiar with the place. We've been asked to help out, in any case.'

'What's it all about?'

'Murder. Two of them. Some madman running around and cutting people's heads off with an axe or something. It's all in the papers today, but maybe you haven't—'

'I haven't seen a paper for three weeks,' said Van Veeteren.

'The latest one – the second, that is – happened yester-day, or rather, the day before. Anyway, we have to send them some reinforcements, and I thought that as you were in the area already, well . . .'

'Thank you very much.'

'I'll leave it up to you for the time being. I'll send up Münster or Reinhart next week. Assuming you haven't solved it by then, of course.'

'Who's chief of police? In Kaalbringen, I mean.'

Hiller coughed again.

'His name's Bausen. I don't think you know him. Anyway, he only has another month to go before he retires, and he doesn't seem all that thrilled to have been handed this on his plate just now.'

'How very odd,' said Van Veeteren.

'You'll go straight there tomorrow, I take it?' Hiller was starting to wind up the conversation. 'That will mean you don't have to double the journey unnecessarily. Is the water still warm enough for swimming, by the way?'

'I spend all of every day splashing around.'

'Really . . . really. Well, I'll phone them and say you'll be turning up tomorrow afternoon. OK?'

'I want Münster,' said Van Veeteren.

'I'll see what I can do,' said Hiller.

Van Veeteren put down the receiver and stood for a while staring at the telephone before pulling out the plug. It suddenly dawned on him that he'd forgotten to buy food. Damn!

What made him think of that now? He wasn't even hungry, so it must have something to do with Hiller. He fetched a beer from the fridge and went out onto the patio and settled back in a deck chair.

Axe murderer?

He opened the can and, pouring the beer into a tall glass, tried to remember if he'd ever come across this sort of violence before. He'd been a police officer for thirty years – more than that – but no matter how hard he searched and ransacked his brain, he couldn't dig out a single axe murderer from the murky depths of his memory.

I suppose it's about time, he thought, taking a sip of beer.

3

'Mrs Simmel?'

The corpulent woman opened the door wide.

'Please come in.'

Beate Moerk did as she was bidden and tried her best to look sympathetic. She handed her light overcoat to Mrs Simmel, who fussed as she arranged it on a hanger in the hall. Then she ushered her visitor into the house, tugging nervously at her tight black dress that had doubtless seen better days. Coffee was served on a smoked-glass table between substantial leather sofas in the large living room. Mrs Simmel flopped down into one of them.

'I take it you're a police officer?'

Beate Moerk sat down and put her briefcase on the sofa beside her. She was used to the question. Had expected it, in fact. People evidently had no difficulty in accepting policewomen in uniform, but coping with the fact that wearing a uniform was not a necessary part of the job seemed to be a different matter. How could a woman wear something fashionable and attractive and still carry out her police duties?

Was that still the bottom line? That it was harder to interview women? Men were often embarrassed, but opened up. Women went straight to the point, but at the same time were less forthcoming.

Nevertheless, she was confident that Mrs Simmel was not going to be a problem. She was sitting on the sofa, breathing heavily. Big and ungainly, her eyes swollen but naïve.

'Yes, I'm a police inspector. My name's Beate Moerk. I'm sorry that I have to inconvenience you so soon after . . . what's happened. Is there anybody staying with you?'

'My sister,' said Mrs Simmel. 'She's just gone down to the store.'

Beate Moerk nodded and took a notebook out of her briefcase. Mrs Simmel poured coffee.

'Sugar?'

'No, thank you. Can you tell me what happened last Tuesday evening?'

'I've already . . . I spoke about it with another police officer yesterday.'

'Chief Inspector Bausen, yes. But I'd be grateful if you could go through it one more time.'

'I don't see why . . . I didn't have anything special to say.'

'Your husband went out at around eight o'clock, I gather you said.'

Mrs Simmel gave a little sob, but regained control of herself.

'Yes.'

'Why did he go out?'

'He was going to meet a business contact. At The Blue Ship, I think.'

'Did he often do business there?'

'Now and again. He is . . . was . . . in real estate.'

'But we understand that your husband was alone in The Blue Ship.'

'He can't have turned up.'

'Who?'

'His business contact.'

'No, evidently not. But your husband didn't come home instead, when this other person didn't put in an appearance?'

'No . . . no, I suppose he thought he might as well have dinner, seeing as he was there anyway.'

'He hadn't eaten already?'

'No, not dinner.'

'Do you know who it was?'

'Excuse me?'

'Who he was going to meet.'

'No . . . no, I never interfere in my husband's business.'

'I understand.'

Mrs Simmel gestured towards the cake dish and helped herself to a chocolate biscuit.

'What time did you expect him home?'

'Around . . . well, about midnight, I suppose.'

'What time did you go to bed yourself?'

'Why do you want to know that?'

'I'm sorry, Mrs Simmel, but your husband has been murdered. We simply have to ask all sorts of questions. If we don't, we'll never be able to catch the man who did it.'

'I suppose it's the same one.'

'The same as what?'

'The one who killed that Eggers in June.'

Beate Moerk nodded.

'There is evidence to suggest that, yes. But there again, it could be that somebody was, er, inspired by that.'

'Inspired?'

'Yes, somebody who used the same method. You never know, Mrs Simmel.'

Mrs Simmel swallowed, and took another biscuit.

'Did your husband have any enemies?'

Mrs Simmel shook her head.

'Many friends and acquaintances?'

'Yes . . .'

'A lot of business contacts you weren't all that well acquainted with, perhaps?'

'Yes, lots.'

Beate Moerk paused and took a sip of coffee. It was weak and wishy-washy. If you did what her hostess had done and added two lumps of sugar, it would have been impossible to say what it was.

'I have to ask you to allow me to ask a few questions that you might find a bit indiscreet. I hope you realize how serious this business is, and that you'll answer them as honestly as you can.'

Mrs Simmel scraped her cup nervously against the saucer.

'How would you describe your marriage?'

'Excuse me?'

'What sort of a married life did you have? You'd been married for thirty years, if I'm not mistaken.'

'Thirty-two.'

'Thirty-two, yes. Your children have flown the nest. Did you still have much contact?'

'With the children, you mean?'

'No, with your husband.'

'Well . . . yes, I suppose so.'

'Who are your closest friends?'

'Friends? The Bodelsens and the Lejnes . . . and the Klingforts, of course. And the family, naturally. My sister and her husband. Ernst's brother and sister . . . And our children, it goes without saying. Why do you want to know about them?'

'Do you know if your husband had a relationship with any other woman?'

Mrs Simmel stopped chewing and tried to look as if she hadn't understood the question.

'With another woman?'

'Or several. If he'd been unfaithful, for instance.'

'No . . .' She shook her head slowly. 'Who might that have been? Who would have had him?'

That was one way of looking at it, of course. Beate Moerk took a drink of coffee in order to suppress a smile.

'Has there been anything lately that you noticed? Anything unusual about your husband's behaviour, I mean.'

'No.'

'Or anything else you can think of?'

'No. What could that have been?'

'I don't know, Mrs Simmel, but it would be very helpful if you could think carefully about the last few weeks. Something might occur to you. Did you go away this summer, for instance?'

'Two weeks in July, that's all. A package holiday, but . . . but we went to different places. I went with a friend to Kos. Ernst went off with a friend of his.'

'To Kos?'

'No, not to Kos.'

'Where to, then?'

'I can't remember.'

'I see . . . And apart from that you've been at home?'

'Yes, apart from the odd day now and then, when we went off in *Vanessa* . . . That's our boat. We sometimes go sailing, and stop somewhere for the night.'

Beate Moerk nodded.

'I understand. But there was nothing special that your husband was worried about lately?'

'No . . . no, I don't think so.'

'No new friends or acquaintances?'

'No . . .'

'He didn't tell you about or hint at anything unusual?'

'No.'

Beate Moerk sighed and put down her pen. She leaned back in the sofa.

'And how was business?'

'Fine,' Mrs Simmel answered, seeming surprised. 'Fine, I think . . .'

As if there were no other possibility, thought Beate Moerk as she dusted a few crumbs from her skirt.

'Do you work, Mrs Simmel?'

She seemed to hesitate.

'I sometimes help my husband at his office now and then.'

'Doing what?'

'This and that . . . smartening the place up. Flowers and cleaning, that sort of thing . . .'

'I'm with you. It's in Grote Plein, is that right?'

Mrs Simmel nodded.

'When were you last there?'

'The last time? Er, that would be in May, I think.'

My word, you are a busy bee! thought Beate Moerk.

She had a look around the house as well, mainly because Bausen had instructed her to do so. Mrs Simmel led the way, puffing and panting, and Beate Moerk found herself feeling almost sorry for her, having to keep up all these large rooms. Mind you, no doubt there was a cleaning lady to help out.

It wasn't easy to see what good it would do, but there again, it was always the same with murder investigations. The aim was to gather facts and information of every kind imaginable – the more the better – and file it all away, ready for when some kind of breakthrough was achieved, at which point the tiniest little detail could suddenly prove to be the key to the whole puzzle . . . case . . . mystery, or whatever you wanted to call it.

Beate Moerk hadn't been involved in a murder investigation for over six years, not since she was a probationer down in Goerlich, and then she hadn't been much more than a messenger: knocking on doors, passing on messages, sitting in freezing-cold cars waiting for something to happen that never did.

But now they were faced with an axe murderer. Her, Kropke and Detective Chief Inspector Bausen. No wonder it all seemed a bit odd. Some big shot or other was evidently being sent to help them out but basically it was their case. Local people naturally expected them to be the ones who sorted it all out.

To arrest this madman.

And when she thought about Kropke and Bausen, she realized that much depended on her for a successful outcome.

'Would you like to see the basement as well?'

She nodded, and Mrs Simmel puffed and panted her way down the stairs.

In June, when the first one happened, she'd been on vacation, in a cottage in Tatrabergen with Janos. She'd broken up with him since then or, at least, put him on ice for a while. She'd missed the first few days of the case, and even if she would never admit it, she'd been fretting about it quite a lot.

Heinz Eggers. She'd read up all about it and put herself in the picture, obviously. She'd taken part in the interviews and interrogations, drawn up outline plans and solved puzzles for the rest of the summer. But they hadn't got very far, she'd be the first to admit. After all those hours of interrogation and consideration, they didn't seem to have dug up even the slightest trace of a suspicion. Both she and Kropke had put in so many hours of overtime by now that they must be due at least an extra month's leave – and she might very well cash that in, provided they'd caught the confounded Axeman first.

That's what they called him in the newspapers: the Axeman.

And now he'd struck again.

Her mind elsewhere, she allowed Mrs Simmel to take her on a guided tour of the house. Six rooms and a kitchen, if she'd counted right – for two people. Only one now. Plus a poolroom and a sauna in the basement. Patio and a large garden facing the woods. Real estate? Bausen had given Kropke the task of digging around in Simmel's company. Not a bad idea, in fact. Surely they would come up with something?

But what the hell could Heinz Eggers and Ernst Simmel possibly have in common?

Needless to say, that was the question that had been nagging away inside her ever since they'd found Simmel's body, but so far she hadn't even managed to hit on anything even resembling a guess.

Or was there no link?

Was it just somebody killing at random?

No motive whatsoever, and two months in between strikes. When he felt like it. Were they really dealing with a madman, as some people maintained? A lunatic?

She shuddered, and the hairs on her arms were standing on end.

Get a grip, Beate! she thought.

She took her leave of Grete Simmel on the paved drive leading into the garage, taking a shortcut over the neat lawn and stepping over the low fence in faux jacaranda. She settled down behind the wheel of her car and considered indulging in a cigarette, but suppressed the urge. She'd gone over four weeks without now, and it would take more than an axeman to break her willpower again.

On the drive, watching her pull away, stood Mrs Simmel, a black, depressed colossus who had suddenly been saddled with a house worth a million, a sailing boat and a real estate company.

And God only knows what else.

The visit had made several things clearer, in any case.

It wasn't Grete Simmel who had been lying in wait with the axe in the woods; Beate Moerk was 100 per cent certain of that.

She was almost equally sure that the victim's wife hadn't hired anybody else to carry out the attack, and that she wasn't involved in any other way. Needless to say, there was no solid evidence to support any of these conclusions; but why not bow to your good judgment and intuition when you've been blessed with an abundance of both qualities?

Why not indeed?

She checked her watch. There was time to go home and take a shower before meeting that big shot, she decided.

4

Van Veeteren parked outside the overgrown garden. He checked that the number on the flaking mailbox by the gate really did correspond with the address he'd noted down on the scrap of paper in his breast pocket.

Yes. No doubt about it.

'You'll find it all right,' Chief of Police Bausen had said. 'There's nothing else like it anywhere in town!'

That was certainly no exaggeration. He got out of his car and tried to peer over the tangled spirea hedge. It looked dark inside there. Heavy, sagging branches of un-pruned fruit trees coalesced at about chest height with the undergrowth – grass three feet high, untamed rose-bushes and an assortment of prickly tendrils of obscure origin – to form a more or less impenetrable jungle. There was no sign of a house from the pavement, but a well-worn path suggested that one might possibly be in there some-where. A machete would have been useful, thought Van Veeteren. The guy must be crazy.

He opened the gate, crouched down and ventured in. After only ten yards or so he found a house wall ahead of him, and a thickset man came to meet him. His face was rugged, wrinkled and heavily tanned – it had been a hot summer. His hair was sparse, almost white, and Van Veeteren thought he looked as if he'd already been retired for some time. Nearer seventy than sixty, if he'd had to guess. But still pretty fit and strong, obviously. His clothes indicated that he was on home territory – slippers, worn corduroy trousers and a checked flannel shirt, with the sleeves rolled up.

'Chief Inspector Van Veeteren, I presume?'

He held out a muscular hand. Van Veeteren shook it and admitted his identity.

'Forgive the garden! I started growing roses and a few other things a couple of years ago, but then I got fed up. Bloody amazing how fast everything grows! I haven't a clue how to sort it out.'

He flung out his arms and smiled apologetically.

'No problem,' said Van Veeteren.

'Anyway, welcome! Come this way; I have a few easy chairs around back. I take it you drink beer?'

'Masses,' said Van Veeteren.

★

Bausen contemplated him over the edge of his glass and raised an eyebrow.

'I hope you'll forgive me,' he said. 'I felt I had to check out what sort of bastard I'd been stuck with. Before we meet the rest of them, that is. Cheers!'

'Cheers,' said Van Veeteren.

He lounged back in the wicker chair and emptied half the bottle in one gulp. The sun had been blazing down all the way there; only an hour, it was true, but he could feel his shirt clinging to his back.

'I think the heat wave's going to last.'

The chief of police leaned forward and tried to find a patch of sky through the network of branches.

'Yes,' said Van Veeteren. 'Nice place you've got here.'

'It's not bad,' said Bausen. 'Once you get out into the jungle, you're usually left in peace.'

That seemed to be the case. A well-camouflaged little nest, no doubt about it. The dirty yellow awning; straggly clumps of bushes and roses climbing up the trellis; the thick, tall grass; a heavy scent of late summer, the buzzing of bees . . . And the patio itself: nine or ten square yards, stone flags and a frayed cord mat, two battered wicker chairs, a table with newspapers and books, a pipe and tobacco. Next to the house wall was a lopsided bookcase full of tins of paint, brushes, plant pots, several magazines and other bric-a-brac . . . a chessboard protruded from behind a few crates of empty bottles. Oh yes, there was something special about this place. Van Veeteren produced a toothpick and stuck it between his front teeth.

'Sandwich?' asked Bausen.

'If I can have something to wash it down with. This is empty, I'm afraid.'

He put the bottle on the table. Bausen knocked out his pipe and rose to his feet.

'Let's see if we can do something about that.'

He disappeared into the house, and Van Veeteren could hear him pottering about in the kitchen and singing something that sounded reminiscent of the bass aria from *The Pearl Fishers*.

Well, he thought, clasping his hands behind his head. This could have got off to a worse start. There's life in the old boy yet!

Then it struck him that there could hardly be more then eight or ten years between them.

He declined Bausen's offer of accommodation most reluctantly, indicating that he might well change his mind later on. In any case, he hoped that his esteemed colleague would keep a door open . . . if this business drags on and on, that is . . .

Instead he took a room at The See Warf. Fourth floor

with a balcony and sun in the evening. View over the harbour, quays and the bay with the open sea beyond. This wasn't too bad a place either, he had to admit. Bausen pointed out to sea.

'Straight ahead you can see Lange Piirs, the lighthouse, but only when the mornings are clear. Last year that meant four days. On top of the cliffs over there is The Fisherman's Friend, a gourmet restaurant. Maybe we can treat ourselves to an evening there, if we can't think of anything better to do.'

Van Veeteren nodded.

'Perhaps it's time to do a bit of work?'

Bausen shrugged.

'If you insist, Chief Inspector.' He checked his watch. 'Oh, damn! They'll have been waiting for us for half an hour, I reckon!'

The police station in Kaalbringen was a two-storey affair at the Grande Place. A front office, canteen, changing rooms and a few cells in the basement; a conference room and four offices on the upper floor. Because of his status as chief of police, Bausen had the biggest office, of course, with a desk and bookcases in dark oak, a worn leather sofa and a view over the square. Inspectors Moerk and Kropke each had a smaller office overlooking the courtyard, and the fourth was occupied by Constables Bang and Mooser.

'Allow me to introduce Chief Inspector Van Veeteren, who's come here to solve the case for us,' said Bausen.

Moerk and Kropke stood up.

'Bausen's the man in charge,' said Van Veeteren. 'I'm only here to help out . . . if and when needed.'

'You'll be needed all right,' said Bausen. 'This is the whole Kaalbringen force. Plus the lesser ranks, of course, although I wouldn't expect too much of them if I were you.'

'Inspector Kropke,' said Kropke, standing to attention.

Idiot, thought Beate Moerk, and introduced herself.

'Inspector Moerk is responsible for all the charm and intuition we have to offer,' said Bausen. 'I would advise you not to underestimate her.'

'I wouldn't dream of it,' said Van Veeteren.

'Right, shall we get going?' Bausen started to roll up his shirtsleeves. 'Is there any coffee?'

Beate Moerk indicated a tray on a table in the corner. Kropke ran a hand through his fair, close-cropped hair and fumbled with the top button of his shirt behind the knot in his tie. He was obviously the one charged with holding forth.

Rookie's up first, presumably, Van Veeteren thought. Perhaps Bausen is teaching him the ropes.

Seemed to be necessary, if he was to be honest.

5

'I thought I'd take the Eggers case first,' said Kropke, and switched on the overhead projector. 'In order to brief Chief Inspector Van Veeteren, and also to summarize the situation for the rest of us. I've made a few transparencies to make it easier . . .'

He looked first at Bausen, then Van Veeteren in the hope of registering an approving reaction.

'Excellent,' said Beate Moerk.

Kropke coughed.

'On June twenty-eight, early in the morning, a man by the name of Heinz Eggers was found dead in a courtyard behind the railway station. He had been killed by a blow to the back of the head from an axe of some kind. The blade had gone through the vertebrae, the artery, everything. The body was found by a newspaper delivery boy shortly after six o'clock, and he had been dead between four and five hours.'

'What kind of a man was Eggers?' wondered Van Veeteren aloud.

Kropke put on a new transparency, and Van Veeteren could read for himself that the victim had reached the age of thirty-four when his life was suddenly brought to a close. He was born and permanently resident in Selstadt a few miles inland, but he had been living in Kaalbringen since April of this year. He had no regular work, not in Kaalbringen, or in Selstadt, or in any other location. He had a lengthy criminal record: drug crimes, assault and battery, burglary, sexual offences, fraud. In all, he had served about ten years in various prisons and institutions, starting when he was sixteen. The local authorities were not aware that he was in Kaalbringen; Eggers had been living in a two-room apartment in Andrejstraat belonging to a good friend of his who was currently serving a comparatively short sentence for rape and threatening behaviour. He'd had plans to settle down and go straight in Kaalbringen, get a steady job and so on, but he had not had much success on that score.

'Where does the information come from?' asked Van Veeteren.

'Several sources,' said Beate Moerk. 'Mostly from a girlfriend.'

'Girlfriend?'

'Yes, that's what she called herself,' said Bausen. 'She

lived in the apartment with him. But she didn't kill him, even if she didn't seem particularly put out by his death.'

'Nobody was,' said Moerk.

'She had an alibi, in any case,' explained Bausen. 'Water-tight.'

'How have you gone about the investigation?' asked Van Veeteren, reinserting the toothpick the other way around.

Kropke turned to Bausen for assistance, but received nothing but an encouraging nod.

'We've interviewed around fifty people,' he said, 'most of them the same sort of dregs of society as Eggers himself. His friends and acquaintances are mostly petty thieves, drug addicts, that sort of thing. His circle of friends in Kaalbringen wasn't all that large since he'd only been here for a few months. A dozen people, perhaps, all of them well known to us. The usual riffraff, you might say, the sort who spend the day on park benches drinking beer. Getting high in one another's apartments and selling their womenfolk in Hamnesplanaden and Fisherman's Square. And then of course we've interviewed masses of people following anonymous tips, all of whom have turned out to have nothing to do with the case.'

Van Veeteren nodded.

'What's the population of Kaalbringen?'

'Forty-five thousand, give or take,' said Beate Moerk. 'A few thousand more in the summer months.'

'What about crime levels?'

'Not high,' said Bausen. 'The odd case of domestic violence now and then, four or five boats stolen in the summer. An occasional brawl and a bit of drug dealing. I take it you're not interested in financial crime?'

'No,' said Van Veeteren. 'Not yet, in any case. Anyway, what theories have you got about this Eggers character? You don't have to give me all the details today. I'd prefer to read up on it and ask if I have any questions.'

Beate Moerk took it upon herself to respond.

'None,' she said. 'We don't know a damn thing. I suppose we had started to think – before the Simmel business, that is – that it must be some kind of inside job. A junkie killing another junkie for some reason or other. A bad trip, or money owing or something of that sort—'

'You don't kill somebody who owes you money,' said Kropke. 'If you do, you'll never get it back.'

'On the contrary, Inspector,' sighed Moerk. Kropke frowned.

Oh, dear, thought Van Veeteren.

'Coffee?' Bausen's question was rhetorical, and he was already passing around mugs.

'If it's true,' said Van Veeteren, 'what Inspector Moerk says, then it's highly probable that you've already interrogated the murderer. If you've sifted through the . . . the dregs, that is?'

'Presumably,' said Bausen. 'But now Simmel has turned up. I think that changes the situation quite a bit.'

'Definitely,' said Moerk.

Kropke put on a new transparency. It was obviously a picture of where Eggers was found – dumped behind some garbage cans in the rear courtyard of an apartment block waiting to be demolished, by the look of it.

'Was he murdered on the spot?' asked Van Veeteren.

'More or less,' said Kropke. 'Only moved a few yards at most.'

'What was he doing there?'

'No idea,' said Bausen. 'Drug dealing, I suppose.'

'What time was it?'

'One, two in the morning, something like that.'

'Was he high?'

'Not especially.'

'Why do they have garbage cans outside an apartment block that's due to be demolished?'

Bausen pondered for a while.

'Dunno . . . I've no idea, in fact.'

Van Veeteren nodded. Kropke poured out some coffee and Beate Moerk opened a carton from the bakery, brimful of Danish pastries.

'Excellent,' said Van Veeteren.

'From Sylvie's, a top-notch bakery and café,' said Bausen. 'I recommend a visit. You'll get a twenty per cent discount if you tell them you're a copper. It's just around the corner from here.'

Van Veeteren removed his toothpick and helped himself to a pastry.

'Anyway,' said Kropke, 'as far as Eggers is concerned, we're rowing against the tide, you might say.'

'What about the weapon?' asked Van Veeteren, speaking with his mouth full. 'What does the doctor have to say?'

'Just a moment.'

Kropke produced a new transparency – a sketch of how the axe blade, or whatever it was, had cut its way through the back of Eggers's neck, passing straight through the vertebrae, artery, gullet – the lot.

'A massive blow?' asked Van Veeteren.

'Not necessarily,' said Beate Moerk. 'It depends on what the blade looks like, and it seems to have been extremely sharp – and thin.'

'Which means that not so much force was needed,' added Kropke.

'You can also see,' said Beate Moerk, 'that it came at quite an angle, but that doesn't necessarily mean anything special. It could indicate that the murderer was quite short, or rather tall. It all depends on how he held the weapon. And what it looks like, of course.'

'Just think how many different ways there are of hitting a tennis ball,' said Kropke.

Van Veeteren took another Danish pastry.

'And it's likely that the weapon was an axe?' he asked.

'Of some kind,' said Bausen. 'I think we'll move on to Simmel now. Maybe Inspector Moerk would like to fill us in?'

Beate Moerk cleared her throat and leafed through her notebook.

'Well, we haven't got very far yet. It was only the day before yesterday, at eight in the morning, that a jogger found him in the municipal woods. He first noticed blood on the path; and when he stopped to investigate, he saw the body just a few yards away. The murderer doesn't seem to have made much of an effort to hide it. He – the jogger, that is – called the police right away. Chief Inspector Bausen and I went to the spot together, and we were able to establish that, well, that we seemed to be dealing with the same killer as last time.'

'Cut down from behind,' said Bausen. 'A bit harder and the head would have been severed altogether. It looked like one hell of a mess.'

'The same weapon?' asked Van Veeteren.

'Ninety per cent certain,' said Kropke.

'A hundred would be better,' said Van Veeteren.

'Presumably,' said Bausen, 'we're not talking about an

ordinary axe. The blade appears to be wider than it's deep. Maybe six or even eight inches. No sign of either end of the blade in Eggers or Simmel, according to the pathologist, at least. And Simmel especially had a real bull neck.'

'A machete, perhaps?' suggested Van Veeteren.

'I've looked into that,' said Bausen. 'I wondered if it might be some kind of knife or sword with a very strong blade, but the cutting edge is straight, not curved like a machete.'

'Hmm,' said Van Veeteren. 'Maybe that's not the most important thing at this stage. What's the link between Eggers and Simmel?'

Nobody spoke.

'That's a good question,' said Bausen.

'We haven't found one yet,' said Kropke. 'But we're looking, of course—'

'Scoundrels, the pair of them,' said Bausen. 'But in different leagues, you might say. I reckon Simmel's business affairs wouldn't stand all that much broad daylight shining on them, but that's something for the tax lawyers rather than ordinary mortals like us. He's never been involved in anything specifically criminal. Not like Eggers, I mean.'

'Or at least, he's not been caught,' said Moerk.

'Drugs?' said Van Veeteren. 'They usually unite princes and paupers.'

'We have no indications of any such involvement,' said Kropke.

It would be no bad thing if we solved this business before a new chief of police takes over, thought Van Veeteren.

'What was he doing in the woods?'

'On his way home,' said Beate Moerk.

'Where from?'

'The Blue Ship restaurant. He'd been there from half past eight until eleven, roughly. There are several witnesses. Went for a stroll through the town, it seems. The last people to see him alive were a couple of women in Fisherman's Square – at about twenty past eleven, give or take a minute or so.'

'What does the pathologist's report say about the time of death?'

'The final version is due tomorrow,' said Bausen. 'As things look at the moment, between eleven and one. Well, half past eleven and one, I suppose.'

Van Veeteren leaned back and looked up at the ceiling.

'That means there are two possibilities,' he said, and waited for a reaction.

'Precisely,' said Beate Moerk. 'Either the murderer was lying in wait by the path, ready to have a go at whoever came past, or he followed Simmel from the restaurant.'

'He might have just bumped into him,' said Kropke. 'By accident, in other words—'

'And he had an axe with him – by accident?' said Moerk.

Good, thought Van Veeteren. I wonder if Bausen has entertained the idea of having a female successor? Although it's not up to him, of course.

6

Four reporters were lying in wait by the front desk, but Bausen was clearly used to sending them packing.

'Press conference tomorrow morning, eleven o'clock sharp. Not a word out of us until then!'

Van Veeteren declined Bausen's offer of a modest meal and a lift back to the hotel.

'I need some fresh air. Thought I'd buy some newspapers as well.'

Bausen nodded.

'Here's my phone number in case you change your mind. I expect I'll be in all evening.'

He handed a business card to Van Veeteren, who put it in his breast pocket. The chief of police clambered into his somewhat battered Toyota and drove away. Van Veeteren watched him go.

Nice fellow, he thought. I wonder if he plays chess as well.

He looked at his watch. Half past five. A couple of

hours' work in his room, and then dinner. That sounded like a good way of passing the time. That was just about the only skill he'd managed to acquire over the years: the ability to kill time.

Well, plus a certain aptitude for finding violent law-breakers, of course.

He picked up his briefcase and set off in the direction of the harbour.

Fourteen cassettes and three folders.

They were all that constituted the material concerning the Eggers case. He tipped them onto the bed and hesitated for a moment. Then he rang reception and ordered a beer. He tucked the folders under his arm and went to sit on the balcony.

It took him several minutes to adjust the parasol so that he wasn't troubled by the evening sun, but once he'd sorted that out and the girl had brought his beer, he sat out there until he'd read every single word.

The conclusion he drew was simple and straight-forward, and perhaps best expressed in Inspector Moerk's words: 'We don't know a damn thing.'

He wasn't exactly looking forward to listening to the recordings of all the interviews. In normal circumstances, if he'd been on home ground, he would have had them typed out as a matter of course; but as things were, it was no doubt best to take the bull by the horns and put the earphones on. In any case, he decided to postpone that chore until later, or even tomorrow. Instead, he moved on to the next murder, as depicted in the newspapers. He'd acquired four – two national ones and two issues of a local rag, today's and yesterday's.

The national dailies had suitably large, fat headlines, but the text was decidedly thin. They evidently hadn't sent any reporters to Kaalbringen yet. No doubt they would turn up at the press conference. The man in charge of the case, Chief Inspector Bausen, had issued a statement but had only revealed the alleged fact that the police were following up several lines of inquiry.

Oh, really? thought Van Veeteren.

The local rag was called *de Journaal,* and the coverage was more substantial: pictures of Bausen, the place where the body was discovered and the victim – albeit one from when he was still alive. And a photograph of Eggers. The headline on the front page said THE AXEMAN STRIKES AGAIN. TOWN TERROR STRICKEN, and on an inside page a couple of questions were highlighted: 'Who'll be the next victim?' and 'Are our police up to it?'

He skimmed through the articles and read the obituary of Ernst Simmel, who was something of a local stalwart and honorary citizen, it seemed – a member of the Rotary

Club, a director of the local football club and on the board
of the bank. He had held several offices previously, before
moving to live in Spain . . . no sooner is he back home than
he's brutally murdered.

De mortuis . . . thought Van Veeteren, and threw the
newspaper onto the floor. What the hell am I doing here?

He took off his shirt and padded into the bathroom.
What was the name of that restaurant?

The Blue Ship?

The assumption that representatives of the national press
would turn up proved to be well founded. As he walked
through the hotel foyer, two middle-aged gentlemen darted
out of the bar. Their ruddy complexions were a telltale
indication of their trade, and Van Veeteren paused with a
sigh.

'Chief Inspector Van Veeteren! Cruickshank from the
Telegraaf!'

'Müller from the *Allgemejne*!' announced the other. 'I
think we've met—'

'My name's Rölling,' said Van Veeteren. 'I'm a travelling
salesman specializing in grandfather clocks. There must be
some mistake.'

'Ha ha,' said Müller.

'When can we have a chat?' asked Cruickshank.

'At the press conference in the police station at eleven o'clock tomorrow morning,' said Van Veeteren, opening the front door.

'Is it you or Bausen who's in charge of the investigation?' asked Müller.

'What investigation?' said Van Veeteren.

The main colour used for the interior decoration of The Blue Ship was red. The bar was no more than half full, and there were plenty of empty tables in the dining room. Van Veeteren was seated right at the back, with no near neighbours; but even so, he hadn't even started his main course before a thin gentleman with gleaming eyes and a nervous smile materialized in front of him.

'Excuse me. Schalke from *de Journaal*. You're that chief inspector, aren't you?'

Van Veeteren didn't respond.

'I was the last person to speak to him. I've been interviewed by Bausen and Kropke, of course; but if you'd like a chat, I'd be happy to oblige.'

He glanced down meaningfully at the empty chair opposite the chief inspector.

'Could we meet in the bar when I've finished eating?' proposed Van Veeteren.

Schalke nodded and withdrew. Van Veeteren started to

work his way listlessly through something described cryptically on the menu as 'Chef's Pride with Funghi and Mozzarella.' When he'd finished his meal and paid his bill, he still had no idea what he'd been eating.

'He sat on the same chair as you're on now,' said Schalke. 'Very much alive. One thing is certain. He had no idea he was going to have his head chopped off. He acted exactly the same as he always did.'

'And how was that?' asked Van Veeteren, sucking the froth off his beer.

'How was that? Well . . . a bit distant and supercilious, to tell you the truth. Not easy to talk to. He was always like that. His mind was sort of . . . elsewhere.'

That doesn't surprise me, thought Van Veeteren.

'He seemed to be trying to flirt a bit with one of the girls sitting over there.'

He pointed.

'Flirt?'

'Well, maybe that's exaggerating it. But he was giving her the eye all right.'

Van Veeteren nodded.

'Are you saying that Ernst Simmel was a . . . philanderer?'

Schalke hesitated, but only for a second.

'Well, not quite that, I don't think. I didn't know him all that well, and he'd been away for several years . . . kicked over the traces now and then, I suppose, but nothing serious.'

'His marriage wasn't all that serious either then, I assume,' said Van Veeteren.

'No . . . You could put it like that, I suppose.'

'And he left here at about eleven?'

'A few minutes past.'

'Which way did he go?'

'That way.' Schalke pointed again. 'Down towards the square and the harbour.'

'Didn't he live in the other direction?'

'You can go either way, in fact. It's just that it's a bit longer via the harbour.'

'You didn't see anybody follow him?'

'No.'

'Why do you think he took the longer route?'

'I don't know. Women, perhaps.'

'Whores?'

'Yes . . . we have one or two. They usually hang about down there.'

'Did you notice anybody else leave the bar after Simmel?'

'No . . . I've been thinking about that, but I don't think anybody did.'

Van Veeteren sighed.

'What questions would you ask if you were in my place?'

Schalke considered.

'God knows! I haven't a clue, to be honest.'

'You don't have any theories about what happened?'

Schalke considered again. It was obvious that he would have loved to come up with a bold hypothesis, but he gave up after a while.

'No, none at all, to be honest,' he said. 'It must be a madman, I reckon . . . Somebody who's escaped from a funny farm, maybe?'

Funny farm? thought Van Veeteren. A well-chosen expression for a scribbler to use, I must say.

'Bausen's been following that up,' he said. 'The only person who's escaped is a confused old lady in her nineties. Has Alzheimer's and goes around in a wheelchair . . .'

'I don't suppose it's her then,' said Schalke.

Van Veeteren drained his beer and decided it was time to go home. He hopped off his bar stool and thanked Schalke for his assistance.

'Is it always as empty as this here?' he asked.

'Good Lord, no!' said Schalke. 'It's usually packed. I mean, it's Friday and all that . . . People are just scared stiff. They daren't go out!'

Scared stiff? thought Van Veeteren as he stood on the pavement outside. Yes, of course they're scared stiff.

Town terror stricken?

It took him barely ten minutes to walk from The Blue Ship to the harbour and The See Warf. Quite a few cars were around, but he saw no more than a dozen or so pedestrians, all of them in groups. The few bars and cafés that were open also seemed to be fairly empty. The Palladium cinema had started its late-evening showing, but he had the impression that it was just as empty in there. Even if the Kaalbringen nightlife was nothing to write home about, the trend was clear enough.

The murderer . . . the executioner . . . the Axeman left nobody unaffected.

Hardly surprising. He stood for a while outside his hotel and wondered if he maybe ought to go to the municipal woods and take a look but decided to wait. No doubt it would be better to do that in daylight.

There were a lot of other things to take care of tomorrow, of course, but as he settled down in bed and switched on the cassette player, it was Inspector Moerk's words that were ringing in his ears.

Nothing. We don't know a damn thing.

An attractive woman, incidentally, he thought. A pity I'm not twenty-five years younger.

By the time he'd heard one and a half interviews, he was sleeping like a log.

7

In his dreams the old images came back to haunt him again. The same images. The same desperate inability to act, the same sterile white-hot fury – Bitte in the corner by the sofa with her arms covered in needle marks and eyes like black, empty wells. The pimp, thin as a rake with jet-black, straggly hair, eyeing him scornfully and sneering. Hands raised, palms up, and shaking his head. And the other man – her face over the shoulders of the naked man. A sweaty, hairy back, heavy buttocks thrusting violently into her and pressing her up against the wall, her legs wide apart and her eyes reflecting his own, seeing what he sees . . . just for a second before he turns on his heel and leaves.

The same images . . . and imposed upon them, penetrating them, the image of the ten-year-old with blonde plaits, roaring with laughter, running towards him along the beach. Arms outstretched, eyes gleaming. Bitte . . .

He woke up. In a cold sweat as usual, and it was several seconds before he remembered, before he got the upper hand . . . the weapon . . . the intense feeling of bliss as he swung it through the air and the dull thud as it penetrated their necks. The lifeless bodies and the blood bubbling out . . .

That blood.

If only that blood would flow over those dream images. Cover them in stains, make them incomprehensible, un-recognizable. Destroy them. Settle the bill once and for all, reduce all debts to zero . . . But even so, it was not about his torture. It wasn't about the images, it was about what the images were based on. The reality behind them. The reality.

Her revenge, not his. That ten-year-old running towards him, whose life had come to a sudden stop. Who was blocked and obstructed in midstride, just as abruptly and inexorably as in the photograph. It was about her and nobody else.

He fumbled for his cigarettes. Didn't want to put the light on. Darkness was what was needed; he didn't want to see anything now. He struck a match. Lit the cigarette and inhaled deeply, resolutely. Immediately felt that warm sensation again spreading through his body, a tidal wave flowing up into his head and making him smile. He thought about his weapon again. Could see it before him in the darkness. He was an exhilarated Macbeth suddenly, and he wondered how long he would have to wait before it was time to let it speak again . . .

8

In the clear light of morning and with a fresh breeze blowing in from the sea, Kaalbringen seemed to have forgotten that it was terror stricken. Van Veeteren had a late breakfast on his balcony and observed the teeming crowds in Fisherman's Square down below. There were obviously more than delicacies from the depths of the sea being sold from the stalls under their colourful awnings – more like everything under the sun. Saturday morning was market day; the sun was shining and life went on.

The clock in the low limestone church struck ten, and Van Veeteren realized that he had slept for almost eleven hours.

Eleven hours? Did that really mean, he asked himself, that what he needed in order to get a good night's sleep was a murder hunt? He contemplated that theory as he tapped the top of his egg. It seemed absurd. And what was that insidious feeling that had taken possession of him this peaceful morning? He'd noticed it when he was in the shower, tried to rinse it away, but out here in the salty air it had returned with renewed strength. Spun esoteric threads of indolence around his soul and whispered seductive words in his ears . . .

It was that he had no need to exert himself.

The solution to this case would come to him of its own accord. Strike him as a result of some coincidence. A gift from the heavens. A deus ex machina!

A mercy devoutly to be wished, thought Van Veeteren. Fat chance!

But the thought was there nevertheless.

Cruickshank and Müller were sitting in the foyer, waiting for him. They had been joined by a photographer, a bearded young man who brandished a flash gun at his face the moment he emerged from the lift.

'Good morning, Chief Inspector,' said Müller.

'It looks like it,' said Van Veeteren.

'Can we have a chat after the press conference?' asked Cruickshank.

'If you write what I tell you to write. One word too many and you'll be banned for two years!'

'Of course,' said Müller with a smile. 'Usual rules.'

'I'll be at Sylvie's between noon and half past twelve,' said Van Veeteren, handing in his room key at reception.

'Sylvie's? What's that?' asked the photographer, taking a new picture.

'You'll have to work that out for yourselves,' said Van Veeteren.

Detective Chief Inspector Bausen took charge of the assembled journalists and immediately stamped his authority on the proceedings. He started by waiting for several minutes until you could have heard a drop of sweat fall in the packed conference room. Then he started to speak, but stopped the moment anybody whispered or coughed and fixed the perpetrator with a beady eye. If anybody dared to interrupt him, he delivered the warning that a repeated offence would result in the sinner's being ejected from the room forthwith by Kropke and Mooser. And he himself would help out if need be.

But he answered calmly and methodically the questions that were put to him, adopting a precisely judged degree of superiority that exposed and established the limited intellectual faculties of the questioner. Always assuming he had any.

The man must have been an actor, thought Van Veeteren.

'When do you think you will have the murderer under

58

lock and key?' asked a red-nosed reporter from the local radio station.

'About ten minutes after we've found him,' said Bausen.

'Have you any theories you're working on?' wondered Malevic, chief reporter on *de Journaal*.

'How else do you think we operate?' asked Bausen. 'We're not working for a newspaper.'

'Who's actually in charge of the investigation?' asked the man sent by the *Neuwe Blatt*. 'Is it you or DCI Van Veeteren?'

'Who do you think?' responded Van Veeteren, contemplating a comprehensively chewed toothpick. He didn't answer anything else, referring all direct questions to Bausen by nodding in his direction. If he was smiling inwardly, nobody could have told that from the expression on his face.

After twenty minutes most of the questions seemed to have been asked, and Bausen began issuing instructions.

'I want the local newspapers and the radio to urge everybody who was in town last Tuesday night between eleven o'clock and midnight, give or take a few minutes, in the area around The Blue Ship, Hoistraat, the steps down to Fisherman's Square and the Esplanade leading to the municipal woods to get in touch with the police from tomorrow onward. We'll have two officers on hand at the station to deal with all the information we receive, and we shall not turn a blind eye if anybody who was out then fails to report to us. Don't forget that we're dealing with an unusually violent killer.'

'But won't you have a vast number of responses?' somebody wondered.

'When you're hunting a murderer, Miss Meuhlich,' said Bausen, 'you have to accept a few minor inconveniences.'

'What do you think, Chief Inspector?' asked Cruickshank. 'Just between you and me.'

'You, me and two others, if I'm not much mistaken,' said Van Veeteren. 'I don't think anything.'

'The Bausen guy seems to like throwing his weight around,' said Müller. 'Do you think you'll be able to work with him?'

'You can bet your life,' said Van Veeteren.

'Have you anything to go on?'

'You can write that we have.'

'But you haven't, in fact?'

'I never said that.'

'How long is it since you last had to leave a case unsolved?' asked Cruickshank.

'Six years,' said Van Veeteren.

'What was that, then?' asked the photographer, curious.

'The G-file . . .' Van Veeteren stopped chewing and stared out of the window.

'Oh, yes, I remember,' said Cruickshank. 'I wrote about that one—'

Two young ladies came in and were about to sit at the next table, but Müller drove them away.

'Sit in the corner instead,' he urged them. 'There's a terrible stink here!'

'Well,' began Cruickshank, 'are we dealing with a madman, or is it planned?'

'Who says that madmen don't plan?' said Van Veeteren.

'Is there a link between the victims?'

'Yes.'

'What is it?'

'. . .'

'How do you know?'

'Give me a Danish pastry!'

'Will there be any more top brass coming?'

'If necessary.'

'Have you any previous experience with axe murderers?' wondered the photographer.

'I know a fair amount about murderers,' said Van Veeteren. 'And everybody knows how an axe works. How long can your esteemed journals afford to do without your services and leave you here in Kaalbringen? Six months?'

'Ha ha,' said Müller. 'A few days, I should think. Unless it happens again, that is.'

'It'll be some time before that, no doubt.'

'How do you know that?'

'Thank you for the coffee,' said Van Veeteren, standing up. 'I'll have to leave you now, I'm afraid. Don't stay up too late, and don't write any rubbish!'

'Have we ever written rubbish?' asked Cruickshank.

'What the hell are we doing here?' wondered the photographer when Van Veeteren had left them on their own.

What the hell am I doing here? thought Van Veeteren, and clambered into the passenger seat next to Bausen.

'It's not a pretty sight,' said Bausen. 'I think I'll stay out here and do a bit of planning.'

Van Veeteren followed the limping pathologist.

'Meuritz,' he said when they had entered the room. 'My name's Meuritz. Actually based in Oostwerdingen, but I generally do one day a week here as well. It's been a bit more than that lately.'

He pulled the trolley out of the deep freeze, and removed the sheet with an extravagant gesture. Van Veeteren was reminded of something Reinhart had said once: There's only one profession. Matador. All the rest are substitutes and shadows.

Bausen was right, no doubt about it. Even if Ernst Simmel hadn't exactly been a handsome specimen of a man while on this earth, neither the Axeman nor Meuritz had done anything to improve the situation. He was lying on his stomach, and for reasons that Van Veeteren didn't fully understand but which were no doubt pedagogical, Meuritz had placed the head at ninety degrees to the neck in an upward direction, so that the incision was clearly visible.

'A pretty skilful blow, you have to give him that,' he said, poking into the wound with a ballpoint pen.

'Skilful?' wondered Van Veeteren.

'Look at this!'

Meuritz held out an X-ray film.

'This is Eggers. Note the angle of entry! Only a couple of degrees difference. They were exactly the same depth, incidentally . . .'

Van Veeteren scrutinized the picture of the maltreated white bones against a black background.

'. . . lands from above, diagonally from the right.'

'Right-handed?' asked Van Veeteren.

'Presumably. Or a left-handed badminton player. Who's used to playing forehands way out on the backhand side, if you follow me.'

'I play three times a week,' said Van Veeteren.

Who was it who had said something about tennis balls not so long ago?

Meuritz nodded and pushed his glasses up onto his forehead.

'Is it the same weapon?' asked Van Veeteren. 'Take that ballpoint out of his throat, if you don't mind.'

Meuritz wiped his pen clean on his white coat and put it in his breast pocket.

'Definitely,' he said. 'I can even claim to be able to describe it – an axe with a very sharp blade, sharpened by an expert no doubt. Five inches deep and quite wide. Maybe six inches, possibly more.'

'How do you know that?'

'It penetrated exactly the same distance in both cases, and then it was stopped by the handle. If the blade had been deeper, the skull would certainly have been severed. Have you seen the things butchers use to cut up bones with?'

Van Veeteren nodded. Began to regret the fact that he'd eaten three Danish pastries at Sylvie's luxury café.

'Time of death?'

'Between half past eleven and half past twelve, roughly speaking.'

'Can you be more precise?'

'Closer to half past eleven – twenty to twelve, if you were to really press me.'

'Have you come across anything like this before?' Van Veeteren indicated the pale blue corpse.

'No. You never stop learning in this business.'

Although it was three and a half days since Ernst Simmel's body had been found, and almost four days since he'd been murdered, the scene of the crime had not lost its attraction. The police had sealed it off with red-and-white tape and warning notices, but a trickle of people was still flowing past this woodland corral, a narrow stream of Kaalbringen citizens who didn't want to miss the opportunity of seeing the white markers in among the bushes and the increasingly dark-coloured patch of human blood on the path.

Constable Erwin Bang had been given the task of maintaining order and keeping the most curious at bay, and he carried out this mission with all the dignity and attention to detail that his 160-pound frame allowed. The moment there were more than two visitors at a time, he would get them moving.

'Come on! Move it! Keep going!'

It seemed to Van Veeteren that Bang was handling the situation as a spot of traffic policing more than anything else. But that was of minor significance, of course.

'Can you keep the spectators at bay so that the chief

inspector and I can take a look in peace and quiet?' asked Bausen.

'Right, that's it. Move along!' bellowed Bang, and flocks of jackdaws and wood pigeons panicked and took to the air. 'Quickly now! This is a crime scene investigation!'

'You can go and have a cup of coffee,' said Bausen when they were on their own. 'We'll be here for about half an hour. I think we can remove the tape and stuff then. You can take it all back to the station.'

'Will do!' said Bang, giving a smart salute. He embarked on his amended duties, and strode off in the direction of the Esplanade and the harbour café.

'Well,' said Bausen, plunging his hands into his pockets. 'That was Constable Bang.'

Van Veeteren looked around.

'Hmm,' he said.

Bausen produced a pack of cigarettes from his pocket. 'Would you like one?'

'No,' said Van Veeteren, 'but I'll have one even so. Can we try a little experiment?'

'Your word is my command,' said Bausen, lighting two cigarettes and handing one of them to Van Veeteren. 'What do you want to do?'

'Let's walk along the path for twenty or thirty yards. Then I'll come back with you following me, and I'll see if I can hear you.'

'OK,' said Bausen. 'But I've tested that already. The path has been trampled down by so many feet, it's damn hard. You won't hear a thing.'

They carried out the experiment, and Bausen's prediction proved to be absolutely correct. The distant murmur of the sea and the rustling of the wind in the trees was sufficient to mask any other noise. Bausen had more or less been able to put his hand on Van Veeteren's shoulder before he'd noticed he was even there.

'And that's how it happened,' said Bausen.

Van Veeteren nodded.

'I take it you've made a thorough search?' he said.

'Of the crime scene? We most certainly have! We've vacuumed every single blade of grass. Not a thing! Just blood, and more blood. It's dry, you see. Hasn't rained for three weeks. No soft ground anywhere, no footprints. No, I don't think we're going to get any leads of that sort. It looks as if he wiped his weapon clean at one spot, but that's all.'

'What about the Eggers case?'

'The same story. We were very interested in a cigarette end for a long time, but it turned out to be two days old. It occupied several officers for a week.'

'Has Meuritz had backup from forensic officers, by the way?' asked Van Veeteren.

'Four of them. Not that I think he needed them. Damn

competent doc, even if he can be a bit difficult to work with.'

Van Veeteren bent down and studied the stained grass.

'Have you heard of Heliogabalus?' he asked.

'The guy with the blood on the grass?'

'That's the one. Roman emperor, 218–222. Killed people because he liked to see red against green. An uncompromising aesthete, no doubt about it. Although blood doesn't keep its colour all that well, it has to be said—'

'No,' said Bausen. 'Not really the right motive in this case, anyway. It must have been pitch-black here last Tuesday night. Two lights in sequence along the path were out.'

'Hmm,' said Van Veeteren. 'We'll eliminate Heliogabalus, then. It's always good to be able to cross a name off the list.'

Some would-be detectives from the general public were approaching from the Rikken direction. Bang must have put in place some kind of barrier down by the harbour, as they'd been left in peace for nearly ten minutes. Bausen checked his watch.

'Half past four,' he said. 'I have a leg of mutton in the freezer. Only needs some roasting. How about it?'

Van Veeteren hesitated.

'If you allow me a couple of hours at the hotel first.'

'Of course,' said Bausen. 'You're welcome at the nest around seven. I hope we'll be able to sit outside.'

9

Beate Moerk slid down into the bath and switched off the light. She allowed herself to be swallowed up by the hot water and imagined that she was inside a womb. That was a recurring thought, and no doubt had some significance.

She felt her waist and hips, and had the impression that she was not putting on weight. A hundred and twenty pounds. She'd run five miles, the last one pretty quickly. It was true some experts maintained that the most efficient speed for burning up calories was sixty per cent of maximum, but what the hell! Surely you would lose a few extra ounces if you really stretched yourself.

That's enough vanity for now. She rested her head on the edge of the bath and let her tiredness grow and spread all over her body. I'm thirty-one, she thought. I'm a thirty-one-year-old female cop. Without a husband. Without children. Without a family, a house, a boat . . .

That was also a recurring thought. She wasn't too worried about a house or a boat. She could also imagine getting by without a husband, for the time being, at least. But children were another matter. A very different matter.

She was living in a different world, in fact. Perhaps it was to get away from that feeling that she liked to fantasize about lying in a womb. Who knows? Of the seven or eight best friends she'd had since she was a teenager, at least five or six of them had masses of children by this time; she was aware of that. Husbands and boats as well, for that matter. Still, thank God, she wasn't still living in Friesen; that had been a necessary condition, of course. She'd never have been able to survive if she'd had to put up with all that went with living there wherever she turned. Her independent and liberated life would have shrivelled away like a . . . like a used condom if she'd been forced to have everybody and everything weighing down on her all the time. With her parents and childhood misdemeanours and the follies of youth like a caste mark on her forehead. Like a contents list writ large that she could never detach herself from! Hell, no, she thought.

But there again, sooner or later she would have to give birth to that child; sooner or later she'd have to toe the line of accepted lifestyles. She'd known that for some years now, but every time she celebrated her birthday, at the beginning of January, she would give herself just one more year. A twelve-month moratorium, she would think. One more round. That wasn't a bad birthday present, and it

would no doubt be on her wish list one more year, at
least . . .

She groped for the soap and found it, then changed the
subject. This was certainly not the time to start thinking
about a husband and children. Besides, the reality probably was that only a policeman would consider marrying
a policewoman, so the choice was a bit limited. Bang,
Mooser, Kropke . . . perish the thought! She started soap-
ing her breasts . . . still firm and bouncy; another recurrent
thought was that one of these days she would start to dis-
like her breasts – the whole of her body, come to that. But
naturally, that was a trauma she shared with all women. A
fact of life, presumably, and one that had to be accepted . . .
Anyway, both Kropke and Mooser were married already.
Thank goodness for that.

But it was none of them she wanted to think about
tonight. Why should she? The person she was going to
devote her attention to for the next few hours was not a
police officer at all. On the contrary. It was that other
man . . .

The Axeman. Him and nobody else.

He's the one I want.

She smiled at the thought. Smiled and switched on the
light with a haste that seemed to her a little sudden.

★

She had done no more than sit down at her desk when the telephone rang. Beside her was a cup of Russian tea, and the only light in the room formed a small oval in which her notebooks basked.

Her mother, of course. Ah, well, might as well get that call over with now rather than being interrupted later.

Would Beate be coming home this Sunday? That was what she wanted to know. Dad would be so pleased. He'd been depressed all week and the doctors had said that . . . but that was something they could come back to, perhaps. What was she doing? Working! Surely she didn't have to get involved in that awful murder business; that was a man's job, surely? Hadn't they got any men in the Kaalbringen police force? What kind of a place was it?

Ten minutes later the call was over, and her bad conscience was gnawing at her like an aching tooth. She was looking out the window, watching the last stages of the sunset as it spread its symbolic light over the whole sky, and made up her mind to go home for a few hours on Sunday evening after all. Perhaps she could spend the night there and take the first train back on Monday morning . . . yes, she had no alternative, of course.

She unplugged the telephone. Just in case. After all, it wasn't impossible that Janos might ring, and she had no desire at all to sacrifice a whole evening to *that* particular bit of bad conscience . . . not for a while yet, at least.

The Axeman.

She opened the two notepads and placed them side by side. Started to study the one on the left.

Heinz Eggers, it said at the top, underscored with a double line.

Born April 23, 1961, in Selstadt.

Died June 28, 1993, in Kaalbringen.

That was indisputable, of course. Below came a long series of notes. Parents and siblings. School education. Various addresses. A list of women's names. A number of dates marking when Eggers had entered or left various penal institutions, mainly prisons, dates of convictions and sentences . . .

Two children with different women. The first, a girl, born in Wodz, August 2, 1985. The mother, one Kristine Lauger. The second, a boy, born on December 23, the day before Christmas Eve she had noted earlier, 1991 – so he was not yet two. Mother's name Matilde Fuchs, address and place of domicile unknown. She devoted a few seconds' thought to this woman, musing on how she appeared to have achieved what Beate herself was striving for. A child without a father – there again, was that really what she was striving for? Besides, Fuchs could just as well be a junkie and a whore who had long since given the unwanted boy away to some other, more suitable guardians. Yes, that was a far more likely hypothesis.

Well? How far had she got with her meditations last night? An important question, no doubt . . . She turned a few pages. There!

What had Heinz Eggers been doing in that courtyard? That was the crux of the matter! Why, to be more precise, was this social outcast, this dropout, in the courtyard at 24 Burgislaan at one o'clock in the morning (or even later) on June 28, 1993?

She knew that was a good question, and even if it was not yet possible to give a definitive answer, she could draw a few conclusions, of course, without exceeding the limits of logic and without sinking into a morass of speculation. Anybody could do that.

First, even if Eggers was a confirmed drug user, one could assume that he was capable of a certain amount of rational thought – there was not a lot of poison in his veins that night; he had died more or less clean and sober (which one might hope, as a good Christian, would stand him in good stead when they started to assess his earthly life on the other side). In any case, Eggers could not possibly have just happened to be at Burgislaan. He must have gone there for some reason. In the middle of the night. On June 28. Alone.

She took a sip of tea.

Second, none of the shady characters Eggers mixed with – and she had questioned all of them very carefully –

had the slightest idea what it was all about, not even his so-called girlfriend, who was evidently sleeping like a log on the night in question after spending the previous day or days drinking vast amounts of wine. When she and Kropke had pressed them even harder, insisted that they make an informed guess, all they could come up with was that Heinz must have had a tip-off. A hint. Information that somebody had something to sell . . . some goods. Drugs of some sort . . . heroin or amphetamines or even hash. Could be anything. Heinz took the lot. And what he couldn't stuff into himself, he would sell to little kids.

Third, ergo, conclusion: The Axeman had arranged to meet him. Eggers was the intended victim and nobody else. The deed was carefully planned and prepared. No room for madmen or lunatics and similar epithets that certain people were throwing around. The only possible category of crime was first-degree murder! Not something done on the spur of the moment, no extenuating circumstances, no junkie who happened to hit another one on the head.

First degree. Not a shadow of a doubt about that, or about what kind of a person the Axeman was – a meticulous, very self-assured criminal who was absolutely clear about what he was doing. Who didn't appear to leave anything to chance, and who . . .

Fourth, who had a motive!

She leaned back in her chair and took a deep drink of tea.

A very single-minded murderer.

She moved on to the other notebook.

Ernst Leopold Simmel.

Not so much data here. Only a few pages. She simply hadn't had the strength to note down the abundance of information Kropke had fished out from such sources as local council records and national registers and company registrations, bankruptcies, shell company dealings, commissions, tax returns, business trips and God only knows what else. She glanced quickly through what she had written, then concentrated on the questions at the end, the ones she'd scribbled down last night before going to bed. The trick was to ask the right questions, as old Wundermaas, her favourite at the police college in Genschen, never ceased to stress. Keep rephrasing them! he used to growl impatiently as he pinned you down with his piercing eyes. The answers can be harder to find than needles in a haystack! So make sure that you're rummaging in the right haystack, at least!

Well, what were the questions to ask about Simmel? The right ones? She took another sip of tea and started thinking.

What was he doing when he went out last Tuesday evening? She knew that.

Why did he go via Fisherman's Square? They could be pretty sure of that.

Why did he take the path through the municipal woods? That was obvious.

When did the Axeman begin following him? A good starting point, perhaps? What about the answers?

From near The Blue Ship? In all probability, yes. He must then have followed him all the way through town, more or less. Yes, what else could he have done?

What does that imply?

She raised her head and looked through the window. The town was stretched out before her. She switched off her desk lamp and suddenly Kaalbringen was illuminated, lit up by myriad lamps that come into their own when night falls. The main thoroughfares and features were clearly marked – Bungeskirke, Hoistraat, Grande Place, the town hall, the tower blocks out at Dünningen . . . The Fisherman's Friend. Yes, that must be the restaurant hanging up there on the edge of the cliff; she hadn't thought of that before. He'd walked past all that; the murderer had walked all the way from The Blue Ship with his victim only a few yards ahead, and there must . . .

There must be witnesses.

That was as obvious as can be. People simply must have

seen the Axeman as he skulked in the shadow of the walls along Langvej and Hoistraat, as he scampered down the steps, as he sneaked across Fisherman's Square . . . There's no other possibility. Whoever he is, he's not invisible. What does that indicate?

Just as obvious was that tomorrow they would open up their doors, and that famous detective the general public would come teeming into the police station; and sooner or later somebody – possibly several people – would turn up and prove to have seen him. They didn't know it was him, obviously; but nevertheless, they'd seen him and now they were reporting that fact. They'd seen him full in the face, they had even said hello to him!

That was the way it was. She put the light on again. In a few days they'd have the name of the Axeman hidden away among the mass of completely irrelevant information; and nobody would know which one it was, and there'd be no way of separating the wheat from the chaff. Or would it be worth sifting through it all? Would anybody regard it as being worth the trouble? Kropke, perhaps.

Shit! she thought. Just the job for Kropke. If that's how it's going to turn out, we might as well acknowledge defeat in advance.

But surely there must be some shortcuts? Cribs? Some way of cutting through the mass of irrelevant data? There must be. So what was the question she could write on the next page with quadruple underscoring?

It was already there.

'Connection???' it said. She stared at it for a while. Then she drew a triangle. Wrote the names Eggers and Simmel in two of the corners. Hesitated for a moment before putting Axeman in the third. Contemplated her handiwork.

What on earth am I doing? she thought. What kind of rubbish is this? What childish drivel!

Nevertheless, the drawing certainly looked plausible. If only I had a computer, she thought, I'd simply feed Simmel into one end and Eggers into the other. The patterns that came up on the screen would sooner or later highlight a point, or produce a bundle of lines that indicated something that made sense. A single name would emerge from the chaos or whatever the mathematical term was, and it would be the name of the Axeman. It would be as easy as that!

Oh, come on, thought Beate Moerk. I'm losing my grip! If there's one thing in this world that I don't understand, it's computers.

She closed her notebooks and saw from the clock that it was too late for that Italian film on the TV that she hadn't really intended watching anyway. No, she was not one for the quantitative approach. Not for her the tedious search through haystack after haystack; Kropke could get on with that, with the help of Mooser and Bang. She had better things to do.

She looked up again, just in time to see the moon glide into the rectangle formed by her window. Full and round . . . Juno! It was a sign, no doubt about it. There were other criteria to be applied to this case. Different assumptions. Intuition! Woman! None of this confounded left side of the brain! Yin, not yang! She sat smiling at the moon. I'm an idiot, she thought. A damn fool! Time to go to bed. Yes, no doubt about it. Lucky that nobody else knows how I'm using my brain. Or rather, abusing it!

She stood up and went into the hall. She slid out of her dressing gown and examined herself in the mirror. Hmm, not too bad, she thought. Could easily be twenty-five, twenty-six, or thereabouts. A pity there isn't a man waiting for me in my bed.

But she certainly didn't want him there tomorrow morning as well!

And when she started to doze off a quarter of an hour later, all that drifted into her subconscious through the darkness were the imaginary images of the murderer. Insofar as there are any imaginary images . . .

The Axeman?

Could they even be sure that it was a man?

That question registered just as she abandoned her

final foothold and submitted to the boundless embrace of slumber. There was no time to consider whether or not Wundermaas would have assigned her to one of the potentially fruitful haystacks.

10

'I sometimes get the feeling there is a guiding hand, despite everything,' said Bausen, handing Van Veeteren a glass.

'God's finger?'

'Or the other one's. Cheers! This is not strong; I didn't want to kill off your taste buds. I thought we could sample a few decent things later.'

They drank and the wicker chairs creaked in sympathy. Van Veeteren lit a cigarette. He'd succumbed to temptation and bought a pack at the news-stand outside his hotel. It was the first one since Erich had left him, so he felt entitled to it.

'Anyway,' said Bausen, producing a shabby tobacco pouch vaguely reminiscent of something Van Veeteren had seen in Ernst Simmel's throat. 'We lead a fairly quiet life here. Lock up a few drunks, clear up the occasional case of assault and battery, confiscate a few bottles of the hard stuff from the boats coming in from the east, and suddenly we're landed with this. Just when I'm about to call it a day. Don't try to tell me that's not a pointer!'

'There are certain patterns,' said Van Veeteren.

Bausen sucked fire into his pipe.

'I've even given the racists a rap on the knuckles.'

'Ah, yes. You have a refugee camp out at Taublitz, if I remember rightly,' said Van Veeteren.

'We certainly do. These characters started stirring up trouble a few years ago, and in November last year there was a gang going around setting fire to things. They burned two huts down to the ground. I arrested eight of them.'

'Excellent,' said Van Veeteren.

'Four of them are busy rebuilding the cabins; can you imagine that? They're working alongside the asylum seekers! They were allowed to choose between two years in jail or community service. Damned fine judge. Heinrich Heine his name was, the same as the poet. And now they've learned their lesson.'

'Impressive,' said Van Veeteren.

'I agree. Maybe it is possible to make human beings out of anybody at all, providing you go for it hook, line and sinker. Mind you, four of them preferred jail, of course.'

'Are you intending to go on October first anyway, no matter what happens?' asked Van Veeteren. 'They haven't approached you about staying on, or anything?'

Bausen snorted.

'No idea. I've not heard any hints yet, in any case. I expect they hope you'll sort this out in a couple of ticks so that they can send me packing in the usual manner when the day comes. I hope so as well, come to that.'

Same here, thought Van Veeteren. He picked up his glass and looked around. Bausen had cleared the table and put a cloth on it, but apart from that, the patio looked the same as the previous time – books and newspapers and junk everywhere. The serpentine rambling roses and the overgrown garden sucked up every noise and impression but their own; you could easily imagine having been trans- ported to some Greene-esque or Conradian outpost. A mangrove swamp at the mouth of some river in the as yet unexplored continent. The heart of darkness, perhaps. A couple of topis, a jar of quinine tablets and a few mosquito nets would not have disturbed the image. But nevertheless, he was in the middle of Europe. A little toy jungle by a European sea. Van Veeteren took a sip of his drink, which smelled slightly of cinnamon, and felt a brief pang of satis- faction.

'Your wife . . . ?' he said. Sooner or later he'd have to ask that question, after all.

'Died two years ago. Cancer.'

'Any children?'

Bausen shook his head.

'What about you?' he asked.

'Divorced. Also two years ago, or thereabouts.'

'Ah, well,' said Bausen. 'Are you ready?'

'For what?'

Bausen smiled.

'A little trip into the underworld. I thought I'd show you my treasure trove.'

They emptied their glasses, and Bausen led the way down into the cellar. Down the stairs, through the boiler room and a couple of storage rooms full of still more junk – bicycles, furniture, worn-out domestic appliances, rusty old garden tools, newspapers (some in bundles and some not), bottles, old shoes and boots . . .

'I find it hard to let anything go,' said Bausen. 'Mind your head! It's a bit low down here.'

Down a few more steps and along a narrow passage smelling of soil, and they came to a solid-looking door with double bolts and a padlock.

'Here we are!' said Bausen. He unlocked the door and switched on a light. 'Stand by to have your breath taken away!'

He opened the door and allowed Van Veeteren to go in first.

Wine. A cellar full of it.

In the dim light he could just make out the dull reflections from the bottles stacked up in racks around the walls.

In neat rows from floor to ceiling. Thousands of bottles, without doubt. He sucked the heavy air into his nostrils.

'Aah!' he said. 'You are rising in my estimation, Mr Chief of Police. This denotes without doubt the pinnacle of civilization.'

Bausen chuckled.

'Exactly! What you see here is what will become my main occupation when I've retired. I've worked out that if I restrict myself to three bottles per week, they'll last ten years. I doubt if I'll want to continue any longer than that.'

Van Veeteren nodded. Why haven't I been doing something like this? he thought. I must start digging the moment I get home!

It might be a bit problematic in view of the fact that he lived in an apartment block, of course, but maybe he could start by purchasing the goods instead. Perhaps he could rent an allotment or something of the sort? He made up his mind to take it up with Reinhart or Dorigues as soon as he was back home.

'Please choose two for us to drink,' said Bausen. 'A white and a red, I think.'

'Meursault,' said Van Veeteren. 'White Meursault, do you have any of that?'

'A few dozen, I should think. What about the red?'

'I'll leave that to the boss of the investigation team,' said Van Veeteren.

'Ha ha. All right, in that case I'll propose a Saint Emilion '71. If my friend the chief inspector doesn't disapprove.'

'I expect I'll be able to force it down,' said Van Veeteren.

'Not too bad an evening, on the whole,' he maintained two hours later. 'It would be no bad thing if life were to be enhanced by rather more of this kind of thing – good food; intelligent conversation; sublime wines, to say the least; and this cheese.' He licked his fingers and took a bite of a slice of pear. 'What do I owe you, by the way?'

Bausen chuckled with pleasure.

'Haven't you figured it out? Put the Axeman behind bars, for God's sake, so that I can grow old with dignity!'

'I knew there'd be a catch,' said Van Veeteren.

Bausen poured out the last drops of the Bordeaux.

'Don't worry,' he said. 'We'll have a whiskey to round it off later. Well?'

'Hmm,' said Van Veeteren. 'It might be better if we take what you have to say first. You've been in it from the start, after all.'

His host nodded and leaned back in his chair. He kicked off his shoes and put his feet up on a wooden crate of empty jars. Wiggling his toes for a while, he seemed to be lost in thought.

'God only knows,' he said after a minute or two. 'I have so many ideas and loose ends buzzing around in my head that I don't know where to start. I've spent most of today wondering if there really is a connection, when you get right down to it.'

'Explain!' said Van Veeteren.

'Of course we're dealing with the same murderer; I take that for granted – for simplicity's sake if for no other reason. The same murderer, the same method, the same weapon. But the link between the victims – that's what I'm a bit doubtful about. I'm a bit afraid of finding out something that we might jump at simply because we've found it. That they were on the same package holiday in Sicily in 1988, or were in the same hospital in October 1979, or some other damn thing.'

'Two people always cross each other's path somewhere or other,' said Van Veeteren.

'Something like that, yes, and the fact that they do doesn't necessarily mean a thing. It can, but it doesn't have to, by any means.'

'Don't forget that we're talking about three paths,' said Van Veeteren. 'The murderer's as well.'

'Yes, fair enough; of course we have to look for the third

link as well if we're going to make a breakthrough. It's just that I have the feeling it might be different in this case.'

'You mean that Eggers and Simmel might have been picked out at random?'

'Possibly,' said Bausen, staring out into the darkness. 'Of course he has picked on Eggers and Simmel on purpose, but it's not certain that they have much to do with him personally. There could be much looser connections, as it were.'

'A list picked out at random from the phone book?' suggested Van Veeteren. 'There are precedents, as you know. Harridge, if you remember him. He shut his eyes and stuck a pin into the Coventry edition of the telephone directory. Then went out and strangled them, one after another.'

'I know,' said Bausen. 'One every Saturday . . . finished off five before they got him. Do you know what scuppered him?'

Van Veeteren shook his head.

'One of the people he'd picked out, Emerson Clarke, if I remember rightly, was a former boxing champion. Harridge simply couldn't cope with him.'

'Tough luck,' said Van Veeteren. 'But he ought to have taken the boxers off his list before he got started.'

'Serves him right,' said Bausen.

They both lit a cigarette and sat in silence for a while

listening to the gentle rustling among the roses. A few hedgehogs had appeared and sniffed around before drinking from the saucer of milk outside the back door, and a few swallows were still sailing back and forth from underneath loose tiles. Perhaps not exactly the sounds and creatures of the jungle, but Van Veeteren still had a distinct feeling of the exotic.

'Of course, we'll be in a different position altogether if he beheads somebody else,' said Bausen.

'No doubt about that,' said Van Veeteren.

A cold wind suddenly swept through the garden.

'Do you want to go indoors?' asked Bausen.

'No.'

'And you don't have any suspicions?'

Bausen shook his head and tasted his whiskey and water.

'Too much water?'

'No. Not even any . . . little glimmers of a suspicion?'

Bausen sighed.

'I've been in this job for more than twenty-five years. Half the population I know by name, and I know how they spend their lives – the rest I recognize by sight. There might be a thousand or two, newcomers and the like, whom I haven't got a finger on, but apart from that . . . For Christ's sake! I've thought about every one of them, I reckon, and come up with absolutely nothing. Not a damn thing!'

'It's not easy to imagine people as murderers,' said Van Veeteren. 'Not until you meet them face-to-face, that is. Besides, he doesn't have to be from here, does he?'

Bausen thought for a moment.

'You might be right there, of course, but I doubt it. I'd stake all I've got on his being one of our own. Anyway, it would be nice to be able to come up with something useful. For Christ's sake, we've spent thousands of hours on this damned Eggers!'

'There's no justice in this job,' said Van Veeteren with a smile.

'Not a trace,' said Bausen. 'We might as well put our faith in the general public. They always come up with something.'

'You may be right,' said Van Veeteren.

Bausen started scraping out his pipe, looking as if he were turning something over in his mind.

'Do you play chess?' he asked.

Van Veeteren closed his eyes in delight. The icing on the cake, he thought.

Better make the most of everything that comes along. It looked suspiciously as if things might get more difficult.

11

It wasn't only the radio station and the local press that had taken Chief of Police Bausen's orders *ad notam*. On Sunday, several national newspapers issued a serious exhortation to the conscientious burghers of Kaalbringen to go to the police without delay with any scrap of information that might possibly lead to the rapid capture of the Axeman.

When Inspector Kropke and Constable Mooser compiled the results of the general public's first day of sleuthing, quite a lot of things were crystal clear. It is true that Kropke had not had time to prepare any overhead projector transparencies before he addressed his colleagues in the conference room that evening, but everything was neatly set out in his notebook with detachable pages and dark-blue leather covers:

1) In the course of the day, forty-eight persons had reported to the police station and testified about various aspects of the evening of the murder. Of

them, eleven had been interrogated previously. Six
of the remaining thirty-seven were considered to be
irrelevant because they were in the wrong part of
town (three), or had been out at the wrong time (two)
or had got the date wrong (one – old Mrs Loewe, a
widow, had been out to buy some cat food on the
Monday morning, and had observed and noted down
several mysterious characters with axes hidden under
their overcoats).

2) The remaining forty-two witnesses, of all ages,
had been without exception in the area – Langvej,
Hoistraat, Michel's Steps, Fisherman's Square,
Harbour Esplanade, municipal woods – at some time
between 2300 and 2400 hours. Everyone's name,
address and telephone number had been meticulously
recorded, and they had also been forbidden by Kropke
to leave the town and its environs for the coming
week, in case any of them should be required to
present themselves for supplementary questioning. (A
measure that smacked very much of abuse of power,
of course, but Van Veeteren suppressed his objections.
He was not in charge of the investigation, after all.)

3) All the witnesses had at some time or other
and in various locations noticed one another, in
accordance with an extremely complicated and
potentially even more involved pattern that Kropke

had failed to program into his PCB 4000, despite repeated attempts. (The fact that this had led to a degree of annoyance and frustration was something Constable Mooser could not have failed to appreciate during the late afternoon, the hierarchy and pecking order of the police force being what it is.)

4) The earlier evidence provided by Miss deWeutz and Mrs Aalger, who had been conducting a conversation in Dooms Alley and had noticed Ernst Simmel walking across the square, had now been confirmed by four new witnesses. Two couples, who had crossed the square at around about 2320, albeit in different directions, had also noticed a lone pedestrian who, now that they came to think about it, could be identified as the deceased property developer.

5) Two teenagers on scooters (as likely as not in circumstances that placed them somewhat to the wrong side of the letter of the law) had ridden across the square towards the Esplanade about a minute later, and claimed to have passed a person who, to all appearances, seems to have been Simmel.

6) A courting couple, of which the lady for certain reasons wished to remain anonymous and therefore preferred to confirm the man's account by telephone rather than appearing in person at the police station, had been sitting, or more likely semi-recumbent, in a

car down by the marina between approximately 2300 and 0100, and at 2330 or thereabouts had seen a man smoking at the edge of the quay, scarcely more than ten yards away from their car. Both were more or less convinced that it was Ernst Simmel.

7) Up in Hoistraat, three new witnesses (to add to the other two) had seen the murdered man on the way from The Blue Ship. In addition, all three had observed one or possibly two unaccompanied male persons; in all probability this was a case of witnesses observing one another.

8) One lone witness had seen an unaccompanied man come out of Hoistraat and walk down Michel's Steps sometime between 2310 and 2315, in all probability Ernst Simmel. It is true that the distance between the witness and the person observed was some twenty yards; but since the man was under a streetlight at the time, the witness had been able to register a fairly clear picture of him. The most interesting aspect of this picture was probably that the man in question had been wearing a hat with a broad brim, which had kept his face shaded. This was one of the facts suggesting that this sighting was actually of the murderer; if that really was the case, it was the only direct sighting thus far. No male person wearing a hat had figured in any of the other reports

submitted by the citizens of Kaalbringen frequenting their town by night.

The name of the witness was Vincent Peerhoovens, and unfortunately he had been somewhat inebriated at the time of his observation and hence not entirely reliable – a fact he freely admitted and one that was confirmed by several of the other witnesses. Nevertheless, his account must naturally be regarded as extremely interesting with regard to further investigations.

9) Perhaps the most significant piece of evidence to emerge on this Sunday – which had been Chief Inspector Bausen's view, at least, when he passed comment on the material summarized by Kropke – came from four young people in their early teens who had been strolling through the woods from the harbour towards Rikken – in other words, the very path the investigation was concerned with. They appeared to have passed by the scene of the murder shortly after 2340. Since Ernst Simmel had been smoking a cigarette down by the marina about ten minutes earlier, according to witness number six, and since none of the young people appeared to have seen him, it could be concluded that when they passed the scene of the crime, the murderer had just struck and was presumably crouching over his victim in the

bushes, waiting for them to go away. (On realizing this, one of the girls had burst into a fit of hysterical sobs – the very girl, incidentally, for whose sake they had avoided contacting the police sooner. Her father was the pastor at the local Assembly of God; and at the time in question, she ought to have been at home in bed at her friend's house [another of the girls in the party of young people] instead of wandering about in the woods with a group of boys.)

Whatever, this piece of evidence suggested that the time of the murder could most probably be fixed at 2340 – give or take a minute or so.

'That's about it, more or less,' said Kropke, closing his note-book.

'We ought to give Meuritz a cigar,' said Van Veeteren. 'It looks as if he was spot-on regarding the time of death. What I want to know is how the murderer managed to cross the square. I mean, there were – let me see – six or seven people there at the critical moment.'

'Eight,' said Kropke. 'At least eight. He probably walked along the arcade. There's a line of columns along the western side of the square, the Waalska Building – I don't know if you've noticed them, Chief Inspector. The lighting is pretty bad there. None of our witnesses went that way.'

'As if built for a murderer,' sighed Bausen. 'Well, gentlemen, what do you think? A good day?'

Mooser scratched himself behind the ear with a pencil and yawned. Kropke studied his notes. Van Veeteren drained the last drops from his cardboard cup and registered that there was a world of difference between stale, lukewarm coffee and white Meursault.

'Hard to say,' he said. 'At least we've acquired a great deal of information. And tomorrow is another day.'

'Monday,' Mooser made so bold as to point out.

'He could have been waiting there in the woods,' said Kropke, who had evidently been following his own line of thought. 'We shouldn't dismiss that possibility out of hand.'

'Nevertheless,' said Van Veeteren, 'I think I'd like to conduct a series of little interviews now. Unless our leader has other tasks lined up for me, of course?'

'None at all,' said Bausen. 'Good police officers know how to keep themselves usefully occupied.'

Mooser yawned again.

12

'You were his legal adviser, is that right?' asked Van Veeteren, taking a toothpick out of his breast pocket.

'More a good friend of the family,' smiled the lawyer.

'One doesn't exclude the other, does it?'

'Not at all.'

Eugen Klingfort's office had the touch of a luxury cabin about it. Bright teak panels with heavy brass fittings here and there. Built-in bookcases with rows of leather-bound volumes, every one of them unopened since they'd left the printer's. A leather-covered filing cabinet, a bar counter that could fold into the desk, a Wassermann/Frisch safe.

The incarnation of bad taste, thought Van Veeteren. The more money they have to satisfy it with, the more ghastly it gets.

'And for how long?' he asked.

'How long? Oh, you mean . . . let's see, twenty-five or thirty years, something like that. Ever since I established myself in Kaalbringen, I think it's fair to say. Would you like a cigar, Chief Inspector?'

'No, thank you,' said Van Veeteren. 'What state were his affairs in?'

'His affairs? What do you mean?'

'I want to know what state Ernst Simmel's affairs were in. You were his financial adviser, after all; I thought we'd agreed on that.'

Klingfort lay back in his chair and let his chins rest on his chest. A bit on the corpulent side, thought Van Veeteren.

'His affairs were in perfectly good shape.'

'And his will?'

'There is no will. He didn't need one. Grete and the children will each get a share of his estate; there are no unusual circumstances.'

'How much are we talking about?'

'Now, listen here, Mr Veeteren—'

'Van Veeteren.'

'—Van Veeteren. I've already wasted enough time on that with Inspector Kropke. If you imagine that I have any intention of going through everything once again just because you are a rank higher, well . . .'

'Well what?' asked Van Veeteren.

'Well, you're deluding yourself.'

'Thank you, Mr Klingfort. I gather there must be something fishy hidden away, but we'll no doubt be able to track it down without your help.'

Eugen Klingfort snorted and lit a cigar.

'Let me make one thing crystal clear to you,' he said after creating a few thick clouds of smoke. 'There isn't the slightest trace of any irregularity with regard to Ernst's affairs or his estate.'

'So you exclude the possibility that the murderer could have had financial motives?' asked Van Veeteren.

'Yes.'

'But were there not people who owed him money?'

'Of course he had debtors. But not the kind of debts you are implying.'

'What am I implying?' asked Van Veeteren, placing his toothpick on the arm of his chair. 'Tell me!'

Klingfort didn't answer, but his face had started to turn somewhat redder.

'What do you think about the murder?' asked Van Veeteren.

'A lunatic,' replied Klingfort without hesitation. 'I've said that right from the start. Make sure you catch him, so that law-abiding citizens can wander about the streets at night without fear of assault.'

'Did you go to prostitutes with him?' asked Van Veeteren.

The question came just as Klingfort was inhaling, and

the lawyer had a coughing fit that Van Veeteren realized must have been quite painful. Klingfort stood up as quickly as his massive frame allowed, and staggered over to the window. When he came back, he took a swig of soda water from the bar shelf.

'What the hell do you mean by that?' he said when he had recovered, trying to bellow. 'This is clearly nothing short of abuse of power.'

'It's public knowledge that Simmel used prostitutes,' said Van Veeteren, unconcerned. 'I just wondered if you could give me any names.'

'Would you please get out now and leave me in peace.'

'Wouldn't dream of it. Sit down and answer my questions. This is a murder inquiry and I have the authority to take you to the station if I want to. Don't get so high and mighty, Mr Klingfort. I'm used to shooting down much higher fliers than I've noticed around here.'

Eugen Klingfort remained standing in the middle of the room with his chins on his chest. He looks like a sick walrus, thought Van Veeteren.

'You're spilling ash on the carpet,' he said. 'Well? I'm waiting for some names of those women.'

'I have . . . I have nothing to do with that side of Ernst's life,' said Klingfort, going back to his desk chair. 'Nothing! I suppose he might have gone off with the odd one of . . .

the usual ones . . . occasionally. I have no doubt the chief of police has their names.'

'I want the ones who are not known to the police,' said Van Veeteren. 'You are comfortably married, Mr Klingfort. Wife, children, your own house – don't you realize that I can make things very difficult for you if you insist on being wilful?'

The solicitor rummaged in his desk drawer. He produced a scrap of paper and scribbled down something, then slid it over to Van Veeteren.

'But I can assure you that this has nothing at all to do with the murder.' He wiped a bead of sweat from his brow. 'Absolutely nothing.'

I didn't think for a moment it had, thought Van Veeteren when he emerged into the street. But a shit needs to be reminded that he's a shit now and then.

'Are you sober today?' asked Bausen, putting the coffee tray on the table and sitting down.

'I'm alluss sober on a Monday,' said Peerhovens. 'I have a job to do, haven't I?'

'Looking after the grocery carts at Maerck's?'

'That's it. You have to take what you can get nowadays.'

Bausen held out a packet of cigarettes and Peerhovens took what he could get.

'Coffee and a cigarette – it's like I alluss said. It pays to stay on good terms with the cops.'

'I hope you haven't made this up in order to get the occasional . . . favour?' said Bausen, leaning forward over the table. Peerhovens jumped and started to look nervous.

'No, no, for Chrissake, Chief Inspector! I'd never dream of lying to the cops! I saw him just as clear as I can see you now . . . coming from Klaarmann's . . . me, that is. I'd been talking with Wauters and Egon Schmidt, if you know—'

Bausen nodded.

'I'd just passed the bookstore, on the way home. I live in Pampas, if you know—'

'I know,' said Bausen.

'Anyway, just as I come around the corner, into Hoistraat, that is, I turn left, of course, and I see a figure hurrying down the steps. He'd come from, well, from The Blue Ship, if you like, and he seemed to be in a hurry.'

'In a hurry?'

'Yeah, he was more or less running down the steps, sort of—'

'Describe him!' said Bausen.

'Well, it all happened a bit quick, but he was wearing one of those thin overcoats that was flapping a bit. And a hat, yeah, a floppy hat, sort of, and it was pulled down so I couldn't see a fuck . . . er, sorry . . . any detail of his face.'

'What colour was his coat?'

'Colour? Well, brown. Or blue, sort of. Pretty dark anyway.'

'And his hat?'

'Even darker. But not black. It all happened very quick, like I said. And I didn't really think about it then, like . . . not until Kovvy told me somebody had killed Simmel.'

'Kovvy?'

'Kowalski . . . Radon Kowalski. The guy that lives underneath me. Good solid guy.'

'When did you hear about it?'

'When? Well, I guess it must have been the next day . . . Yes, that's it . . . late afternoon. We bumped into each other on the stairs, and that's when he told me. 'Have you heard that the Axeman's killed Ernst Simmel?' he said.'

'And even so you waited until yesterday before you went to the police,' said Bausen sternly. 'Why?'

Peerhovens stared down at his coffee cup.

'Well . . . I . . .' he said. 'I don't know, really. I suppose I thought it wasn't anything important. And I'd been a bit under the weather, but then I heard on the radio—'

'How much had you drunk last Tuesday evening?'

'Hard to say . . . not easy to say,' said Peerhovens. 'I mean, I'd been at Klaarmann's for a few hours, so I suppose I'd had quite a bit. Wauters had brought a bottle of his own as well.'

'I'm with you,' said Bausen. 'And you wouldn't recognize this person if you were to see him again?'

Peerhovens shook his head.

'What did he look like, by the way? Big or small . . . well built or thin?'

'No, no, I didn't have chance to ob . . . observe that. Somewhere in between, I suppose. No, I wouldn't recognize him.'

Bausen nodded.

'What about his hat and coat? Not them either?'

Peerhovens hesitated and was given a cigarette.

'Thanks. No,' he said eventually. 'I can't really say I would.'

Bausen sighed. He stood up and left Vincent Peerhovens to his fate. At least he's bright enough to see that he'd be running a risk, he thought.

Having seen the Axeman, that is.

'Marie Zelnik?' asked Beate Moerk.

She could see that the woman on the red sofa must actually be several years younger than she was herself, and that gave her a dubious feeling of insecurity. On the one hand, it aroused a sort of dormant protective urge; but on the other, she was forced to restrain her antipathy and distaste. Repress her repugnance.

The animosity seemed to be mutual. Marie Zelnik leaned back with one leg crossed over the other in such a way that her leather skirt pointedly revealed most of her thigh. She was smoking, and examining her nails.

'I'd just like to ask you a few questions.'

'Go ahead.'

'You earn you living as a prostitute, is that right?'

'Among other things, yes.'

'What else do you do?'

No answer.

'I'd like you to tell me a bit about Ernst Simmel. I understand he was one of your clients, wasn't he?'

'What do you want to know?'

'Everything that might be of use to the investigation. How long have you . . . been in contact with him, for instance?'

'About six months, roughly . . . since he came back.'

'How often?'

She shrugged.

'Not all that often. Once a month, or even less. He went more often with Katja.'

'Katja Simone?'

'Yes.'

'We know about that. Inspector Kropke has spoken to her already.'

'So I heard.'

She stubbed out her cigarette and lit another one immediately. Disgusting, thought Beate Moerk.

'What was he like?'

'Simmel? Your average sort of John.'

Beate Moerk made a note.

'How did he usually make contact?'

Marie Zelnik thought that one over.

'Most times the same day,' she said. 'Never made an appointment . . . phoned from the pub and asked if he could come around.'

'And could he?'

'Sometimes.'

Beate Moerk was searching for questions to ask. She realized that for once, she could have been better prepared and wondered what she was really trying to find out.

'When did you last meet?'

'A week before he died, or thereabouts.'

'How did he seem?'

'As usual . . . horny as hell, not much staying power.'

To her surprise, Beate Moerk realized she was blushing.

'Did he used to tell you things?'

'What kind of things?'

'About his life – his family, for instance? His wife?'

'Never.'

'You didn't ask?'

'Why should I?'

'And he . . . paid with no problems?'

What an idiotic question! Beate Moerk could feel herself losing control now. She'd better make sure she got out of here without doing anything rash.

'Of course he paid.'

Marie Zelnik looked at her with some amusement. Beate Moerk had another go.

'And there was nothing special about him? Anything you think . . . might have been connected with his murder? That we ought to know about?'

'Such as?'

'I don't know,' Beate Moerk admitted. 'How much do you charge?' The question slipped out before she could stop herself.

'That depends,' said Marie Zelnik.

'Depends on what?'

'How they fuck me, of course. There are all kinds of variations, but maybe you don't know about that, Inspector. I only take men, by the way.'

You disgusting little bitch! thought Beate Moerk. Thank your lucky stars that I didn't set Bausen onto you! She sat for a while trying to think of more questions to put to this arrogant hussy, but nothing came to mind.

'Many thanks,' she said, getting to her feet. 'This has been a most interesting conversation. Most interesting. If

I weren't on duty, I'd probably throw up all over your fake carpet.'

At least that had gone some way towards restoring the balance, she told herself.

13

He had slept late on Tuesday.

He deserved it. A week had passed since he'd put an end to Ernst Simmel in the woods, and there was no sign that the police were onto his trail. No sign at all.

He'd never thought they would be. He'd known from the beginning that the first two murders would cause him relatively few problems. Number three was a different matter altogether, however. People had realized what was happening. It wasn't simply a one-off, as they'd imagined when they found Eggers. Not some impulsive murderer who went after just one unfortunate victim, but one with several names on his list.

Several would have to have their heads cut off before justice was done.

The images still came to him in his dreams, and just as he had expected, it was number three who stood out now – the man who was still alive and whose turn it was next. It wasn't a very clear image, however: There weren't such strong memories of him, no on-the-spot snapshot. Perhaps that corner of the sofa, though, when he'd sat there with his cool, somewhat superior air – the young, well-dressed, upper-class puppy who always got by, thanks to his breeding and social status. Who floated up to the surface when others were dragged down. Dry shod and hair neatly combed.

Who landed on his feet when others were killed by the fall. God, how he hated this self-serving aristocracy! The worst of them all . . . When he compared this one with the others, he could see it in letters of fire. He was the instigator. He carried the greatest blame; he would receive the harshest punishment. That was another reason why he needed to be extra careful this time. He must do something to make clear his significance beyond all shadow of a doubt – something extra, which had been part of his plan from the very start. Not in order to make people understand – they wouldn't in any case – they'd be horrified, perhaps, but they wouldn't understand. No, it was for his own sake.

And for hers.

He spent the morning being practical. Polished the cutting edge until it was almost impossibly sharp. Then wrapped it in the muslin rag and hid it in the usual place. Burned the coat and hat in the open fire; it was time for different disguises now. Sat for a long time at the kitchen table, smoking and thinking about how to approach it, and eventually decided on the artistic touch to make this time special. It would be bound to involve a degree of risk but very little, he told himself. Very little, and from the point of view of news value, it was most attractive. He didn't doubt for a second that this time he would dominate both television and the newspapers – for a day at least. Perhaps several.

Surprising thoughts, these. In no way had this been his motive, but perhaps it was as somebody had said: A man much prefers to die in the arena than at home in bed! So much depends on the battle itself. The actions and the drama.

Or was there something he'd misunderstood when it came to the crunch? No matter what, it couldn't be denied that the whole business had acquired a dimension that he hadn't foreseen from the start . . . hadn't taken into account. An unbidden stimulus and the sweet taste of temptation that naturally had nothing at all to do with the basic problems.

With life. With death.

With necessity.

★

In the evening he went out for a walk. Partly to recon-
noiter the area he had in mind, partly to satisfy and come
to terms with an obscure need to wander around town. His
town.

Kaalbringen. The community stuck fast to the diagonal
running from the flat plains and up to the high coast in the
east. The rounded bay, the spit of land pointing a finger at
the open sea, the busy entrance to the harbour with the
quays and breakwaters, the marina with restless luxury
yachts and cabin cruisers rubbing against jetties and moor-
ing posts . . . He spent quite a while up in the ruined
Monastery of St. Hans, with the wind and the seagulls
screaming and dancing all around him; he looked down at
the streets, the squares and the muddle of houses. The
churches: St. Bunge, St. Anna and St. Pieter; copper, copper
and red brick. The two hotels with their backs to the land,
chests towards the sea: The See Warf and the old Bendix;
the municipal woods cutting through the buildings like
a sharp-edged sword; the private houses in Rikken and
Werdingen. On the other side, hardly visible in the afternoon haze, the apartment blocks at Pampas, Vrejsbakk and
the industrial estate looking like a miniature model on the
other side of the river.

His Kaalbringen. With a sudden flash of insight, he
realized that he hadn't felt for a very long time as closely
attached to the town as he did now. In these circumstances.

Perhaps there was a meaning and a source of comfort in that . . . He was the Axeman. The town down below was in his grip of iron. Down below people were now going out in the evenings in groups, or locking themselves in. His shadow weighed heavy and dark. If the town was on the lips of people all over the country, it was no doubt thanks to him.

And this was the unexpected dimension. So far from the real force behind it all. The motive.

Could he have anything against that? He didn't think so. Perhaps he was even pleased, in some mysterious way.

Brigitte. Bitte.

It was only when the lights went on down below that he noticed the onset of dusk. He put his hands in his pockets and started strolling slowly back to town. He thought for a while about his time schedule . . . gave himself two days, no more. Tomorrow evening, or the one after; the rhythm was not without significance.

It was important to listen to the inner voice.

14

'There is a little tiny connection,' said Beate Moerk, 'but it's not much to go on.'

'What's that?' wondered Kropke, without turning his head from his computer.

'Both Eggers and Simmel had only recently arrived in Kaalbringen. Well, Simmel was coming back again, of course. But in any case, neither of them was here a year ago, for instance.'

Van Veeteren folded up his newspaper and left his seat in the window bay.

'When did Eggers turn up?' he asked. 'Was it May, or—'

'More like the beginning of April, and at first he used to travel back and forth quite a bit. Simmel moved back into his house in February.'

'And what conclusions do you draw from that?' asked Kropke.

'None at all,' said Beate Moerk. 'I just thought it might be worth noting, nothing else.'

Van Veeteren rummaged around in his pocket for a toothpick, but in vain. 'It might not be a bad idea,' he muttered. 'I think I'll make a house call now.'

House call? thought Kropke when the door had closed behind the chief inspector. What the hell does he mean by a house call?

On the way he called in on Bausen, who was busy emptying his desk drawers.

'Burning your boats, are you?'

'Yes. I don't want to leave anything compromising. Kropke can be a pedantic devil, you know.'

'No new brainstorms?'

Bausen shook his head.

'It's been ten days now. They say that if you don't clear up a case inside two weeks, you'll never solve it.'

'Lots of time,' said Van Veeteren. 'Have you spoken to that Mandrijn fellow?'

'Mandrijn? Yes, of course. Why?'

'There was just something I thought of,' said Van Veeteren. 'I hope you haven't forgotten that you promised me a chance at revenge tonight.'

'You're very welcome,' said Bausen. 'Try the Nimzo-Indian defence; then you're bound to win.'

'I'll bring a bottle with me. I don't want to steal any more of your pension.'

Bausen threw out his arms.

'If you insist, Chief Inspector.'

Van Veeteren cleared his throat and rang the doorbell.

If I carry on wandering around and interviewing people haphazardly, he thought, I'm bound to meet him sooner or later.

Always assuming it was somebody local, that is, and Bausen was pretty certain it was; and when he eventually came face-to-face with him, he would know, not an ounce of doubt about it. That's the way it generally was. That was what gave him his strength and the upper hand – his ability to know when he was face-to-face with the criminal. His intuition was almost like a woman's, and he was hardly ever wrong.

Hardly ever . . .

He rang the bell again. Footsteps could be heard in the newly built house, and then a figure came into view through the frosted-glass door.

'Just a moment!'

The door opened. Dr Mandrijn had been taking a nap,

it seemed. Or possibly involved in some mid afternoon love tryst. His black hair was ruffled, his dressing gown was gaping open, his bare feet were highlighted by the wine-red marble floor.

About thirty-five years, was Van Veeteren's immediate assessment. Successful physician and head of family. Intelligent eyes. Not especially athletic, shoulders somewhat hunched. Nearsighted, perhaps? He flourished his ID.

'Chief Inspector Van Veeteren. Have you ten minutes to spare?'

'What's it about?'

He ran his hand through his hair and fastened his belt.

'Murder,' said Van Veeteren.

'What . . . oh, yes,' said Mandrijn, coughing. 'The Axeman again? A ghastly business. Come in, by all means.'

Van Veeteren looked around the high-ceilinged, white-painted room. A large picture window looked out onto a virgin lawn. Particles of dust danced around in the rays of sunshine angled across the room. He could see that the garden would eventually be pretty.

'Did you build it yourself?'

'Well, I designed it and did all the fittings at least. It's not finished yet, as you can see, but it's possible to live here. I was up all night painting the ceilings. That's why I was having an afternoon nap. I'm on call at the hospital tonight.

What do you want to know? I spoke to another officer last week—'

'Yes, Chief of Police Bausen. I'd just like to ask a couple of complementary questions.'

Mandrijn gestured towards one of the two armchairs in the room, and Van Veeteren sat down.

'I understand that you rented the Simmels's house while they were away in Spain,' he began. 'Let me see, that must have been . . . from 1988 onward; is that right?'

'August 1988, yes. We both got jobs at the hospital at the same time, Catrine and I; she's my wife. Fresh out of medical school, both of us, and of course, we didn't know if we wanted to stay here or not. It seemed ideal to rent a house instead of buying one, or building a new one.'

'Do you have any children?'

'Two. They're at the day nursery,' he said, sounding a bit apologetic. 'Catrine's on duty today. Can I offer you anything?'

Van Veeteren shook his head.

'So you've decided to stay on in Kaalbringen.'

'We certainly have. We think it's wonderful here. The only thing is, we'd counted on staying for another six months in the Simmels's place.'

'So they came back sooner than expected?'

'Yes. The intention was that they wouldn't come back at all, but they said we could have the house for five years.

I assume he intended selling the place once they were established down there.'

'Where?'

'Where? In Spain, of course.'

'Do you have the Simmels's address in Spain?'

'No . . . no, the contact man was Klingfort, the solicitor. Why do you ask?'

Van Veeteren didn't answer. He asked another question instead.

'What was your impression of Mr and Mrs Simmel?'

Mandrijn looked out the window.

'Just between you and me?' he asked after a while.

'Yes.'

'I wasn't impressed, I have to say. I don't suppose they meant any harm, but they weren't very nice . . . well, a bit vulgar, I suppose you could say. Rich but cheap. No class, if you're allowed to say that nowadays. Especially him, of course.'

'Why did they come back?'

Mandrijn shrugged.

'I've no idea. They told us at the beginning of December that they intended coming back home, and they wanted us out of the house by February first. Pretty short notice, in fact. A damnably bad way of going about things, to be blunt about it, but we didn't want to stir things up. We'd already bought a plot, so all we needed to do was to start building.'

Van Veeteren pondered for a moment.

'Do you have any theory of your own about why Ernst Simmel was murdered?'

If he says it was a Lunatic or No Idea, that will be the fiftieth time in a row, he thought. Mandrijn took his time, rubbing away at one of his ear lobes.

'Yes,' he said, astonishing Van Veeteren. 'I've thought a lot about that. I think quite simply that it was somebody who couldn't bear to see him around Kaalbringen again. He was a real bastard, Chief Inspector. A real bastard.'

You don't say, thought Van Veeteren.

He made a detour on the way home. He felt a distinct need to stretch his legs, and to put some distance between himself and the case. Maybe also to escape . . . perhaps it wasn't all that surprising. Nothing to get agitated about. He explored a few roads he'd never been on before – not difficult around here, of course; found himself in unknown places and out-of-the-way havens, and eventually finished up on a ridge with a bird's-eye view of the town down below.

This was the countryside, not the urban environment. He followed the edge of the forest in an easterly direction, towards the restaurant Bausen had spoken about. Wandered lonely as a cloud up here, his hands clasped behind his back and the wind in his face. Some of the trees had already started to shed their leaves, thanks to the dry summer, and it suddenly struck him that there was some kind of promise in the air, or perhaps a portent. Pure imagination, of course, but premonitions are like that. When he came to the ruined monastery, he sat down with a cigarette and some unformulated questions; and it was only when he heard a dog barking in the distance that he stood up and started walking down the steps in the hillside – carved directly out of the limestone, slippery and not easy to walk on.

This would be an ideal place to have an accident, Van Veeteren thought.

When he reached the bottom, he found himself next to the graveyard – St. Pieter's Church, if he remembered rightly – the graveyard that looked out over the sea. It must have been levelled and terraced at some point in the past when they started to use it, he thought, and he spent a little time wondering what it was really like down there in the loose, artificial earth among all the caskets and cavities. He noticed the outline of The See Warf on the other side of the graves, and decided to take the most direct route.

He threaded his way through the graveyard, zigzagging along the raked gravel paths. As he passed the gravestones, he read a year here, a name there; but it was not until he'd passed through them all and was about to open the gate and leave the cemetery from the other side that he noticed him: Chief Inspector Bausen's burly figure, head bowed, standing by one of the memorial stones.

What had he said? Two years ago?

He couldn't be sure if the chief of police was actually praying. He found that hard to believe; but in any case, there was something solemn and spiritual about his expression – serene, even – and for a brief moment he felt a pang of envy. He decided on the spur of the moment not to announce his presence. To leave the chief inspector in peace by his grave.

How on earth can I envy a man who is mourning the death of his wife? he thought as he passed through the gate. Sometimes I don't even understand myself.

Back in his hotel room he lay down on his bed with his feet on the footboard. Lay there and stared up at the ceiling with nothing more in mind than smoking and giving free rein to his thoughts.

He was back in the habit: smoking, as usual, when work was getting on top of him. When an investigation was not flowing along the channels he'd dug out, or wished he had.

When everything came up against a brick wall, when the breakthrough never came.

Nevertheless, that's not really how it felt.

He thought about Bausen's two-week rule. If it was right, they had five days left. He'd spent a week in Kaalbringen by this time, and when he tried to sum up his input into the investigation so far, he got no further than the uncomfortably round number of zero.

Zero, zilch.

I can't stand hanging around here another five days, he thought. I'm going home on Sunday! Hiller will just have to send somebody else – Rooth or deBries or any other bastard he feels like. Nobody gains by my hanging around here any longer!

Living out of a suitcase in a hotel. Drinking the chief of police's wine, and being beaten at chess! The renowned Chief Inspector Van Veeteren!

The only thing that could change matters, he told himself, was the possibility Bausen had floated a few days back.

If he struck again. The Axeman.

Not much chance of that, according to the experts they'd called in. If he strikes again, we'll get him!

But there again . . . At the same time, he had this remarkable feeling that all they needed to do was wait. To hang in there. That this remarkable case would be solved, or solve itself, in some way that thumbed a nose at all the rules, and that neither he nor anybody else would be able to stop or influence . . .

After thinking these rambling thoughts and smoking four (or was it five?) cigarettes, Van Veeteren went to stretch out in the bathtub. He spent an hour pondering how to develop a Russian or Nimzo-Indian opening. Much more tangible, of course, but he didn't reach any conclusions on this either.

15

When Beatrice Linckx had parked and locked her car in Leisner Allé, the clock in the Bunges church tower struck eleven p.m. She'd been on the road since four in the afternoon, having skipped the final evaluation session of the conference, and now there were only three things she was longing for.

A glass of red wine, a hot bath, and Maurice.

She glanced up at their apartment on the third floor, saw that the light was on in the kitchen, and concluded that he was waiting up for her. It was true that she hadn't been able to get through to him when she'd tried to phone on the way home, but he knew she was due back tonight. No doubt he'd opened a bottle of something, and maybe he'd have some toasted sandwiches up his sleeve as well. Onion rings, mushrooms, fresh basil and cheese . . . She took her bags out of the trunk and crossed the street, stiff after the long journey but looking forward to what lay ahead . . . keen to get into the apartment. To come home.

What Beatrice Linckx hadn't the slightest inkling of was that the kitchen light had been on for more than twenty-four hours and that although Maurice was in fact up there, he was by no means in the state she'd expected. Nor were there any toasted sandwiches, and nobody had opened a bottle of wine to breathe – and she wouldn't be able to snuggle down into that hot bath for many hours yet. When she eventually did so, it would be in a neighbour's bathtub, and in a state that she would never have been able to foresee.

The door was unlocked. She pressed down the handle and went in.

Afterward, a lot of people wondered about her behaviour. She did as well. Given the circumstances, pretty well anything might be regarded as normal; but even so, you had to ask questions.

She switched on the light in the hall. Stared at Maurice for a few seconds, then picked up her bag again and backed out through the door. Closed it and went back downstairs. Hesitated for a moment when she emerged onto the sidewalk, then crossed the road and sat in her car again.

Sat there hugging the steering wheel and trying to heave the heavy stone of forgetfulness over the opening to her consciousness. Trying to rewind time, just a few hours . . . back to when she was happy and unaware . . . the hours before, the unsullied normality . . . the road, the cars, the oncoming headlights, the Waldstein Sonata over her loudspeakers, the rain on the windshield, the mint pastilles in the bag on the empty seat beside her . . . looking forward to coming home.

She hadn't seen anything. Still hadn't gone up to the apartment. She sat in the car and rested for a while before going up to see Maurice . . . to the sandwiches and the wine; her warm red dressing gown; the sofa and the plaid throws; Heyman's String Quintet; candles in the designer candle-stick . . . sitting here waiting . . .

Nearly two hours later she wound down the window. The evening air and a veil of drizzle crept in and brought her back to reality. For the second time, she picked up her bags and crossed the street. Didn't look up at the apartment now. Knew that all she could expect to find in store for her was Maurice, and at ten minutes past one she had calmed down sufficiently to phone the police and inform them that the Axeman had dispatched another victim.

TWO

10-24 SEPTEMBER

16

'It's the bishop that's in the wrong place,' said Bausen.

'I can see that,' said Van Veeteren.

'F6 would have been better. As it is now, you'll never manage to get it out. Why didn't you use the Nimzo-Indian defence, as I suggested?'

'I've never mastered it properly,' muttered Van Veeteren. 'There's more oomph in the Russian—'

'Oomph, yes,' said Bausen. 'So much oomph it whips up a damn gale and blows big holes through your own lines. Do you give up?'

'No,' said Van Veeteren. 'I'm not dead yet.' He checked his watch. 'Good Lord! It's nearly a quarter past one!'

'No problem. Night is the mother of day.'

'You have no more pieces than I have, after all—'

'Not necessary by this stage. My h-pawn will become a queen in another three or four moves at most.'

The telephone rang, and Bausen went indoors to answer it.

'What the hell?' he muttered. 'At this time in the morning . . .'

Van Veeteren leaned forward and studied the situation. No doubt about it. Bausen was right. It was hopeless. Black could force the exchange of both castles and central pawns, and then the h-file would be wide open. His remaining bishop was stuck behind his own pawns on the king's side. Bad play, really shitty play – he could have accepted a loss if he'd been black, but when he had the white pieces and was able to use the Russian opening, there was no excuse. No excuse at all.

Bausen came rushing out.

'Call it a draw, for God's sake!' he yelled. 'He's done it again!'

Van Veeteren leaped to his feet.

'When?'

'I don't know. They phoned in five minutes ago. Come on for Christ's sake! This is an emergency!'

He plowed his way through the undergrowth with Van Veeteren after him, but stopped at the gate.

'Oh, shit! The car keys . . .'

'Are you really thinking of driving?' said Van Veeteren. 'You've drunk at least three pints!'

Bausen hesitated.

'We'll walk,' he said. 'It's only a few hundred yards.'

'Let's go!' said Van Veeteren.

Constable Bang had been first on the scene, and had succeeded in waking up the whole apartment block in the space of a few minutes. When Bausen and Van Veeteren came around the corner, lights were on in every window and there were masses of people milling about on the stairs and landings.

Bang had placed himself in the relevant doorway, however, so there was no risk of unauthorized persons trampling all over the crime scene, at least. In firm but friendly fashion Bausen started ushering the neighbours back into their own apartments, while Van Veeteren turned his attention to the young woman sitting on the floor at Bang's feet, shivering. It looked as if she'd discovered the body and called the police.

'My name's Van Veeteren,' he said. 'Would you like something to drink?'

She shook her head. He took hold of her hands and noted that they were icy cold and trembling.

'What's your name?'

'Beatrice Linckx. We live together. His name's Maurice Rühme.'

'I know,' said Bausen, who had cleared away all the

neighbours. 'You can go with Mrs Clausewitz for the time being, and she'll give you something hot to drink.'

A chubby woman was peering at the scene from behind him.

'Come along, little Beatrice,' she said, holding up a yellow blanket. 'Come on. Auntie Anna will look after you.'

Miss Linckx clambered to her feet and went with Mrs Clausewitz as bidden, albeit unsteadily.

'There's goodness in the world as well,' said Bausen. 'We mustn't forget that. Shall we take a look? I've instructed Bang to keep the rabble at bay.'

Van Veeteren swallowed and peeked in through the door.

'God Almighty!' said Chief Inspector Bausen.

The body of Maurice Rühme was lying just inside the door, and at first glance it looked as if every single drop of blood had left it. The wall-to-wall carpet in the hall, some four or five square yards, was so thoroughly soaked that it was barely possible to guess its original colour. Van Veeteren and Bausen remained in the doorway.

'We'd better wait for the crime scene boys,' said Van Veeteren.

'There are some footprints there,' said Bausen, pointing.

'Yes, I can see them.'

'The same blow, more or less . . .'

That seemed to be right. Rühme was lying on his stomach with his arms underneath him, as if he'd fallen forward but not managed to stop himself. His head was still attached, but it looked as if it had very nearly been severed as well. His face was turned to one side and slightly upward, and his wide-open eyes appeared to be staring at a point level with Bausen's knees, more or less. Not only blood had flowed out of the opening in his neck, but also some undigested bits of food, by the look of it . . . and something fleshy that was still attached somewhere. Van Veeteren assumed it must be his tongue.

'He must have been here for some time,' said Bausen. 'Have you noticed the smell?'

'Twenty-four hours at least,' said Van Veeteren. 'Shouldn't the forensic team be here by now?'

'Five minutes, I'd guess,' said Bausen, checking his watch. 'It seems I was right about the weapon, at least.'

That was the novelty this time. In the case of Maurice Rühme, the murderer had not been content with one blow – after slashing through his neck and killing him instantly, he'd dealt him another blow. This time to the base of his spine, and he'd left the weapon embedded there.

It looked as if it was firmly entrenched. The handle was pointing diagonally upward, like some sort of grotesque phallus, back to front; and from the little of what could be made out of the blade, it seemed to be more or less as Bausen and Meuritz had supposed.

Short handle. Wide but shallow blade. A butcher's implement, evidently, of the highest quality.

'God Almighty!' said Bausen again. 'Can you really face standing here and looking at this?'

'No,' said Van Veeteren.

17

The expressway was endless.

Endless and endlessly grey. To be sure, it was only another forty miles to the turnoff for Bokkenheim and Kaalbringen, but even so, he wished he had the chance to excise the next half hour from his life. Avoid having to sit here behind the wheel and drive for mile after mile, minute after minute, with gloom and weariness building up behind his eyes like a bank of clouds. Dark and insidious.

He'd got up early. Synn and the boys were still asleep when he left. The quarrel they'd had last night prevented him from waking her up. Even as he backed the car out of the drive, he knew it was wrong.

Though it was possible she'd been doing the same thing. Only pretending to be asleep while he crept around the bedroom packing a suitcase. How could he know?

In any case, he would obviously have to call her the moment he arrived. He didn't want it to be like this. Couldn't put up with being at loggerheads, disagreeing about everything, all the unspoken antagonism – not between him and Synn. Others might be able to live with it, but not them! That was the way it was, they'd always agreed on that. Him and his lovely Synn . . .

Perhaps she'd been right, after all. Perhaps he might have been able to refuse.

'They've found another one in Kaalbringen,' Hiller had said. 'VV needs somebody to bellow at, or he won't be able to solve this case. You'd better go, Münster!'

He didn't really have any objections as such, and that was the snag. He should have. There were at least three detectives of similar standing, all of them bachelors – Reinhart, Rooth and Stauff: Hiller could have sent one of them instead.

But he'd chosen Münster.

Who'd agreed without blinking an eye. Without worrying that he'd be separated from Synn and the boys for . . . well, how long? Nobody could say. A few days? A week? Even longer? Until they had this Axeman under lock and key?

Once he'd said yes, of course, it was much harder to back out of it. Even Synn had acknowledged that eventually, but of course he ought to have thought about that from the start. That's as far as they'd got last night, and then it was stalemate. Synn had gone to bed, he'd stayed up, and he knew deep down that she was right. He did now, in any case, sitting in the car and feeling sick and driving far too fast through this unbearably grey pointlessness.

I don't want to get away from her, he thought. I want to get closer to her. Go back, not back off.

The fact that Van Veeteren had no doubt specifically picked him to help him could naturally be considered rather flattering in other circumstances, but right now, that was not much of a consolation.

I know I'm a good police officer, he thought. I only wish I was as good a husband and father as well. It sounded pretty pathetic, undeniably, and he pulled a handkerchief from his trouser pocket and blew his nose.

BOKKENHEIM, KAALBRINGEN 29, it said on the sign. He'd covered another five miles.

He found The See Warf without needing to ask for directions. Chief Inspector Van Veeteren wasn't in at the moment, he was informed, but there was a room reserved in Münster's name. Next door to the chief inspector. Had he come in connection with the latest horrible murder? they asked.

He admitted as much. And picked up his bag and hurried up the stairs.

The moment he closed his room door behind him, he darted over to the telephone. He had to wait forever before the switchboard gave him an outside line, but when he eventually heard the ringing back home, he noticed to his surprise that his heart was thumping. It reminded him of his teens, when he used to call redheaded Marie, the pharmacist's daughter, for help with his French homework. Very odd . . . but there again, perhaps it wasn't?

It was Bart who answered. Mom's gone out, he was informed. No, Bart didn't know where she was or when she'd be back; Aunt Alice was looking after them. When would Dad be coming home?

'As soon as I can,' he said. 'Say hi to Marieke and your mom. Tell Mom that I'll call her later and that I love her.'

'How gross!' said his six-year-old son, and hung up.

Münster sighed, but he did feel a bit better. Time to face the music, he supposed.

But I'd be of much more use if I could first have an afternoon nap for a couple of hours with my arms around my wife, he also thought.

18

'If Mooser would shut the door, we can start,' said Bausen.

Kropke switched on the overhead projector.

'I think it would be simplest if we were to try to map out the series of events, insofar as we know it, to sum up the situation and flesh out the bare bones for Inspector Münster.'

'Thank you,' said Münster.

'The murder victim,' said Bausen, 'is one Maurice Rühme, aged thirty-one, a doctor up at the hospital specializing in orthopaedics and back injuries. He's been working there since March. I'd like to point out for the benefit of our guests' – he eyed Van Veeteren and Münster in turn – 'that the name Rühme is not exactly unknown here in Kaalbringen. Isn't that right, Kropke?'

'Jean-Claude Rühme is a consultant at the hospital,' said Kropke. 'He also conducts a private practice at his house up the hill. I think he does various things for the National Health Board as well.'

'Maurice is one of two sons,' said Bausen. 'The other one is in the Seldon Hospice in Kirkenau . . . mentally deficient since a childhood accident. Incurable.'

'What kind of accident?' asked Münster, and Van Veeteren made a note on his pad.

'Fell headfirst from the pulpit in St. Pieter's,' explained Beate Moerk. 'Fifteen feet straight down onto the stone paving. Even I know that . . . it's part of the local folklore, you could say.'

'Hmm,' said Bausen. 'Anyway, Maurice Rühme was found dead in his apartment at 26 Leisner Allé by Beatrice Linckx, his live-in girlfriend – thirty years old, psychologist, works down the road in Kirkenau.'

'Really,' said Van Veeteren.

Bausen paused, but there was no further comment.

'She found him shortly after eleven at night last Thursday, the day before yesterday, in other words, when she got home from a three-day seminar in Kiel. She appears to have had a very nasty shock – went out and sat in her car for two hours before reporting it to us. Bang was on duty, and received the call at 0111.'

'That's correct,' said Bang.

'Van Veeteren and I got there just after twenty past,' said Bausen, 'and it was obvious to us that our friend the Axeman had struck again. Perhaps Detective Chief Inspector Van Veeteren might like to take it up from there?'

'All right,' said Van Veeteren, taking the toothpick from his mouth. 'The most interesting thing is the weapon, I assume. Forensics are still busy with it, but he left it behind this time, which might suggest that he's finished now and doesn't intend to chop anybody else's head off. That's only a hypothesis, of course. In any case, it's a damn effective weapon – lightweight and easy to handle, and incredibly sharp.'

'A child could kill with that thing,' said Bausen.

'Rühme had been lying in the hall for quite some time when we arrived,' said Van Veeteren. 'Is that a box of Danish pastries I can see behind Constable Bang?'

'Mooser, would you go downstairs and order some coffee,' said Bausen, and Mooser departed without more ado. Bang opened the carton and sniffed noisily at the contents.

'Today's,' he said.

'Anyway,' Van Veeteren continued, 'even if Meuritz hasn't delivered his last word yet, we can safely assume that Rühme had been lying there dead for at least twenty-four hours by the time we got to the scene.'

'Late on Wednesday evening,' said Bausen. 'I think we can take it that was when he struck. We have that witness as well—'

'Mr Moen,' said Beate Moerk. 'I must say he seemed remarkably clearheaded, given the circumstances.'

'Can we take the forensic details first?' said Bausen. 'Kropke, I assume you've talked to the lab?'

Mooser returned with a tray and started distributing mugs of coffee.

'Yes,' said Kropke. 'They're not finished yet – with the weapon, that is. All the marks on the floor, in the blood, were almost certainly made by Miss Linckx. Footprints, the marks made by her suitcases – they haven't found anything that didn't come either from him or from her. As for the weapon, it appears to be a special tool used by butchers and is several years old, it seems. No manufacturer's stamp or anything like that – he probably filed that away – but with a bit of luck we should be able to trace where it came from . . . in a few days, they thought.'

'Why the hell did he leave it behind?' asked Bausen. 'Can somebody tell me that?'

'Hubris,' said Beate Moerk. 'Wanted to prove he was cleverer than we are, that we'll never catch him.'

'Presumably correct,' said Van Veeteren, but Münster wasn't clear which of Inspector Moerk's assumptions he was referring to.

'Let's have a few more facts before we start speculating,' said Bausen. 'How did it happen, Detective Chief Inspector?'

'The blow came from above, in all probability,' said Van Veeteren. 'Went in more or less in the same place as in the earlier cases . . . with the same result. He evidently died instantaneously.'

'From above?' said Kropke. 'Doesn't that sound a bit unlikely? There were no signs of a struggle, were there? Or of resistance, as I understand it?'

Bausen exchanged a look with Van Veeteren, then cleared his throat and leaned forward over the table.

'We think,' he said, 'the chief inspector and I, that you could do it more or less like this, and you can make up your own minds: One, the murderer rings the doorbell. Two, Rühme goes to open it. Three, he recognizes the murderer and invites him in. Four, the murderer crosses the threshold and drops something on the floor—'

'A scrap of paper, a coin, could be anything,' said Van Veeteren by way of explanation.

'—five, Rühme bends down to pick it up, and six, the murderer strikes!'

Silence all around the table. The only sound to be heard was Constable Bang chewing away on a piece of Danish pastry. Inspector Kropke loosened his tie and looked doubtful.

'Good,' said Beate Moerk eventually. 'I think you're right – but not a coin. It could have rolled anywhere.'

'Correct,' said Van Veeteren. 'Not a coin. In any case, he had time to pick up whatever it was before making his escape.'

'He planted the axe in Rühme's back as well,' said Bausen. 'He doesn't seem to have been in much of a hurry.'

'Didn't he get any blood on himself?' asked Mooser.

'That's possible, but not enough for him to have left any traces if he did,' said Bausen. 'There are no signs of blood on the stairs or anywhere else.'

'Hmm,' said Van Veeteren. 'A pretty professional job all around, it seems; but I don't think we should put too much faith in the assumption that Rühme recognized him. There are masses of possible alternatives—'

'He could have forced him down onto his knees with a gun, for instance,' said Beate Moerk.

'For instance,' said Van Veeteren.

'The witness,' said Bausen. 'Let's examine Mr Moen's evidence a little more closely. It's crucial that we don't mess things up here.'

'Absolutely,' said Van Veeteren.

'We've spoken to him, both Inspector Moerk and I,' said Bausen, 'with somewhat different outcomes, I suppose you could say. Anyway, his name is Alexander Moen, and he lives in the apartment above Rühme and Linckx. He claims he noticed somebody coming in the front door of the apartment block shortly before eleven on Wednesday evening, and then saw the same person hurrying out again some fifteen minutes later. For the whole of that time, Moen was sitting at the table in his kitchen, looking out over Leisner Park and the avenue waiting for and then listening to the eleven o'clock news on the radio.'

'There's no reason to doubt that,' said Beate Moerk. 'It's part of his evening ritual to sit there listening. He's been doing it for the last thirty years, it seems.'

'There wasn't an eleven o'clock news until 1972,' maintained Kropke.

'Really?' said Van Veeteren. 'Anyway, I don't think it matters much. Can we get his description of this man? That's the interesting bit, of course. Bausen first.'

'OK, I talked to him that same night,' said Bausen. 'He awoke for the same reason as all the other tenants, hmm –' He glanced at Bang, who was still busy with the Danish pastries.

'– and evidently couldn't get back to sleep. Stood there on the stairs in his slippers and dressing gown at three-thirty in the morning, and was keen to give evidence.'

'He's ninety-four years old,' said Beate Moerk, to put Münster in the picture.

'Anyway,' said Bausen, 'he claimed that he'd seen a man enter the building from the direction of the park—'

'Door lock?' asked Münster.

'Hasn't been working for several days,' said Kropke.

'—and go in through the front door. He was wearing

some kind of tracksuit, dark with lighter markings. Tall and thin and carrying a parcel, or a bundle – well, he eventually decided that it was a bundle. He didn't see anything of the man's face because it was in the shadows all the time, but he thinks he had a beard – and quite long hair. Anyway, a quarter of an hour passed, or thereabouts, and then the man came out again and hurried into the park. That was more or less all, but it took more than half an hour to extract it.'

'The bundle?' asked Kropke. 'Was he still carrying the bundle when he came out again?'

'Moen doesn't remember that. He was uncertain about practically every detail, and to start with, he wasn't even sure of the day; but when we were able to link it up with what had been said on the news, we eventually concluded that it must have been that Wednesday night. The question is: Was it the murderer he saw? I have to say that I'm very doubtful.'

'Even if it was the Axeman,' said Van Veeteren, 'what he had to say might not be all that helpful. Inspector Moerk?'

'Well,' said Beate Moerk, sucking at her pencil. 'I don't know. I spoke to him this morning. I had the impression that he was a bit absentminded, but when we came to the point, he seemed to be clearer. Isn't that the way it usually is? They're generally more sure of the details than they are of the whole picture, as it were. My father's in the early stages of dementia, so I have some idea about how it works.'

'OK,' said Kropke. 'What did he have to say?'

'The same as he told the chief inspector to start with,' said Beate Moerk. 'Same times, same bundle – it's just the description that was different.'

'What did he tell you, then?' asked Mooser.

'That it was quite a short, sturdy person – powerful, rather. He sticks to the bit about the tracksuit, but he says he didn't see the man's hair because he had a hat pulled down over his eyes.'

'Did you remind him about what he'd said earlier?' asked Kropke.

'Yes, but he couldn't really remember what he'd said. It was in the middle of the night, and he was tired. I suspect the chief inspector is right: We're not going to get much useful information out of this gentleman.'

'Which doesn't prevent us from keeping a weather eye open for joggers, whether or not they're carrying a bundle,' said Van Veeteren. 'It's as long as it is short. Incidentally, Meuritz hasn't yet established the time of death. We shall see if he died during the eleven o'clock news or not. In Simmel's case, he could pinpoint the time to the exact minute; don't forget that!'

He broke the toothpick in two and gazed meaningfully at Bausen's pack of cigarettes.

'Well, that's it,' said Bausen. 'Any ideas? You can say whatever you like. We'll go through the strategy after lunch, but right now, anything goes. Well, what do you think?'

Bang belched. Kropke glowered at him, leaving no doubt as to what would happen to him once Bausen was no longer in charge, assuming that Kropke would be the one who took over, that is. Van Veeteren leaned back in his chair until it creaked. Münster sighed.

'At least one thing's obvious,' said Beate Moerk eventually. 'Regarding the motive, that is. Maurice Rühme is the Axeman's third victim, and he's the third one who moved to Kaalbringen this year. Don't try to tell me this isn't significant.'

19

It had started quite promisingly, in fact, but after ten minutes it was the same old story. The DCI's 5–1 lead was transformed via 6–6 and 7–10 to the usual and satisfying score of 9–15. In subsequent sets, Münster's greater mobility and better precision reaped their reward. His short, angled strokes interspersed with long, high lobs were triumphant as always. It was the same old story, and perhaps Van Veeteren was not in peak condition after the last few days' cigarettes and wine. In any case, after 6–15, 8–15 and 5–15, he'd had enough; and they handed possession of the court over to two young men who had spent the last few minutes watching them with a degree of scorn.

'The light is poor in this hall,' muttered Van Veeteren, and they ambled back to the changing rooms.

'Very,' said Münster.

'Not much of a floor either. Easy to slip.'

'Exactly,' said Münster.

'Hard to play with borrowed rackets as well.'

'Hopeless.'

'But we'll have another joust the day after tomorrow even so,' Van Veeteren decided. 'We need to keep in training if we're to solve this case.'

'You could be right,' said Münster.

The dining room at The See Warf was practically empty when they sat down at a window table. Only Cruickshank and Müller were adorning a table not far away, accompanied by a man and a woman from TV6. Van Veeteren had spoken to all four of them at the press conference a few hours previously, and none of them showed any sign of wanting to disturb their dinner.

'Nobody seems to be venturing outdoors any more in this town,' said Van Veeteren, looking around him. 'People are a bit illogical. This last time, he actually struck in somebody's home – Rühme's, that is.'

Münster agreed.

'I've started to believe it's a pretty weird business, this thing we're mixed up in,' said Van Veeteren, helping himself to salad. 'They do excellent fish here, by the way, especially the turbot, if you are inclined that way.'

'How do you mean, weird?' asked Münster politely.

'God knows,' said Van Veeteren, chewing away. 'Just a feeling – but I generally have my hunches.'

Münster leaned closer to the windowpane in order to see through the reflections. The sea looked dark and choppy out there. The weather had changed during the morning; banks of cloud came scuttling in from the north-west in rapid succession and one shower had followed hard on the heels of another all day. The boats in the marina were tossing about in the high waves, and Münster suddenly felt tuned to the raging of the elements, Nature's own protest at the deeds and sayings of mankind – murderers roaming around unrestrained and all that crap.

Or was it his relationship with Synn? He still hadn't been in touch with her and was starting to be annoyed by the DCI's smug musings. Still, he had a fair amount of experience, and this is how things usually went – and he hoped that everything would be back to normal when he could get through to her. It seemed selfish, to say the least, sitting here and fretting about his private life while people were expecting him to do all he could to set traps for the Executioner, or the Mad Axeman, or whatever name happened to be in vogue at the moment.

'I can't work out what his motive is,' said Van Veeteren. 'He must have a hell of a good reason for going out there and cutting three people's heads off.'

'You don't believe it's a madman, then?'

'Not for a minute,' said Van Veeteren. 'On the contrary, I think we're looking at some very carefully planned acts. His intention has been to kill these three men – Eggers, Simmel and Rühme – and that's what he's done. We won't nail him unless we can find the motive, Münster. The motive!'

'And there aren't any more names on his list?'

Van Veeteren took a sip of beer and gazed out to sea.

'God knows,' he said again. 'We must sit down and take a good look at this, Münster. There are several different possibilities, and I want us to make up our minds what our priorities are going to be.'

'What possibilities?' asked Münster, as was no doubt the intention.

'Well,' said Van Veeteren, 'off the top of my head I can only think of two. The first is, of course, that there is a clear and distinct link between the victims, that he's had an all-important reason for murdering these three particular individuals. As yet, we don't know what that link is, but it could very well be that as soon as we do, everything will fall into place. We'll have him in a little box.'

Münster nodded.

'Moerk's idea?' he said.

'Of course,' said Van Veeteren. 'That's the only one we've discovered so far. All three of them arrived in Kaalbringen this year, that much is certain. It could be a coincidence, of course, but I don't think so. There's an opening here, but where the hell does it get us?'

'Not very far,' said Münster.

'No,' sighed Van Veeteren. 'We need something more.

Although it may be that they've nothing more in common than the link with the murderer. Obviously, you'd expect the local police to find out what the connection is before we do, but if this is all there is, well . . . that means—'

'—that we'll see everything as clear as day as soon as we find him,' interrupted Münster. 'But not until then.'

'Not a damn thing until then,' said Van Veeteren. 'Would you like dessert, or just coffee?'

'Just coffee,' said Münster.

'Just let things take their course, then,' said Münster, trying not to sound impatient. 'Sooner or later we'll fall over something. Or else he'll strike again. How many new arrivals are there, by the way? He might be after all of them.'

'About fifty this year, Bausen says. But let's hope the motive is a bit more specific than that. I think we should cross our fingers and hope the press doesn't latch on to Moerk's thesis. It could be a bit awkward, providing police protection for all incomers; we've got enough panic as it is. No, let's solve this like greased lightning, Münster; I think that would be best for all concerned! I want to get home as soon as possible.'

Same here, thought Münster. He toyed with the idea of suggesting a changing of the guard, that Reinhart and

Rooth should come and relieve them; but of course, that was not very realistic. No, it would doubtless be best to consider themselves citizens of Kaalbringen for the immediate future, and if only he could get a call though to Synn, as he'd already established, he was sure he'd be able to put up with everything fate threw at him.

'What's the other possibility?' he remembered to ask.

'Huh,' said Van Veeteren, scratching the back of his neck. 'That it's all a bluff, pure and simple. *The ABC Murders* – have you read it?'

Münster shook his head.

'The murderer launches a whole series of murders to camouflage the fact that there's only one victim he has his sights on. He kills them in alphabetical order, but it's only the C murder that is significant – from his point of view, that is.'

'I see,' said Münster. 'So Eggers and Simmel might be red herrings, as it were? The victim who really counts is Rühme. A bit far-fetched, I'd have thought.'

'It could be Eggers or Simmel as well – the main character, that is – don't forget that! That would be even more far-fetched.'

'But would he keep going afterward? No, I think that's psychologically impossible.'

'Not impossible,' said Van Veeteren. 'Less credible, perhaps. The one who matters might also be number six, or number thirteen, although I'm inclined to think this isn't an ABC affair.'

'What is it, then?' Münster ventured to ask after a pause.

Van Veeteren stirred his coffee slowly with a toothpick.

'A murderer,' he said deliberately, 'who is a perfectly normal citizen of this town, and who had a damn good reason to kill Heinz Eggers, Ernst Simmel and Maurice Rühme. All of them men, all of them recent arrivals.'

Great, thought Münster. So now we know.

'How many candidates are there?' he asked.

'I've done a few sums,' said Van Veeteren. 'If we leave out the women—'

'Can we do that?'

'No,' said Van Veeteren, 'but we'll do it all the same. And the elderly, and children, which we're not really permitted to do either. Well, that leaves us with about fifteen thousand people.'

'Excellent,' said Münster. 'Can we ask all male citizens between the ages of fifteen and seventy-five to turn up at the station and produce an alibi?'

'Of course we can,' said Van Veeteren. 'I've no doubt that Kropke would be delighted to feed them all into his computer. Should be ready by around Christmas, I would think.'

'A shortcut might not be a bad idea,' said Münster.

'That's what we're going to find,' said Van Veeteren, finishing off his coffee. 'That's why we're here.'

'Really?' said Münster. 'I was beginning to wonder . . .'

'Who do you think we should concentrate on?' asked Van Veeteren as Münster reached for the door handle.

'Meaning what?'

'Well, even if this isn't an ABC affair, it might be an idea to off-load a couple of the murders. Concentrate on just one of them, as if the others had never happened. That way you avoid diluting your concentration. If we solve one, we no doubt solve them all. Three flies with one thwack.'

Münster approved.

'Maurice Rühme, in that case,' he said. 'No point in poking around old corpses when there's a fresh one at hand.'

'My view exactly,' said Van Veeteren. 'You'll go far, one of these fine days.'

'Just now I'll settle for going to bed,' said Münster. 'Good night, sir!'

20

As soon as she woke up, she went down to the news-stand and bought the newspapers.

It was part of the Sunday ritual, and she could normally count on walking there and back by the time the kettle had boiled. Today it took four times as long. Mrs Sorenson stopped her outside the front door and wanted her worries put to rest, Mr Markovic had opinions to shout down from his balcony, and Miss deMaar at the news-stand refused to hand over the papers until she had been given a detailed report on how the murder hunt was progressing. A family that had only recently moved in, husband and wife and two blubbering children, had views about the competence of the police and their duty to protect ordinary, decent citizens; and when she finally managed to get away, it was only by referring to the important interrogations she was due to conduct after lunch.

'Interrogations! Really?' growled the janitor, Mr Geurtze, who had materialized out of nowhere. 'That's something, I suppose. And when do you expect to find the next victim?'

It was impossible not to notice his sarcasm. But there again, she reminded herself that Mr Geurtze never did have anything nice to say. Not since somebody set fire to the rabbit hutches at his allotment a few years ago. She could see his point, in fact; in his world, good had surrendered unconditionally to evil. There was no reason for him to expect anything but unpleasantness and ugly stuff. It was one way of avoiding disappointment.

Perhaps that wasn't a stupid stance to adopt – not if you were a lonely old man with a weak bladder, cataracts and heart fibrillation. On the other hand, if you were a woman in her prime, perhaps you ought to try for a more balanced view of life.

Stupid old bastard, was Beate Moerk's conclusion as she locked the door behind her.

The line taken by the newspapers was more or less consistent. Two and a half months had passed since the first murder, twelve days since the second, three since the last one – surely it was high time the police spoke out? What leads did they have? What theories were they working on? Had they any concrete suspicions? The general public had a right to be informed!

Nevertheless, the criticism was not as cutting as what she'd been subjected to at the news-stand. Their faith in Bausen and the two experts summoned from outside to assist appeared to be more or less unshaken. The chief of police had evidently succeeded yet again with his spin and tactical ploys at the press conference the day before.

The speculation and guessing games were all the more wholehearted for that.

Who was this macabre demon?

A madman? A psychotic butcher? A perfectly normal citizen of Kaalbringen with a wife and children and a law-abiding lifestyle?

The latter was, of course, the most attractive possibility from a journalistic point of view – the idea that it could be anybody at all! Somebody sitting opposite you on the bus. Somebody you chatted to in the line at the post office. One of the supply teachers at the high school. A series of psychologists from various factions pontificated; one news-paper had an article in its Sunday supplement about a number of similar cases, most of them foreign and several decades old. Rolliers, the Nice murderer; Günther Katz, the grim reaper from Vermsten; Ernie Fischer, who butchered women in 1930s Chicago – not to mention the Boston Strangler and various other stars in the criminal firmament.

As there had been no clear guidance from those in charge of the investigation, the garden of speculation was in full bloom. The *Neuwe Blatt* gave prominence to the so-called Leisner Park theory, which was based on the fact that in at least two of the killings (Simmel and Rühme), the murderer had probably come from or through that park; and so he must live in one of the apartment blocks in that area. C. G. Gautienne wrote in *den Poost* that 'the accelerating tempo of the murders quite clearly indicates another outrage at the beginning of next week, Tuesday or Wednesday at the latest . . .'; whereas the *Telegraaf* informed its readers of the most effective way of protecting themselves from the Axeman, as well as passing on the prophecy of their resident astrologer, Ywonne: The next victim would probably be a forty-two-year-old man in the building trade.

Beate Moerk sighed.

De Journaal, finally, Kaalbringen's local voice in the media world, naturally devoted more space to the murders than any other newspaper – no less than eighteen pages out of thirty-two – and perhaps expressed the general unrest and the mood of the town in its front-page headline – eight columns wide and in war-is-declared typography:

WHO'LL BE THE NEXT VICTIM?

Beate Moerk dropped the newspapers on the floor and slumped back into the pillows and closed her eyes.

What she would most have liked to do, if she had been

free to respond to her body's signals, was pull the bedspread over her head and go back to sleep.

But it was eleven o'clock. High time to go out for a jog. A couple of miles west along the shore, then three or four back through the woods. It was still windy, but the rain seemed to be holding off. The wind would be behind her on the way out – that was the most important thing. Most of the time, you weren't affected by the wind in the woods.

'Don't go out on your own, whatever you do!' her mother had instructed when she phoned yesterday. 'Don't assume that he doesn't attack women, and don't fool yourself that your being a police officer will make any difference!'

If it had been anybody else who'd said that, she might have been tempted to pay some attention, but as it was, it was years ago that she had learned the trick of letting her mother's advice go in one ear and out the other. If by any chance she happened to remember any of the words spoken, it was mainly because she wanted to find justification for ignoring them.

So, let's get jogging! Obey her body's pleas to stay in bed and rest for a few more hours? No, not on your life!

A quarter of an hour later she was dressed and ready. She pulled the zipper of her tracksuit top as high as it would go, and tied the broad red headband around her hair.

She checked how she looked in the mirror. It'll do.

Fear not the devil or the fairies.

Weather, wind or wicked weapon-wielders.

Dusk closed in rapidly. It fell like a stage curtain, more or less, and when she entered her apartment it was almost pitch-dark, even though it was only seven o'clock. Her body was tired and aching now. Two hours of jogging and stretching followed by four hours of interrogation at the police station, then working out a programme for the coming week with who would do what – needless to say, it all had its effect. Who could ask for more, even from a woman in her prime?

Even so, she refused merely to flop into bed. Despite the protest from her body, she prepared an evening meal of an omelette, some greens and a lump of cheese. She washed up and made coffee. Two hours at her desk in peace and quiet – that was what she wanted. Two hours of solitary majesty, with darkness and silence forming a protective dome around her thoughts and ideas, around her note-pad, notes and speculations – it was during these evening sessions that she would solve the case. It was here, lost in thought at her desk, that Inspector Beate Moerk would seek out, identify and outsmart the Axeman!

If not tonight, then very soon, no question about it.

Was there any other cop in this country who had a more romantic attitude towards her job than she did? Hardly likely. Whatever, there was another rule she was loath to abandon, even though she was not at all clear where she had got it from: Any day you fail to carve out even a short time to spend doing what you really want to do is a wasted day.

How very true.

The triangle looked more impressive than ever. Three names, one in each corner. Eggers – Simmel – Rühme. And a question mark in the middle.

A question mark that needed to be scrubbed out in order to reveal the name of the murderer, a name that would be on people's lips forever. On the lips of Kaalbringen citizens, at least. People never forget an evildoer. Statesmen, artists and much admired performers disappear in the mists of time, but nobody forgets the name of a murderer.

Three victims. Three male incomers. All of them as different as could be – was it possible to imagine bigger differences?

A dropout, drug addict and jailbird.

An established, wealthy, but not especially attractive self-employed man.

A young doctor, the son of one of the town's most prominent worthies.

The more she stared at these names, at her notes, her

guesses and her doodles, the more obvious it became that the murder of this third victim had not provided even the shadow of a new lead.

On the contrary. The more there are, the worse it gets, it seemed.

By a quarter to eleven, she realized that she could barely keep her eyes open any longer. She switched off the light, brushed her teeth and crept into bed.

Tomorrow would be another day. She would work hard. Patiently churning through questions and answers, questions and answers . . . Perhaps it was this humdrum procedure that would eventually produce the goods. The masses of facts and minutes and tape recordings might eventually crystallize to produce a point, an accumulation of points, which could provide the basis for asking the most important question of all.

Who is he?

And it could all indicate a possible answer.

But she would much have preferred to be able to conjure up the face of the murderer, outline for outline, feature for feature. To have persuaded the dark hours of the night to carve out a portrait, a finished picture to place on the desk of the chief of police tomorrow morning.

A shortcut. A shortcut eliminating all those boring investigations.

How much more preferable?

21

Jean-Claude Rühme lived up to his prototype. A broad-shouldered man in his sixties, with a white lion's mane and sharp but totally petrified features. A cross between a human being and a monument, Van Veeteren thought. Or was it just sorrow that immobilized his face?

He received Van Veeteren in his study, sitting at his dark-coloured desk with red and ochre marquetry. He stood up and raised himself to his full height when he shook hands.

'I hope you will forgive me, Mr Van Veeteren, but I haven't been sleeping well since the accident. Please take a seat. Would you like something to drink?'

His voice was deep and resonant.

'A glass of soda water,' said Van Veeteren, 'if it's not too much trouble. May I express my sympathy, Dr. Rühme.'

The doctor barked an instruction into the intercom, and within half a minute a maid appeared with two bottles on a tray.

'I am grateful for the few days' grace you have allowed

me,' said Rühme. 'I'm ready to answer your questions now.'

Van Veeteren nodded.

'I'll be brief, Doctor,' he said. 'There are actually just a few specific questions I want to ask you, but before I do so I would beg you . . . most urgently . . . to bring to bear all your intelligence and intuition in order to help us. I prefer to regard the murder of your son as an isolated case, distinct from the others.'

'Why?'

'For several reasons, mainly to do with technical aspects of the investigation. It's easier to concentrate on one thing at a time.'

'I understand.'

'If anything at all occurs to you regarding a motive – who might have had a reason for wanting to get your son out of his way – I urge you not to hesitate. You can contact me at any time of day or night. Perhaps you already have an inkling?'

'No . . . no, no idea at all.'

'I understand that sorrow can numb the mind, but if anything should occur to you, then . . .'

'Of course, Mr Van Veeteren, I assure you that I shall telephone you. I think you said that you had some specific questions?'

Van Veeteren took a swig of soda water. He fumbled for a toothpick but thought better of it.

'How would you describe the relationship between you and your son?'

Dr. Rühme reacted by raising his eyebrows a fraction of an inch. That was all.

'Thank you,' said Van Veeteren. 'I understand.'

He jotted down a few nonsense scribbles in his notebook and allowed the seconds to pass.

'No,' said the doctor eventually. 'I don't think you understand at all. Maurice and I had a relationship based on great and mutual respect.'

'That's exactly what I have just noted down,' said Van Veeteren. 'Are you married, Dr. Rühme?'

'Divorced twelve years ago.'

'So your son must have been . . . nineteen at the time?'

'Yes. We waited until he'd flown the nest. Separated the very month he started his medical studies in Aarlach.'

'He has lived in Aarlach ever since, is that right?'

'Yes, until he took up his post at the hospital here in March.'

'I see,' said Van Veeteren. He stood up and started pacing slowly around the room with his hands behind his back. Stopped in front of a bookcase and contemplated some of the titles . . . walked over to the window and looked out at the well-tended lawns and bushes. Dr. Rühme glanced at his watch and coughed.

'I'm due to see a patient in twenty minutes,' he said. 'Perhaps you might be so kind as to ask the rest of your questions, assuming there are any more.'

'When did you last visit your son in Leisner Allé?'

'I've never been there,' said Rühme.

'Your opinion of Beatrice Linckx?'

'Good. She's visited me here several times . . . without Maurice.'

'A messenger?'

Dr. Rühme made no reply.

'Your son started his medical studies in 1982 – eleven years ago. When did he take his exams?'

'Two years ago.'

'Nine years? That's quite a long time, isn't it, Dr. Rühme?'

'Some people take longer.'

'How long did you need?'

'Five years.'

'Were there any special reasons in Maurice's case?'

Dr. Rühme hesitated, but only for a moment.

'Yes,' he said.

'Would you mind telling me what they were?' asked Van Veeteren.

'Cocaine addiction,' said Dr. Rühme, clasping his hands

on the desk in front of him. Van Veeteren made another note.

'When was he clean?'

'It came to my notice in 1984. He stopped totally two years later.'

'Any legal repercussions?'

The doctor shook his head.

'No, nothing like that.'

'I'm with you,' said Van Veeteren. 'Everything could be arranged, no doubt?'

Rühme did not reply.

'And this post at the hospital, the kind of post that everybody covets – that could also be . . . arranged?'

Rühme rose to his feet.

'Those were your words, not mine. Don't forget that.'

'I don't forget all that easily,' said Van Veeteren.

'Many thanks, Chief Inspector. I fear that I don't have time to answer any more questions just now . . .'

'No problem,' said Van Veeteren. 'I don't have any more to ask.'

'I've come to talk a bit more about your son,' said Bausen. 'Maurice . . .'

'He's dead,' said Elisabeth Rühme.

Bausen took her arm.

'Do you like walking in the park?'

'I like the leaves,' said Mrs Rühme. 'Especially when they're no longer on the trees, but they haven't started falling properly yet. It's still September, I believe?'

'Yes,' said Bausen. 'Did you meet Maurice often?'

'Maurice? No, not all that often. Sometimes, though . . . but she, Beatrice, often comes with flowers and fruit. You don't think she'll stop coming now that . . . ?'

'Of course not,' said Bausen.

'I feel lonely at times. I prefer to be alone, of course, but it's also nice when somebody comes to visit . . . Funnily enough, I usually think how nice it was afterward. When somebody's been to see me, and it's over and done with, I mean. I can feel somehow exhilarated . . . fulfilled; it's hard to explain.'

'When did you last see Maurice?' asked Bausen.

Elisabeth stopped and took off her glasses.

'I must clean them,' she said. 'I can't see properly through them. Do you have a handkerchief?'

'I'm afraid not,' said Bausen.

She put them back on.

'When did you last see Maurice?' Bausen asked again.

'Hard to say. Are you a police officer?'

'My name's Bausen. I'm the chief of police here in Kaalbringen. Don't you recognize me?'

'Of course I do,' said Elisabeth Rühme. 'Your name's Bausen.'

He carefully steered her back towards the nicotine-yellow pavilion.

'It's beautiful here,' he said.

'Yes,' she said. 'Especially after the leaves have fallen.'

'Your other son . . . Pierre?'

'He's ill. He'll never get better. Something happened in the church, don't you know about that?'

'Yes, I do,' said Bausen.

'I haven't seen him for ages,' she said pensively. 'Perhaps he can be a doctor now . . . instead of Maurice. Do you think that could be arranged somehow?'

'Perhaps,' said Bausen. A nurse wearing a white bonnet was approaching them.

'Thank you for the walk and the chat,' said Bausen. 'I'll ask Beatrice to come and see you next week.'

'Thank you,' said Elisabeth Rühme. 'It's been nice to take a walk with you. I hope I haven't been any trouble.'

'Not at all,' Bausen assured her. 'Not at all.'

So much for Doctor Rühme and his posh family, he thought as he walked to the parking lot, scraping out his pipe.

22

'Let's walk it,' Beate Moerk had suggested. 'No point in taking a car for five hundred yards.'

And so he strolled though the streets of Kaalbringen alongside this lady police inspector, and suddenly found himself thinking about Marie behind the counter at the pharmacy again. She just popped up in his mind, and he preferred not to think about why. His two telephone calls to Synn hadn't sorted out all the problems, but it looked as if they were on the right track. Obviously, everything would be back to normal if only he could get away from Kaalbringen. If only he could see her again soon.

Obviously.

The inspector's hair wasn't red. On the contrary. Dark brown, bordering on black. He was careful not to come shoulder to shoulder as they walked. Keeping a decent distance apart needed quite a lot of his concentration, in fact; and when they eventually reached their destination, he had only a vague memory of what they'd been talking about on the way there.

No great loss, he thought. They'd probably discussed mainly the names of streets and squares they'd passed through . . . but obviously, he'd been surprised. His sense of balance wasn't quite as it should be, it seemed; he felt a nagging worry that wouldn't go away. Not the best starting point for detective work, definitely not. Something gnawing away inside him. What the hell was the matter with him?

'Here we are,' she said. 'There's the entrance, and that's Leisner Park over there, as you can see.'

Münster nodded.

'Shall we walk up, then?' he suggested sardonically.

'Of course,' she said, eyeing him somewhat perplexedly.

Beatrice Linckx bade them welcome and gave them a thin smile. There was a new carpet on the floor in the hall, Münster noted. No trace of any blood, but he had no doubt it was all still there in the wood underneath.

You can't obliterate blood, Reinhart always said. You cover it up.

And then there was something about Odysseus washing his hands and the constant return of the waters of the sea that he couldn't recall exactly just now.

Pale sunlight filtered into the large living room through the tall windows, and her fragility was more obvious here. She looked composed and alert, but the surface was thin – no more than a layer of overnight ice, he thought, and hoped that Inspector Moerk was sensitive enough to recognize the signs and not fall through it.

Afterward, it was clear to him that he needn't have worried. This was Beate Moerk's interview. She was the one holding the reins, and she made sure she didn't lose control; they hadn't agreed on how to split the questioning, but the further they got, the more the teacups were emptied and refilled and the heap of light-coloured biscuits (which Miss Linckx had apparently bought from the corner shop) dwindled away, the more his respect for Inspector Moerk grew. He couldn't have done it any better himself, certainly not, and he found his role quite sufficient and rather relaxing, sitting there in the corner of the sofa and slotting in an occasional question here and there.

Totally sufficient. It wasn't just her hair and her appearance. She seemed to be a damned efficient police officer as well.

'How long had you been living with Maurice, in fact?'

'Not all that long.'

Beatrice Linckx brushed a strand of hair from her face. From right to left, a recurrent gesture.

'A few years?'

'Yes. We met in September 1988. Moved in together a year later, roughly.'

'Four years, then?'

'Yes.'

Not all that long? Münster thought.

'Were you born in Aarlach?'

'No, in Geintz, but I'd lived in Aarlach since I was twelve.'

'But you didn't meet Maurice Rühme until 1988. By then he'd already been living there for . . . six years, if I'm not much mistaken?'

'Aarlach is not a small town, Inspector,' said Beatrice Linckx, with a new, pale smile. 'Not like Kaalbringen, although we must have seen each other in the hustle and bustle occasionally, of course. We discussed that very thing, in fact.'

'Do you know anything about what he was doing during those years before you met?'

She hesitated.

'Yes,' she said. 'I know some things. But we didn't speak about it. He didn't want to, and it was a closed chapter.'

'I understand. No old friends from that time either? Who are still around, I mean.'

'Not many.'

'But there are some?'

Beatrice Linckx thought for a moment.

'Two.'

'Would you mind giving us their names?'

'Now?'

'Yes, please.'

Beate Moerk handed over her notepad and Miss Linckx scribbled down a few words.

'Telephone numbers as well?'

'Yes, please,' said Beate Moerk. Beatrice Linckx left the room and returned with an address book.

'Thank you,' said Beate Moerk when she had the notepad returned. 'Do you find it unpleasant when we poke our noses into your affairs like this?'

'You're only doing your job, I assume.'

'Why did you move to Kaalbringen?'

'Well . . .' She hesitated slightly again. 'Maurice was quite negative at first, of course. I don't know if you are aware of his relationship with Jean-Claude, his father, that is?'

Beate Moerk nodded.

'I suppose it was me who talked him around, I'm afraid. Well, it was to do with work, of course; I assume you realize that. The posts were advertised at the same time – the very same day, in fact – and I expect I thought . . . that it was a sign, as it were. Maurice thought it was something different.'

'What were you doing in Aarlach?'

'Maurice had a temporary post in the long-term ward. Not exactly his speciality. I was working at three or four different schools.'

'And out of the blue you each found your dream job in Kaalbringen?'

'Maybe not dream jobs, but a big improvement, even so. More in line with our level of education, you might say.'

Beate Moerk turned a page of her notebook and thought for a moment. Miss Linckx poured some more tea. Münster stole a glance at the two women. Tried to imagine Synn sitting in the third, empty armchair, but couldn't quite manage it – the same age, all three, more or less, he thought; and he wondered why that thought had occurred to him. Perhaps it was about time he asked a question – was that what Inspector Moerk was waiting for?

'Perhaps we should get down to the nitty-gritty,' he said, 'so that we don't need to take up too much of your time, Miss Linckx.'

'By all means.'

'Have you any idea at all about who might have killed your fiancé?'

The question was a bit brutal, perhaps. He saw that Moerk gave him a quick glance, but the reply came without the slightest hesitation.

'No. I haven't the slightest idea.'

'Did he have any enemies?' asked Beate Moerk, taking over again now that he'd smashed the door down. 'Somebody you know who didn't like him for one reason or another?'

'No, I think he was quite well liked by most people.'

'Anybody he was on bad terms with? At work, perhaps?' asked Münster, but Beatrice Linckx merely shook her head.

'Before we leave,' said Beate Moerk, 'we'll ask you for a list of your closest friends and the colleagues Maurice had most to do with, but perhaps you could tell us about the most important ones right now?'

'Who might have murdered him, you mean?'

For the first time there was a hint of hostility in her voice.

'Most murders are committed by somebody quite close to the victim,' said Münster.

'What are you getting at?' said Beatrice Linckx, and red patches started to grow on her cheeks. 'I can't think of a single name . . . I haven't the slightest suspicion. I took it for granted that we were dealing with this madman . . . isn't that the case? I mean, he's already killed two people who had nothing at all in common with Maurice.'

'I'm sorry, Miss Linckx,' said Beate Moerk. 'I'm afraid we have to ask you all kinds of questions, and some of them might appear to be bizarre or impertinent. Would you please promise that you'll contact us the moment you think of even the slightest little thing that could have to do with the murder?'

'A telephone call, somebody who said something that seemed a bit odd, if Maurice ever acted strangely in some way or other,' added Münster.

'Of course,' said Beatrice Linckx. 'I don't want to criticize the police in any way. Obviously, there's nothing I want more than for you to catch him.'

'Good,' said Münster. 'Speaking of colleagues, by the way – Dr. Mandrijn, is he somebody Maurice had much to do with? He works at the hospital as well.'

She thought about it.

'A bit, I think,' she said. 'But not much . . . I'm not sure who he is, but Maurice did mention his name once or twice.'

Inspector Moerk made a note, and chewed at her pen.

'You work at the Seldon Hospice, is that right?' she asked.

'Yes.'

'As a welfare officer?'

'As a psychologist, rather—'

'Do you come into contact with Pierre, Maurice's brother?'

Beatrice went over to the window and looked out over the park before answering.

'Nobody comes into contact with Pierre,' she said at length. 'Nobody at all.'

'I understand,' said Beate Moerk.

When they came out, they found that it had started raining again; and when she suggested they should have a beer at The Blue Ship, he agreed without a second thought. It was true that they'd downed so much tea that their need of fluid intake was fulfilled for some considerable time to come; but it was a good idea to become acquainted with this establishment as well. If his memory served him correctly, it was from there that the second victim, Ernst Simmel, had embarked on the last stroll he would ever take in this life.

He opened the door and bowed somewhat chivalrously. What the devil am I doing? he thought.

'Are you married?' she asked when they had sat down.

Münster took out his wallet and showed her a photograph of Synn.

'She's pretty,' said Beate Moerk. 'Good, I don't need to worry.'

'Two kids as well,' said Münster. 'What about you?'

'No to both questions,' said Beate Moerk with a smile. 'But that's only temporary.'

'Cheers,' said Münster, and smiled as well.

23

'Cocaine?' wondered Bausen.

'It's a link, in any case,' said Kropke. 'To Eggers, that is.'

'Doubtful,' said Münster.

'A weak link, in that case,' said Van Veeteren. 'Cocaine is an upper-class drug; don't forget that. I doubt if Heinz Eggers and his mates used to sit around and get high on anything as sophisticated as that. Not their line, as simple as that.'

Bausen agreed.

'But we have to follow it up, of course. Mind you, given the number of people on drugs nowadays, it's probably no more than a normal statistical probability.'

'Two out of three?' asked Inspector Moerk.

'A bit high perhaps, I grant you. But of course we must look into it. We don't have much else to do, let's face it.'

'How far is it between Selstadt and Aarlach?' asked Münster.

'A hundred, hundred and twenty miles, I suppose,' said Bausen.

'A hundred and eleven and a half,' said Kropke.

'Just checking to make sure you were awake,' said Bausen. 'Van Veeteren?'

Van Veeteren stopped rolling a coin over his knuckles.

'Well,' he said. 'I think it's as important as it damn well can be for us to get Rühme's time in Aarlach mapped out as accurately as possible. I've spoken to Melnik, the chief of police there, and he's promised to put two men onto it – probably has already, in fact. He'll send us a report as soon as he's done, in any case – in a few days, I hope. A week, perhaps.'

'And then what?' asked Kropke.

'We'll have to see,' said Van Veeteren. 'If nothing else, we can pick out all the names and run them against all the material we have on Eggers and Simmel. That could be a job for you, Kropke, and your computer?'

Kropke frowned for a moment, but then his face lit up.

'All right,' he said. 'Not a bad idea, I suppose.'

'OK,' said Bausen. 'The neighbours, Mooser? How has that gone?'

Mooser leafed slightly nervously through his papers.

'We've been in touch with all of them but two – twenty-six in all. Nobody's seen a damn thing – between ten last

Wednesday night and two the next morning, that is. Those were the times we said, weren't they?'

'That's correct,' said Bausen. 'Meuritz guesses it was some time around about then. He was reluctant to be more precise than that on this occasion – not possible, I assume. I can't help feeling he's had a damn great stroke of luck, our dear friend the Axeman. In Simmel's case he followed him all the way through town, more or less, but with Rühme he just strolls across the street and into the apartment block. Rings the doorbell and cuts his head off. And nobody sees him. No witnesses.'

'Apart from Moen,' said Beate Moerk.

'Ah, yes,' said Bausen with a sigh. 'Moen and Peerhovens . . . one of them aged ninety-five years and the other'd made a night of it and was less than sober.'

'Ah, well,' said Van Veeteren. 'No doubt we'll nail him before long. I think I sniff the traces of a scent—'

'What do we do first?' asked Beate Moerk.

Bausen leafed through his notebook.

'You and . . . Münster, perhaps?'

Münster nodded.

'You take the hospital. Colleagues, and anybody else who strikes you. See what you can get out of them. You have a blank check.'

'Good,' said Beate Moerk.

'Kropke and Mooser . . . I think we need to extend the

neighbourhood a bit. Knock on a few doors around Leisner Park as well. Kropke can draw up a plan. Take Bang with you – he needs a bit of exercise – but for God's sake, write down your questions in advance. And Kropke keeps pressing ahead with Simmel and Spain as well, of course. Nothing's turned up there yet, I don't suppose?'

Kropke shook his head.

'A lot of crap, but nothing significant.'

'DCI Van Veeteren and I ought to take a closer look at the axe,' said Bausen. 'The guys in forensics are a bit vague, but their best guess is that it's a specialist tool used in the butchery trade, made around ten or twelve years ago. We've got the names of four possible manufacturers – and ten or so possible retail outlets. It doesn't sound very promising, of course, but I suppose we'd better waste a day on it, even so. And then we have Simmel's son and daughter coming here tomorrow. Mustn't forget them, even if I wouldn't put a lot of money on them either, but still, you never know. Any questions?'

'Who's going to do the friends and acquaintances?' asked Münster. 'Rühme's, that is.'

'You two,' said Bausen. 'But the hospital first. You have the list, don't you?'

'Shouldn't we send somebody to Aarlach?' asked Beate Moerk. 'That must be the place where we're most likely to draw out a lead, surely?'

'DCI Melnik wouldn't appreciate any outside interference, I can assure you of that,' said Van Veeteren. 'But he can establish the age of a lump of dog shit if he's feeling inspired.'

'Really,' said Beate Moerk. 'One of those, is he?'

'I have some appointments with a few of Simmel's lady friends as well,' said Van Veeteren. 'I'm looking forward to that very much.'

Phew! thought Beate Moerk as she left the police station. What a miserable bunch.

'How far is it to the hospital?' asked Münster.

'A long way,' said Moerk. 'We'll take your car.'

24

He looked around. Then sat down at one of the empty tables on the glazed-in terrace, ordered a glass of stout and spread out *de Journaal* in front of him. He breathed a sigh of cautious satisfaction. It was some time since he'd last been to The Fisherman's Friend.

He took several long draughts of beer, then started to read what they'd written about the case. Not without a degree of satisfaction. This was the fifth day after the latest murder, and the coverage was still more than two pages. There was very little new information; the theories were becoming increasingly absurd, as far as he could judge . . . the silence on the part of the police was bound to irritate the journalists, no doubt, and it looked as if several of them were losing faith.

No wonder, he thought, and gazed down at the harbour. No wonder. A solitary trawler was making its way out towards the open sea from down below. The sea and the sky were an identical shade of grey; the sun appeared unwilling to show itself today. It looked disconsolate.

Disconsolate? For a brief moment he wondered why that particular word had occurred to him.

He had killed three people and the police didn't have a single lead, as far as he could tell. It would have been interesting to see what they wrote in the other papers as well, but they'd been sold out. For obvious reasons, to be sure. He took another draught of beer and allowed the brewer's wort to force tears into the corners of his eyes. No, if he understood the situation rightly, he was as safe as ever.

Beyond reach and beyond punishment.

It felt somewhat remarkable, no doubt about that, although on the other hand, it was more or less what he'd reckoned on . . . wasn't it? Had he reckoned on anything at all, in fact? Was there an afterward? Had he thought about this period? The long drawn-out epilogue, or whatever it was?

He watched the gulls circling around the top of the cliff. They sometimes came so close that their wing tips brushed against the window . . . and he suddenly recalled how he'd been sitting up here one day when one of them had flown straight into the windowpane. At full speed, without checking. It had presumably had a clear view ahead, and death against the cold glass must have come as a complete shock to the poor bird. No notice, no premonitions . . . just like the blow from the axe, it seemed to him, and he sat for quite a while thinking about that bird and the smear of blood and innards it had left clinging to the pane, which he was able to conjure up in his mind's eye, for some reason. And then he thought about the woman for whose sake all this was taking place . . . about her, whose death had not come as a shock at all – it was more a case of a fruit becoming ripe – and he wondered if it really was all over now, everything. If everything had been restored to its rightful place, justice achieved, and if there was any possibility of her being able to give him a sign. And if so, where that could happen . . .

There was probably more than one place, now that he came to think about it.

And about how he would cope with this new emptiness that seemed to have replaced the previous one, and sometimes felt like an enormous vacuum inside him. Insistent and almost endless. But inside him.

I have dug a hole in order to fill another one, he thought. And this new one is so much bigger. Give me a sign, Bitte!

'A spectacular place,' said Van Veeteren, looking around.

'The terrace is best,' said Bausen. 'You're sitting on top of the world, as it were.'

Van Veeteren sat down. Thought fleetingly about The

Blue Ship. It was quite empty up here as well, but perhaps it was different in the evenings. At the moment, there was only a solitary gentleman with a newspaper by the picture window, and a few women in hats just in front of the grand piano. A waiter dressed in black bowed and handed over two menus bound in leather.

'Lunch,' said Van Veeteren. 'Now it's my turn. Get enough inside you to keep you going for a while. We all work best on a full stomach – think best, at least.'

'I wasn't born yesterday,' said Bausen.

'I can't take any more of this,' said Beate Moerk. 'If I have to talk to another single doctor, I'll strangle him.'

'Go back to the car and wait,' said Münster. 'I'll deal with this Mandrijn person – he's due in five minutes.'

'Is he the one who lived in Simmel's house?'

Münster nodded.

'OK,' said Beate Moerk. 'Give him what he deserves. I'm going to lie down on the back seat under the blanket.'

'Good,' said Münster.

'My name is Inspector Kropke,' said Kropke.

'Funny first name,' said the woman, with a yawn. 'But come in, even so.'

'So you lived next door to the Simmels in Las Brochas?'

'I certainly did.'

'Did you mix with them socially as well?'

'I wouldn't say that.'

'Why not?'

She raised her eyebrows a little.

'Why not? Because we had no desire to mix with them, of course. We met at the occasional party, naturally, but the bottom line was that they didn't have any style. My husband had quite a lot to do with Ernst, but I could never make her out.'

'Her?'

'Yes, the wife . . . Grete, or whatever her name is.'

'Were there any . . . improprieties as far as the Simmels were concerned?'

'Improprieties? What do you mean by that?'

'Well, did you hear anything . . . did they have any enemies, was there anything illegal, for instance? We're trying to find a motive, you see—'

'My dear Inspector, we don't go ferreting about for such things in Las Brochas. We leave everybody in peace there. Lots of people have moved there precisely to get away from all the interfering authorities who can't stop sticking their noses into other people's business.'

Style? thought Kropke.

'So that's the way it is,' he said. 'Maybe you think we

shouldn't give a toss about tracking down murderers and that kind of thing?'

'Don't be silly. Go and do your job. That's what you're paid to do, after all. But leave honest folk in peace. Was there anything else?'

'No, thank you,' said Kropke. 'I think I've had enough.'

'Name and address?' said Bang.

'Why?' asked the twelve-year-old.

'This is a police investigation,' said Bang.

'Uwe Klejmert,' said the boy. 'The address is here.'

Bang noted it down.

'Where were you on the evening of Wednesday, September eighth?'

'Is that last week? When the Axeman murdered Maurice Rühme?'

'Yes.'

'Then I was at home.'

'Here?'

'Yes. I watched *Clenched Fist* till ten o'clock. Then I went to bed.'

'Did you notice anything unusual?'

'Yes, my sister had made my bed.'

'Nothing else?'

'No. Did he scream?'

'Who?'

'Rühme.'

'I don't think so,' said Bang. 'I didn't hear anything, in any case, and I was the first on the scene. Are your parents not at home?'

'No,' said the boy. 'They're at work. They'll be home around six.'

'All right,' said Bang. 'Tell them to report to the police if they think they might have some significant information.'

'Signi . . . ?'

'Significant. If they've seen or heard anything odd, that is.'

'So that you can nail the Axeman?'

'Exactly.'

'I promise,' said Uwe Klejmert.

Bang put his notebook away in his inside pocket, and saluted.

'Aren't you going to ask me why Sis made my bed?'

'All right,' said Bang. 'Why did she? I've never heard of a sister making the bed for anybody.'

'She'd borrowed my Walkman and broke the ear-phones.'

'Typical sister,' said Bang.

★

'Do you have a pleasant time at your hotel in the evenings, you and DCI Van Veeteren?' asked Beate Moerk.

'Very pleasant,' said Münster.

'Otherwise I could offer you a toasted sandwich and a glass of wine.'

'Tonight?'

'Why not?' said Beate Moerk. 'But I'm afraid I wouldn't be able to avoid talking shop.'

'That's no problem,' said Münster. 'I have a feeling we ought to get this case solved pretty damn soon.'

'My own feeling precisely,' said Beate Moerk.

25

She swooped down on him just outside the entrance, and he realized she must have been standing there, waiting. Hidden by the privet hedge that ran all the way along the front of the hotel, presumably. Or behind one of the poplars.

A tall and rather wiry woman in her fifties. Her dark flower-patterned shawl was tied loosely around her hair and fell down over her high shoulders. For a brief moment he thought she might be one of his teachers from high school, but that was no more than a fleeting impression; he could never remember names and, in any case, it wouldn't have been possible.

'Detective Chief Inspector Van Veeteren?'

'Yes.'

She put her hand on his arm and looked straight at him from very close quarters. Stared him in the eye, as if she were very nearsighted or were trying to establish an unusual level of intimacy.

'Could I speak to you for a few minutes, please?'

'Of course,' said Van Veeteren. 'What's it about? Shall we go inside?'

Is she mad? he wondered.

'If you could just walk around the block with me. I prefer to talk out of doors. It'll only take five minutes.'

Her voice was deep and melancholy. Van Veeteren agreed and they started walking down towards the harbour. They turned right into Dooms Alley, in among the topsy-turvy gables, and it was only when they had entered the deep shadow that she started to present her problem.

'It's about my husband,' she explained. 'His name's Laurids and he's always had a bit of a problem with his nerves . . . nothing he couldn't get over; he's never been put away or anything like that. Just a bit worried. But now he no longer dares to leave home . . .'

She paused, but Van Veeteren said nothing.

'Ever since last Friday – that's almost a week now – he's stayed home because he's frightened of the Axeman. He doesn't go to work, and now they've told him he'll be fired if he goes on like this—'

Van Veeteren stopped in his tracks.

'What are you trying to tell me?'

She let go of his arm. Stared down at the ground as if she were ashamed.

'Well, I thought I'd track you down and ask how it's

going . . . I told him about it, and I do think that he would dare to go out again if I could go back home with some kind of reassuring or soothing comment from you.'

Van Veeteren nodded. Good God! he thought.

'Tell your husband . . . what's your name, by the way?'

'Christine Reisin. My husband's called Laurids Reisin.'

'Tell him he has no need to be afraid,' said Van Veeteren. 'He can go back to work. We're very hopeful we can nail this murderer in . . . six to eight days at most.'

She looked up and eyed him from close quarters again.

'Thank you, Mr Van Veeteren,' she said eventually. 'Very many thanks. I feel I can rely on you.'

Then she turned on her heel and vanished into one of the narrow alleys. Van Veeteren stood there watching her.

How easy it is to fool a woman, he thought. A woman you've only known for five minutes.

The episode stuck in his mind, and as he stood in the shower, trying to scrub her out of his memory, it became clear to him that Laurids Reisin would hang over him like a bad conscience for as long as this investigation lasted.

The man who daren't leave home.

Somebody was on the way to losing his job – and his dignity, no doubt – simply because Van Veeteren and the others – Münster, Bausen, Kropke and Moerk – couldn't track down this damn murderer.

Were there more like that, perhaps? Why not?

How much collective fear – terror and dread – was in existence at this moment in Kaalbringen? Assuming it was possible to measure such things . . .

He stretched out on his bed and stared up at the ceiling.

Counted.

Six days since the murder of Maurice Rühme.

Fifteen since Simmel.

Eggers? Two and a half months.

And what did they have?

Well, what? A mass of information. An absolute abundance of details about this and that – and no pattern.

Not the slightest trace of a suspicion, and no leads at all.

Three men who had recently moved into Kaalbringen.

From Selstadt, from Aarlach, from Spain.

Two were drug abusers; one of those had given it up several years ago. The weapon was under lock and key. The murderer had handed it over to them himself.

Melnik's report? Hadn't arrived yet, but was that anything to count on? The material they had on Eggers and Simmel, and what little they had on Rühme, had so far turned up no similarities at all, apart from the way they'd died, the way he'd gone about it. No name in the background to link them together – nothing. Would anything turn up in Aarlach? He doubted it.

Damnation!

He didn't even have a hunch, and he usually did. Not a single little idea, nothing nagging away inside his brain, trying to draw attention to itself – nothing odd, no improbable coincidences, nothing.

Not a damned thing, as they'd said.

It was as if the whole of this case had never really happened. Or had taken place on the other side of a wall – an impenetrable, bulletproof glass pane through which he could only vaguely make out a mass of incomprehensible people and events, dancing slowly in accordance with some choreography that made no sense to him. All the different, pointless and meaningless connections . . .

A course of events with one single, totally blind, observer. DCI Van Veeteren.

As if it didn't affect him.

And then Laurids Reisin.

There again, wasn't it always like this? he asked himself as he fumbled around in his pockets for his pack of cigarettes. Wasn't this just the usual familiar feeling of alienation that occasionally used to creep up on him? Wasn't it . . . ?

The hell it was! He cut his train of thought short.

Produced a cigarette. Lit it and went to stand by the window. Looked out over the square.

Darkness was closing in over the town. The shops had closed for the day, and people were few and far between; the stall holders outside the covered market were busy packing up their wares, he noted. Over there in the arcade a few musicians were playing for deaf ears, or for nobody at all. He raised his gaze and eyed the churchyard and the path up to the steep hill on the edge of his field of vision; he looked farther left: the tower blocks in Dünningen. To the right: the municipal woods, Rikken and whatever it was called, that other district. Somewhere or other . . .

. . . somewhere or other out there was a murderer, feeling more and more secure.

We have to make a breakthrough now, thought Van Veeteren. It's high time.

So that people dare to go out – if for no other reason.

Bausen had already set up the board.

'Your turn for white,' said Van Veeteren.

'The winner gets black,' said Bausen. 'Klimke rules.'

'All right by me,' said Van Veeteren, moving his king's pawn.

'I brought up a bottle,' said Bausen. 'Do you think a Pergault '81 might help us to get out of the shit?'

'I couldn't possibly think of any better assistance,' said Van Veeteren.

'At last!' he exclaimed an hour and a half later. 'Dammit all, I thought you were going to wriggle your way out, despite everything.'

'Impressive stuff,' said Bausen. 'A peculiar opening . . . I don't think I've come across it before.'

'Thought it up myself,' said Van Veeteren. 'You have to be on your toes, and you can never use it more than once against the same opponent.'

Bausen drank to his health. Sat quietly for a while, gazing down into his empty glass.

'Damn,' he said. 'This business is starting to get on my nerves, to be honest. Do you reckon we're going to crack it?'

Van Veeteren shrugged.

'Well . . .'

'Keysenholt phoned half an hour before you showed up,' said Bausen. 'You know, the regional boss. Wanted to know if I was prepared to go on. Until we'd cracked the case, that is . . .'

Van Veeteren nodded.

'The snag is that he didn't actually ask me to keep going. Just asked what I thought about it. Wanted me to make the decision. Damn brilliant way to bow out, don't you think? Condemn yourself as incompetent, then retire!'

'Well, I don't know –' said Van Veeteren.

'The trouble is, I don't really know myself. It wouldn't be very flattering to give yourself a few extra months and then mess it up all the same. What do you think?'

'Hmm,' said Van Veeteren. 'A bit awkward, no doubt about it. It might be best to nail the bastard first, perhaps?'

'My view exactly,' said Bausen. 'But I have to give this blasted Keysenholt some kind of answer. He's going to phone again tomorrow—'

'Will it be Kropke who takes over?'

'Until the end of the year, at least. They'll no doubt advertise the post in January.'

Van Veeteren nodded. Lit a cigarette and pondered for a moment.

'Tell Keysenholt you don't understand what he's babbling about,' he said. 'The Axeman will be behind bars within six to eight days, give or take.'

'How the hell can I claim that?' said Bausen, looking doubtful.

'I've promised to solve it before then.'

'Three cheers for that,' said Bausen. 'That makes me feel much better, of course. How do you intend going about it?'

'I'm not sure,' said Van Veeteren. 'But if you were to

bring up a decent – let me see – a decent Merlot, I'd set up the pieces while you're away. No doubt we'll hit on an opening.'

Bausen smiled.

'A homemade one?' he asked, rising to his feet.

'They're usually the best.'

Bausen disappeared in the direction of his wine cellar.

So that's how easy it is to fool an honest old chief of police, thought Van Veeteren. What on earth am I doing here?

26

'But if . . .' said Beate Moerk, scraping a blob of candle wax off the tablecloth. 'If Rühme opened the door because he recognized the murderer, that ought to mean that we have his name somewhere on our lists.'

'Good friend or colleague, yes,' said Münster. 'Do you have anybody in mind?'

'I'll go get my papers. Have you finished eating?'

'Couldn't eat another crumb,' said Münster. 'Really delicious . . . a scandal that you live on your own.'

'In view of the fact that I can make toasted sandwiches, you mean?'

Münster blushed.

'No . . . no, in general, of course. A scandal that the men . . . that nobody has got you.'

'Rubbish,' said Beate Moerk, heading for her study.

What a brilliant conversationalist I am, thought Münster.

★

'If we say that it's a man, that means precisely ten possibilities, in fact.'

'Not more?' said Münster. 'How many are left if we assume that he lives here in Kaalbringen?'

Beate Moerk counted them up.

'Six,' she said. 'Six male friends or colleagues. A bit thin, I'd say.'

'They'd only recently moved here,' said Münster. 'They can't have all that big a circle of friends yet. Who are the six?'

'Three colleagues they occasionally saw socially . . . and three couples, it seems.'

'Names,' said Münster.

'Genner, Sopinski and Kreutz – they're the doctors. The friends are Erich Meisse, also a doctor, incidentally, and . . . hang on a minute. Kesserling and Teuvers. Yes, that's the lot. What do you think? Meisse is a colleague of Linckx's, I think.'

'I've met them all, apart from Teuvers and Meisse. I wouldn't have thought it was any of them, but that's no guarantee of anything, of course. Even so, shall we say it must be . . . Teuvers?'

'All right,' said Beate Moerk. 'That's that solved, then. There's just one little snag, though—'

'What's that?'

'He's been away for three weeks. Somewhere in South America, if I'm not much mistaken.'

'Oh, shit,' said Münster.

'Shall we say it was somebody he didn't know, then?'

'That might be just as well. Not any of these, at least. It could have been a celebrity as well. Somebody everybody recognizes, I mean. The finance minister or Meryl Streep or somebody . . .'

'Would you open your door for Meryl Streep?' asked Beate Moerk.

'I think so,' said Münster.

Beate Moerk sighed.

'We're not getting anywhere. Would you like some coffee?'

'Yes, please,' said Münster. 'If you make it, I'll wash the dishes.'

'Excellent,' said Beate Moerk. 'I hope you didn't think I'd turn the offer down.'

'Not for a second,' said Münster.

'Are you used to this sort of thing?'

'Depends what you mean by used to,' said Münster.

'How many murderers do you generally track down per year?'

Munster thought for a moment.

'Ten to fifteen perhaps . . . although we hardly need to track down most of them. They turn up of their own accord, more or less. Come and give themselves up, or it's just a matter of going around and collaring them – a bit like picking apples, really. Most cases are sorted out within a few weeks, it's fair to say.'

'Cases like this one, though? How often do they crop up?'

Münster hesitated.

'Not so often. One or two a year, perhaps.'

'But you solve them all?'

'More or less. Van Veeteren doesn't like unsolved cases. He's usually impossible to live with if it drags on too long. As far as I know, there's only one case that he's had to shelve – the G-file. Must be five or six years ago now. I think it's still nagging him.'

Beate Moerk nodded.

'So you think he'll be the one who cracks this one as well?'

Münster shrugged.

'Highly likely. The main thing is that we get him, I suppose. There'll be enough glory to go around for all of us. Don't you think?'

Beate Moerk blushed. She turned her head away and ran her hand through her hair, but Münster had noted her reaction.

Aha, he thought. An ambitious young inspector. Maybe fancies herself as a private detective?

'Have you any theories of your own?' he asked.

'Of my own? No, of course not. I think about it a lot, naturally, but I don't seem to get anywhere.'

'That's how it usually looks,' said Münster.

'Meaning what?'

'That you think you're just marking time and getting nowhere; then suddenly, off you go – some little detail starts to grow and becomes significant, and then it goes very quickly.'

'Hmm,' said Beate Moerk. She stirred her coffee and scraped at another blob of candle wax with her nail.

'Do you mind if I make a confession?' she said after a pause.

'Go ahead,' said Münster.

'I think . . . think it's exciting, being in the middle of it all. I mean—'

'I know,' said Münster.

'—I realize my first thought ought to be that it's terrible and awful, and I should be out there hunting down this mad Axeman because he's a horrific criminal, and because honest people need to be able to sleep at night. And I do think that, of course, but . . . but I have to admit that I quite enjoy it as well. That's pretty perverse, don't you think?'

Münster smiled.

'I don't think so,' he said.

'You think the same!' exclaimed Beate Moerk, and suddenly, for one giddy fraction of a second, something happened inside Münster's head – the unfeigned look on her face as she said it, the fresh, slightly childlike expression in her face – genuine, pure; he didn't really know why, but it gave him a jolt, in any case, and reminded him of something that . . . that belonged to another chapter of his life. Something he'd already read. Enjoyed and given in to. Of course, he ought to have been expecting it and, needless to say, he was. There had been something about that walk through the town, the beer at The Blue Ship, their conversation in between the interviews – playful and almost wanton – something that was so banal and so obvious that he quite simply didn't dare put it into words.

'Well,' he said. 'I have thought . . . in the beginning, that is. You get your fingers burned.'

It wasn't that she was trying to lead him on. On the contrary, really. Presumably, he tried to convince himself, it was the knowledge that he was married, the knowledge that Synn existed that had caused her to let herself go a bit, allowed him to come close to her – because she knew she was safe.

Safe? What about him, though?

'A penny for your thoughts.'

He realized that she was looking at him again, and that his mind must have wandered off for a few seconds.

'I . . . don't know really,' he said. 'The Axeman, I suppose.'

'What does your wife think about your job?'

'Why do you ask?'

'Answer first.'

'What Synn thinks about my job?'

'Yes. That you have to be away from home. Now, for instance.'

'Not much.'

'Did you quarrel before you left for here?'

He hesitated.

'Yes, we quarrelled.'

Beate Moerk sighed.

'I knew it,' she said. 'I'm asking because I want to know if it's really possible to be a police officer and be married as well.'

'Possible?'

'Tolerable, then.'

'That's an old chestnut,' said Münster.

'I know,' said Beate Moerk. 'Can you give me a good answer, though, as you've been in the job for some time?'

Münster thought it over.

'Yes,' he said. 'It must be possible.'

'As easy as that, is it?'

'It's as easy as that.'

'Good,' said Beate Moerk. 'You've taken a weight off my chest.'

Münster coughed and wished he could think of something sensible to say. Beate Moerk was watching him.

'Maybe we should change the subject?' she said after a while.

'That would probably be safest,' said Münster.

'Shall we look more closely at my private thoughts? About the Axeman, that is.'

'Why not?'

'Unless you think it's too late, of course.'

'Too late?' said Münster.

The only thing that's preventing her from seducing me is herself, he thought. I hope she's strong enough . . . I wouldn't want to look myself in the eye tomorrow morning.

'Would you like any more wine?'

'Good God, no,' said Münster. 'Black coffee.'

27

'Melnik has gallstones,' said Kropke.

'What in hell's name . . . ?' said Van Veeteren. 'I'm not surprised, actually.'

'That's why the report's been delayed,' explained Bausen. 'He phoned from the hospital.'

'Did he phone himself?' asked Van Veeteren. 'Good for him . . . Well, what shall we do today, then?'

The chief of police sighed.

'You tell me,' he said. 'Continue gathering information, I suppose. Before long every single citizen of Kaalbringen will have had a say in this case. Not a bad collection of documents. Perhaps we can try to sell them to the folklore archives when we've finished—'

'If we ever finish, that is,' muttered Kropke. 'How's it going with the axe?'

Van Veeteren put a cigarette and a toothpick on the table.

'Not very well,' he said. 'Although I don't suppose it

matters much. I doubt that we'll find the shop that sold it – if they sell gadgets like that in shops, anyway. And as for asking some shop assistant to recall who bought an axe a dozen or fifteen years ago, assuming it was the man himself who did, no, I think we'll give the axe trail a rest.'

'What about Simmel's children?' wondered Inspector Moerk, looking up from her papers.

'Led us nowhere,' said Bausen. 'They haven't had much contact with their parents for the last ten years or so, neither him nor her – Christmases and big birthdays, and that's about it. You could say that puts them in a good light. Only visited them once in Spain as well.'

Van Veeteren nodded and put the toothpick in his pocket. Kropke stood up.

'Anyway,' he said, 'I think I'll go to my office and write a few summaries. Unless the boss has anything else for me to do.'

Bausen shrugged.

'We'll just keep plodding on, I suppose,' he said, with a look in Van Veeteren's direction.

'Yes,' said Van Veeteren, lighting the cigarette. 'For Christ's sake, don't think this is anything unusual. It's hard going, we have no sensible leads, no real suspicions, only a hell of a lot of information, but things will start moving sooner or later. It'll come if only we have a bit of patience.'

Either that or it won't, he thought.

'Did Melnik say when he'd be ready with the report?' asked Moerk.

'Not precisely,' said Kropke. 'A few more days, he thought. He seems to be a persnickety bastard—'

'You can say that again,' said Van Veeteren.

'OK,' said Bausen. 'Let's get going with . . . whatever it is we're busy doing!'

Hmm, what am I busy doing? wondered Münster.

The village of Kirkenau was not large. A railway station, a clump of houses in a valley by the river Geusse that had formed a longish lake in this part of the rolling, fertile countryside. Van Veeteren couldn't see any shops, or a post office or a school, and the gloomy-looking stone church by the roadside looked as godforsaken as the rest of the place.

The road to Seldon Hospice was in the other direction, up from the valley through a belt of sparse coniferous woods; ten minutes by car, roughly, and when he parked outside the walls, he wondered if it was really an old sanatorium. The air felt fresh and oxygen rich, and it was no problem resisting the temptation to smoke a cigarette before going in through the gates.

*

Erich Meisse was tall and thin, and baldness had set in early, making it difficult to estimate his age. Probably no more than thirty-five, in any case, Van Veeteren thought; they would have the exact age somewhere if it should prove to be of any importance. Meisse shook hands, gave the detective chief inspector a broad smile and invited him to take a seat in one of the Kremer armchairs in front of the French windows.

'Tea or coffee?' he asked.

'Coffee, please,' said Van Veeteren.

The doctor left the room. Van Veeteren sat down and looked out over the grounds: a large, well-tended and slightly undulating lawn with gnarled old fruit trees dotting it here and there, raked gravel paths and solid-looking white-painted wooden benches. Next to the wall a few little greenhouses; a gardener or someone of the sort was pushing a wheelbarrow full of compost or something of the sort, and farther away, to the left, two nurses dressed in black emerged from a low yellow wooden pavilion with rather a different vehicle, more like a wagon.

He swallowed.

Two creatures were sitting in the wagon, and it took him several seconds before it dawned on him that they were, in fact, two human beings.

★

'We don't accept just any patients here,' explained Dr. Meisse. 'We only take the worst cases. We have no illusions about curing anybody; we simply try to give them a reasonably decent life. Insofar as that's possible . . .'

Van Veeteren nodded.

'I understand,' he said. 'How many patients do you have?'

'It varies,' said Meisse. 'Between twenty-five and thirty, approximately. Most of them spend the rest of their days here; that's the point, really . . .'

'You're the last port of call?'

'You could put it like that, yes. We have a philosophy . . . I don't know if you are familiar with Professor Seldon's ideas?'

Van Veeteren shook his head.

'Ah, well,' said Meisse with a smile, 'maybe we can talk about that some other time. I don't suppose you've come here to discuss the treatment of severe psychiatric cases.'

'No.' Van Veeteren cleared his throat and took his notebook out of his briefcase. 'You were good friends with Maurice Rühme . . . even when you were in Aarlach, if I understand correctly?'

'Yes, I got to know him about . . . five years ago, more or less, through my wife. She and Beatrice – Beatrice Linckx, that is – are old childhood friends, well, school friends, in any case.'

'When did you first meet Maurice Rühme?'

Dr. Meisse pondered a moment.

'I'm not absolutely sure when I was first introduced to him, but we'd started to meet socially by the winter of 1988–89, in any case . . . now and then, at least.'

'Miss Linckx also works out here, is that right?'

'Yes, she's been with us for six months or so.'

Van Veeteren paused.

'Did you fix this job for her?'

But Dr. Meisse only laughed.

'Oh, no,' he said. 'I'm afraid I don't have much influence in such matters, unfortunately. I put in a good word for her, I suppose. Why do you ask?'

Van Veeteren shrugged but didn't answer.

'What do you know about Rühme's cocaine addiction while he was in Aarlach?'

Meisse turned serious again, and ran his hand over his bald head.

'Not very much,' he said. 'No details. Maurice preferred not to talk about it. He told me a little bit one night, when we'd had a fair amount to drink; I think that was the only time it was ever mentioned. He'd got over it, in any case. I reckoned he had a right to draw a line underneath it.'

'Were you acquainted with Ernst Simmel and Heinz Eggers?'

The doctor gave a start.

'With . . . ? The other two? No, of course not. I don't understand—'

'And what about Rühme?' asked Van Veeteren, cutting him short. 'Can you see any connection between him and the other two?'

Dr. Meisse produced a handkerchief and dried his forehead as he pondered that.

'No,' he said after a while. 'I have thought about it, of course, but I haven't been able to come up with any link at all.'

Van Veeteren sighed and looked out the window again. He wondered if there was anything sensible he could ask the young doctor about as he watched a trio approaching the building from the direction of the greenhouses. A man and a woman walked on either side of a hunched figure, supporting her – for it was a she; he could see that now – with their arms around her hunched back. She seemed to be dragging her feet through the gravel, and it sometimes looked as if her helpers were lifting her up and carrying her. It suddenly dawned on him that he recognized the man. The tall, thin figure, the thick dark hair – Dr. Mandrijn, no doubt about it. He watched the three of them for a bit longer before turning to Dr. Meisse.

'What does Dr. Mandrijn do here?'

'Dr. Mandrijn?'

Van Veeteren pointed.

'Oh, of course, Mandrijn. That's a relative of his . . . a niece, if I remember rightly. Brigitte Kerr. One of our most recent guests. She arrived only a month or so ago, poor girl—'

'What's the matter with her?'

The doctor flung out his arms in an apologetic gesture.

'I'm sorry. I'm afraid there are some things I can't discuss. Professional secrecy you know, not only—'

'Crap.' Van Veeteren cut him short again. 'It's true that I don't have any papers with me, but it will be only a matter of time if I decide to relieve you of that commitment to secrecy. May I remind you that this is a murder investigation.'

Meisse hesitated.

'Just give me an indication,' said Van Veeteren. 'That will be sufficient. Are drugs involved, for instance?'

The doctor looked up at the ceiling.

'Yes,' he said. 'To a large extent. But she's not in my group, so I don't know all that much about it.'

Van Veeteren said nothing for a while. Then he looked at his watch and rose to his feet.

'Many thanks for your time,' he said. 'I'll have a word with Miss Linckx as well. May I just ask you one final question?'

'Of course,' said Meisse, who leaned back in his chair and smiled again.

Van Veeteren paused for effect.

'Who do you think killed Maurice Rühme?'

The smile vanished.

'What . . . ?' said Meisse. 'Who . . . ? I've no idea, of course. If I had the slightest idea of who the Axeman was, I'd have told the police long ago, obviously!'

'Obviously,' said Van Veeteren. 'I'm sorry I had to take up so much of your time.'

This place seems to have a remarkable ability to attract people to it, he thought, after he'd left Dr. Meisse in peace and was instead looking for Miss Linckx's office. How many people had he come across, in fact, with some kind of connection with this gloomy, isolated institution?

He started counting, but before he'd gone very far, he bumped into Miss Linckx in the corridor, and decided to abandon that line of thinking until after he had interviewed her.

As he drove out of the parking lot an hour or so later, he was thinking mostly about what sort of an impression she had made on him. The beautiful Beatrice Linckx. And if it really was as she maintained, that her relationship with Maurice Rühme had truly been based on the strongest and most solid trinity as she claimed – respect, honesty and love.

In any case, it didn't sound so silly, he thought, and started remembering his own broken-down marriage.

But he'd hardly got as far as recalling Renate's name when he drove into a cloudburst, so he turned his attention to trying to see through the windshield and stay on the road instead.

28

The confession came early in the morning. Apparently, Mr Wollner had been waiting in the drizzle outside the police station since before six, but it wasn't until Miss deWitt, the clerk, opened up just before seven that he was able to get in.

'What's it all about?' she asked, after she'd sat him down on the visitors' sofa with brown canvas cushions, hung up her hat and coat and put the kettle on in the canteen.

'I want to confess,' said Mr Wollner, staring down at the floor.

Miss deWitt observed him over the top of her frameless spectacles.

'Confess to what?'

'The murders,' said Mr Wollner.

Miss deWitt thought for a moment.

'What murders?'

'The axe murders.'

'Oh,' said Miss deWitt. She felt a sudden attack of dizziness that she didn't think was connected with the meno-pausal flushes she'd been suffering from for some time now. She held on to the table and closed her eyes tightly.

Then she got a grip on herself. None of the police officers would turn up until about half past seven, she was sure of that. She eyed the hunched-up figure on the sofa and established that he didn't have an axe hidden under his clothes, at least. Then she came out from behind the counter, put a hand on his shoulder and asked him to accompany her.

He did as he was bidden without protesting, allowing himself to be led through the narrow corridors and into the innermost of the two cells, the one that could be locked.

'Wait here,' said Miss deWitt. 'An officer will come to interrogate you shortly. Anything you say might be used in evidence against you.'

She wondered why she'd said that last sentence. Mr Wollner sat on the bench and started wringing his hands, and she decided to leave him to his fate. She considered phoning Mooser, who was duty officer, but decided not to. Instead she made the coffee and waited for Inspector Kropke, who duly put in an appearance at seven-thirty on the dot.

'The Axeman has confessed,' she said.

'What the hell . . . ?' said Kropke.

'I've locked him into the cell,' said Miss deWitt.

'What the hell?' repeated Inspector Kropke. 'Who . . . who is it?'

'I don't know,' said Miss deWitt. 'But I think his name's Wollner.'

After thinking it over, Kropke decided that it would be best to wait for one of the DCIs to appear, and so it was twenty minutes to nine before the first interrogation of the presumed murderer could take place. Those present, apart from Kropke and the chief of police, were Inspector Moerk and Constable Mooser.

To be on the safe side, they recorded the proceedings on two tape recorders, partly with an eye to possible requirements if the case eventually went to court, and partly so that the two experts who had been called in from outside, Van Veeteren and Münster, could be sure of an opportunity to form a correct opinion of the circumstances.

BAUSEN:	Your full name, please.
WOLLNER:	Peter Matthias Wollner.
BAUSEN:	Born?
WOLLNER:	February 15, 1936.
BAUSEN:	Address?
WOLLNER:	Morgenstraat 16.
BAUSEN:	Kaalbringen?

WOLLNER:	Yes.
BAUSEN:	Are you married?
WOLLNER:	No.
BAUSEN:	Everything you say may be used in evidence against you. You have the right to remain silent if you wish. Would you like a solicitor to be present?
WOLLNER:	No.
BAUSEN:	Why have you come here?
WOLLNER:	To confess to the murders.
BAUSEN:	The murders of Heinz Eggers, Ernst Simmel and Maurice Rühme?
WOLLNER:	Yes.
BAUSEN:	Tell us how you did it.
WOLLNER:	I killed them with my axe.
BAUSEN:	What kind of axe was it?
WOLLNER:	I've had it for several years. A butcher's tool, I think.
BAUSEN:	Can you describe it?
WOLLNER:	Sharp. Quite light. The blade went in very easily.
BAUSEN:	Where did you get hold of it?
WOLLNER:	Bought it when I was abroad four or five years ago.
BAUSEN:	Where?

WOLLNER: Italy. I can't remember what the town
was called.

BAUSEN: Why did you murder Eggers, Simmel
and Rühme?

No reply.

KROPKE: Why don't you answer the question?

No reply.

BAUSEN: Can you give us more details of how
you went about it?

WOLLNER: Which one?

BAUSEN: Maurice Rühme, for instance.

WOLLNER: I rang the bell and he opened the
door . . . I killed him.

MOERK: Why?

WOLLNER: That's why I went there.

BAUSEN: Describe exactly what you did.

WOLLNER: I said I'd hurt my back. Dropped my
watch on the floor. As I couldn't bend
down to pick it up, the doctor did it for
me . . . I hit him with the axe on the
back of his head.

KROPKE: Were you acquainted with Dr. Rühme?

WOLLNER: I was a patient of his.

MOERK: Did he know you were coming?

WOLLNER: Yes.

MOERK: Are you saying that he received patients at his home at that time of night?

WOLLNER: I had to push.

BAUSEN: What was Rühme wearing?

WOLLNER: Polo shirt . . . greyish-green. Black trousers, dark-coloured socks . . .

BAUSEN: What time was it?

WOLLNER: About eleven.

KROPKE: What was Ernst Simmel wearing when you killed him?

WOLLNER: White shirt and tie. Jacket and trousers. Brown shoes, I think. It was dark.

BAUSEN: That's right, dammit . . . What do you think, Moerk?

MOERK: I find it difficult to believe you, Mr Wollner. Why did you do it?

WOLLNER: I'm prepared to take my punishment.
Pause. Short break in the tape.

BAUSEN: You claim that you killed three people, Mr Wollner. Now you'd damn well better tell me why! We have better things to do than sit here listening to self-punishing types who crave a little attention.

MOERK: But . . .

WOLLNER:	I killed them because they were evil people.
BAUSEN:	Evil?
WOLLNER:	Evil people.
BAUSEN:	Was that the only reason?
WOLLNER:	It's reason enough.
KROPKE:	Why those particular three?

No answer.

BAUSEN:	What were you wearing that evening when you killed Ernst Simmel?
WOLLNER:	What was I wearing?
BAUSEN:	Yes. How were you dressed?
WOLLNER:	I can't really remember . . . Hat and coat, I think.
MOERK:	And when you killed Rühme?
WOLLNER:	Tracksuit.
BAUSEN:	Why did you leave the axe in Dr Rühme's body?
WOLLNER:	He was the last.
BAUSEN:	The last? Aren't there any more evil people?
WOLLNER:	Not as far as I'm concerned. I'm prepared to take my punishment.
BAUSEN:	You're not thinking of murdering anybody else?
WOLLNER:	No.

KROPKE: Why have you come here today of all days?

WOLLNER: I was forced.

BAUSEN: Forced? What is your job, Mr Wollner?

WOLLNER: I'm a janitor.

MOERK: Where?

WOLLNER: At The Light of Life.

KROPKE: The church, do you mean?

WOLLNER: Yes.

            Pause. Whispers and the scraping of chairs.

BAUSEN: Is there anybody who instructed you to commit these murders, Mr Wollner?

WOLLNER: I have a mission.

BAUSEN: Given to you by whom?

            No answer.

MOERK: God, perhaps?

WOLLNER: Yes.

            Silence.

BAUSEN: We'll take a break here. Mooser, get rid of this bastard and lock him up again. We'll erase this tape later.

'Well,' said Bausen. 'What do you think?'

'As mad as a hatter,' said Kropke.

'He's lying,' said Moerk.

'What about the details, though?' said Kropke. 'How could he know so many details?'

Beate Moerk shrugged.

'The media, presumably . . .'

'Have the papers printed anything about the clothes?' wondered Mooser.

'Dunno. We'll have to check. But they've certainly printed quite a lot.'

'It wouldn't surprise me a bit if it turned out to be him,' said Kropke. 'The Light of Life crowd are as weird as they come.'

'No doubt,' said Bausen. 'But how weird? They're not in the habit of wandering around killing people, are they?'

'Where are our guests today?' wondered Kropke, trying to look knowing.

'DCI Van Veeteren is questioning some relative or other of Rühme's, I think,' said Bausen. 'No doubt Münster will turn up soon.'

Beate Moerk coughed.

'I'll wager fifty guilders not a word's been published about the clothes,' said Kropke.

'Why do you think I asked him?' snorted Bausen.

'A religious lunatic,' mumbled Beate Moerk. 'No, I don't believe it. Anyway, isn't it usual for loonies like this to turn up? Confessing to anything and everything?'

'I assume so,' said Bausen. 'We'll have to ask our experts, when they eventually appear.'

'Good morning,' said Münster, walking in through the door. 'Has anything happened?'

'Nothing much,' said Beate Moerk. 'We have an Axeman locked up in a cell, that's all.'

'It's not him,' said Van Veeteren two hours later. 'Let him go or send him to the loony bin. But present him with a bill for wasting police time as well.'

'How can you be so certain?' asked Kropke.

'I've been around for a while,' said Van Veeteren. 'You get to know these things. But go ahead and grill him if you need some practice. What does the chief of police think?'

'I agree with you, I suppose,' said Bausen. 'But I'm not a hundred per cent convinced . . .'

'He seems to know too many details,' said Moerk. 'How can he know what Rühme was wearing?'

Van Veeteren shrugged.

'I don't know. There are lots of possible explanations.'

'What, for example?' asked Kropke.

'Well, the usual tendency to talk accounts for a lot. Miss Linckx might have been gossiping to somebody, for instance.'

'Doubtful,' muttered Kropke. 'I still think we should look into this a bit more closely first. We've been on this case for several months now, and when a suspect eventually turns up, I don't think we should dismiss him out of hand.'

'Do what you like,' said Van Veeteren. 'I have other more important things to do, in any case.'

'OK, OK,' said Bausen. 'We'll give him another grilling then.'

'Hi!' said Bang. 'Oh, I'm sorry. I didn't realize there was an interrogation in progress. Hi, PM!'

'Hello,' said Wollner.

'What the hell?' groaned Kropke.

'Are you two acquainted?' asked Bausen.

'Depends,' said Bang. 'Neighbours, that's all. What's he doing here?'

Wollner stared at the floor.

'Bang,' said Bausen, trying to retain control of his voice. 'Don't tell us that you've been discussing your work with this, er, gentleman in the recent past?'

Constable Bang shuffled awkwardly and started to look worried.

'Do you mean about the Axeman?'

'Yes, I mean the Axeman,' said Bausen.

'I suppose I might have,' said Bang. 'Does it matter?'

'You could say that,' said Bausen.

'Fucking idiot,' said Kropke.

'Ah, well,' said Bausen. 'He cost us the best part of a day. I apologize for not trusting your judgment.'

'Best never to trust anybody's judgment,' said Van Veeteren.

'One day here and there doesn't make much difference,' said Kropke. 'That's what we're always doing anyway – wasting time.'

'Do you have anything constructive to suggest?' wondered Bausen.

Kropke didn't respond.

'What time is it?' asked Mooser.

'Nearly four,' said Bausen. 'Perhaps it's time to wind up today. Or does anybody have any ideas?'

Van Veeteren snapped a toothpick. Mooser scratched the back of his neck. Münster stared up at the ceiling. What a shithouse of an investigation! he thought. I'm going to be stuck here for the rest of my life. I'll never see Synn and the kids again. I might as well resign on the spot. I'll drive back home tonight, and that's that.

Inspector Moerk entered the room with a bundle of papers in her hand.

'What's this? A wake?' she asked. 'It's come.'

'What has?' asked Kropke.

'The report from Aarlach. What's his name? Melnik? A solid bit of work, by the look of it – thirty-five pages.'

'Is that all?' wondered Van Veeteren.

'Let me have a look,' said Bausen, taking hold of the documents. He leafed through them.

'Well, it's a chance, I suppose,' he muttered. 'I think we can regard this as our homework. I'll copy it, and then we can all read it before tomorrow's meeting.'

'Good,' said Van Veeteren.

'You mean we're going to work this Saturday as well?' wondered Mooser.

'We'll go through it tomorrow morning,' Bausen decided. 'Everybody who finds an Axeman gets a medal. You'll all get a copy within the half hour.'

'Does that include me?' asked Mooser.

'Of course,' said Bausen. 'We're all in the same club here.'

'What club is that?' asked Mooser.

'The headless chickens' alliance,' said Bausen.

29

'I think I need a walk,' said Van Veeteren as they left the sports hall. 'Can you take my bag back to the hotel?'

'Of course,' said Münster. 'What do you think of the Melnik report?'

'Nothing until I've read it,' said Van Veeteren. 'If you buy me a beer in the bar tonight, we can talk about it then – a nightcap at about eleven, is that a deal?'

'Maybe,' said Münster.

'A warm wind,' said Van Veeteren, sniffing the air. 'Even though it's coming from the north. Unusual . . . nature's out of joint somewhere. I think I'll stroll along the beach.'

'See you later,' said Münster, scrambling into the car.

In the foyer he bumped into Cruickshank, who was on his way to the bar with a few evening papers under his arm.

The other reporters had disappeared some days ago; only Cruickshank was still around, for some reason.

'Good evening. Anything new?'

Münster shook his head.

'Why do they keep you here day after day?' he asked. 'I don't suppose you've written anything for a week now.'

'It's at my own request,' said Cruickshank. 'Things are a bit nasty on the home front.'

'Really?' said Münster.

'My wife won't have me in the house. Can't say I blame her either, although it's not very stimulating hanging around this dump day in, day out. I'm trying to write a series of articles about refugees, but that's mainly to prevent me from going up the wall.'

'Oh, dear,' said Münster.

'What about you?' asked Cruickshank. 'I don't suppose you're having a fun time either?'

Münster thought for a moment before replying.

'No. I wouldn't say fun was the word.'

Cruickshank sighed and shrugged.

'I thought I'd sit in the bar for a while. You're welcome to join me.'

'Thanks,' said Münster. 'I have some reading to do first, later on perhaps.'

Cruickshank slapped him on the back and headed for the bar. There was a distinct whiff of brandy, Münster noticed as he walked past. A necessity for survival, no doubt. He went to reception and collected his key.

'Just a minute,' said the girl, reaching down behind the counter. 'There's a message for you as well.'

She handed him a white envelope that he slipped into his pocket. When he got to his room, he slit it open with a pen and read the contents:

Hi!

I've just been reading through the Aarlach
report. Something struck me.

Pretty bizarre, but I need to check it out.

I'll be at home when I've finished jogging
at about eight. Ring me then.

Love,

B.

He checked his watch. Twenty past seven. Could there really be something in the report? he wondered, fingering the pile of pages on his bedside table. That would be a blessing worth praying for.

I'd better get reading, in any case. But first a call to Synn.

Van Veeteren continued along the Esplanade and past the west pier before going down to the sands. Twilight had started to fall, but there was probably another hour of light left; growing weaker, it was true, but good enough for him to keep his bearings, he thought. The warm wind was even more noticeable down on the beach, and he considered for a moment taking his shoes off and strolling barefoot through the sand – the warm sand next to the wall. But he decided against it. The sea seemed apathetic, as it had done during the weeks he'd spent in the cottage; the waves were choppy but uninterested, devoid of life . . .

We've had enough of each other, the sea and I, he thought, and he became conscious of a mood he recognized from his childhood summers. When he longed to be back at home, longed to be inland, as he used to put it in those days. When he dreamed of eternity shrinking, so that he could overview it. He wanted to put a frame around everything that was timeless and infinite and seemed to grow and grow under the skies along the coast . . .

Was that what he was feeling now as well?

Was the bottom line that it was more difficult to handle things by the sea? Did this endless grey mirror make everything incomprehensible and impossible to master? Make this case so totally hopeless? Reinhart claimed that it was in this very place – where land, sea and sky come together – that everything acquired its true weight and significance.

Its name and attributes.

Hard to say. Perhaps it was just the opposite. In any case,

he was aware that thoughts and ideas drifted and became blurred. When he gazed straight ahead along the slightly curved coastline, which eventually melted into a darkening haze way beyond the west pier, it seemed more difficult than ever to concentrate and focus on something specific. As if everything were being sucked up, vanishing into eternity and the timeless darkness. Yes, Reinhart was wrong, no doubt about it. It was a hindrance, this damn sea.

On the other hand, it did increase one's sensitiveness, it had to be admitted. The process was open in both directions . . . no deadlocks to check either impulses or conclusions. Input and output. It was a matter of retaining perceptions and impressions long enough for him to be able to register them, at least for a moment.

What about the case? The Axeman? What were the perceptions that had blown in with the warm winds?

The wind was back to front. Something was wrong. He'd had that feeling for quite a while, and it was even more noticeable out here on the silent, firm sand. When he thought back, he realized that something had come up during his conversation with Beatrice Linckx. He couldn't quite remember what it was, hadn't known at the time either – an expression she'd used, something she'd said in passing, possibly the inherent relationship between the words themselves. An unusual combination. That had been enough, and he had sensed something.

Something that Bausen had said during their latest game of chess as well – the chief of police had moved a pawn and created an advantage for himself, despite the fact that it was precisely the move that Van Veeteren had foreseen and wanted him to make.

He'd lit his pipe and said something.

That was unclear as well. Highly unclear – a sudden whiff of something that had dispersed and disappeared just as quickly as it had come, but had nevertheless left a trace in his memory.

Good grief! he thought, and spat out a chewed-up toothpick. What kind of garbled thinking was this? What precision! This must be how it feels when Alzheimer's disease becomes full-blown.

But on the other hand – he was now building lightning-fast bridges between the extremes – the most significant sign of senile dementia was not that you lost your memory. On the contrary! The portals of memory were open wide and allowed everything to enter. No filtering. Everything.

Like the sea. Like the waves. And so it was a matter of choosing. Everything or nothing.

Who was it, then? Who was the Axeman? How much longer would he have to hang around this godforsaken place before he could finally put the handcuffs on this damn games player. What was the combination of words that Beatrice Linckx had let slip? What had Bausen said?

And Laurids Reisin? Sitting at home somewhere weighing the assurance his wife had passed on from the police. Was that anything to rely on? What had he promised? Six to eight days? When was that? Had he already overstepped that limit, in fact?

No doubt. Van Veeteren sighed.

A jogger, a woman in a red tracksuit, suddenly jumped down from the Esplanade about twenty yards ahead of him. Her dark hair was tied up with a ribbon the same shade as her jacket. She continued to the water's edge, to the firm sand, then turned westward, and after only a few seconds, the distance between them had doubled. There was something very familiar about her, and it took him a few moments to work out who it was.

Inspector Moerk, of course!

What had Bausen said about her that first day, at the police station?

Beauty and intuition? Something like that; in any case, whatever it was, he agreed with it wholeheartedly.

He sighed and put his hands in his pockets. Felt the pack of cigarettes, and argued with himself for a while. Oh, all right, he decided, and by the time he had lit a cigarette, Beate Moerk had vanished into the darkness.

Swallowed up.

Darkness, he thought, and took a deep drag. The only thing big enough to enclose an ocean.

Not a bad idea. He must remember to take it up with Reinhart one of these days.

But maybe the ocean is bigger after all, he realized almost immediately. No doubt it's morning on another shore. There's always another shore.

30

She parked in the usual place on the other side of the smokehouse. Locked the car and opened the zip of her tracksuit top slightly. It was warmer than she'd noticed earlier in the day; she would certainly be sweating a lot.

She set off, and immediately the heated excitement she felt in her mind spread all over her body, down to her legs and feet. The pace she was setting was completely mad so early in the run. She would pay for this, but it was somehow irresistible. She simply had to run fast now. Run fast and stretch herself to the limit in order to get her mind working clearly . . . to burn away the nervousness and excessive tension – this vibrant, almost hysterical feeling of approaching triumph. Of being about to have the solution in her grasp.

The breakthrough had arrived. Well, that might be overstating it, perhaps, but if she could complete the train of thought, the one that had been roused to life by the Melnik report and which now, after the first check, had proved to be . . . well, what?

There was nothing to contradict it, at least – nothing at all. Although what the implications were was another matter altogether.

She jumped down onto the beach and continued running to the water's edge. The wind was warmer than ever down here, and she wished she'd been wearing thinner clothes.

Nothing to contradict it, then. On the contrary. A lot supported it – everything, perhaps. If only she could spell out her thoughts to Münster tonight, calmly, in peace and quiet, no doubt it would all become clear-cut.

Dusk was falling, and she wondered if she really ought to run the full course today as well. It would probably be quite dark in the woods on the way back, but there again, she was familiar with every inch . . . knew every root and every low branch by now; it would be a botched job if she shortened the run, and Beate Moerk didn't like botched jobs.

And Münster wouldn't phone until after eight. There was plenty of time.

The lactic acid arrived early. No wonder, she thought, and slowed down a little at last. It was unnecessary to make herself so weary that she ended up staggering through the woods.

A newspaper headline appeared in her mind's eye:

WOMAN POLICE INSPECTOR CATCHES AXEMAN!

And an introductory paragraph along the lines of: 'Despite the presence of criminal experts from outside, it was Kaalbringen's own Beate Moerk who solved the case of the axe murderer, which has made headlines all over the country. Our town is deeply grateful to her, now that our citizens can once again walk the streets at will and sleep peacefully in their beds at night.'

It was not possible to control the flush of satisfaction, and she stepped up the pace again.

However, she didn't have very long to take pleasure in what was written about her before another heading came into her mind, totally unexpected. This time it was the title of a book, a book she'd never read, but she could remember holding it in her hand during a book sale back home in Friesen many years ago. It was an English book.

The Loneliness of the Long-Distance Runner.

She lurched to one side and almost fell on the sand.

How on earth had the title of this book floated up to the surface of her mind just now?

She dropped the thought and glanced over her shoulder. The beach was deserted. Just as empty behind her as in front of her. She checked the time. Twenty-five past seven – a few more minutes and she'd come to the big rock and the tunnel under the road. Then the gentle climb into the woods, and back home . . .

Beate Moerk solves the riddle of the axe murderer!

The Loneliness of the Long-Distance Runner.

As she approached the top of the last hill, she felt very tired. The lactic acid was making her thighs ache, and her heart was pumping salvos of blood into her throat . . . nearly at the top now. Pure willpower: clench your fists, grit your teeth and force yourself up those last few yards. Then, once over the top, it's downhill again – a chance to take it easy, let your body recover, prepare for the last lap, the gently sloping stretch through the beech wood down to the smokehouse and the parking lot . . .

Thinking about the easy finish, the waiting car and a hot shower carried her to the top and gave her a good start on the downward slope; but even if she'd been a little less tired, and even if the light had been a bit more favourable that warm September evening, it is highly unlikely that she would have noticed the dark steel wire in time.

It was stretched across the track at just below knee height and right at the bottom of the hill – just where the leaves of a lime tree added another layer to the gathering darkness. She fell headlong to the ground, and before she had even registered what was happening, he was over her.

31

'I think we'll have to ask the press to leave us on our own for a while,' said Van Veeteren, putting his hand on Cruickshank's shoulder. 'But I can take your chair.'

Münster looked up. Van Veeteren had the Melnik report under his arm, and he looked determined. The network of burst blood vessels had changed from red to blue. The bags under his eyes had prominent black edges. Positive signs, no doubt about it.

'Godammit!' said Cruickshank. 'So the breakthrough has come after seven hard years? May I be the first to congratulate you. What's his name?'

'Who?' asked Münster.

'The Axeman, of course,' said Cruickshank.

'You can have a ringside interview tomorrow morning,' Van Veeteren promised him. 'Provided you're a good boy and go to bed now.'

Cruickshank swallowed the remains of his whiskey and water and stood up. Swaying noticeably and looking as if he might be forced to make an emergency landing on the chair again, he managed to recover. He shook his head and cleared his throat. 'All right,' he said. 'Gentlemen's agreement. Good night, gentlemen. You know my room number.'

He thanked Münster for his company, and walked unsteadily out of the bar.

'Poor devil,' said Münster.

'Why?' asked Van Veeteren. 'I'll have a large beer, please.'

'Well?' said Van Veeteren, sucking the foam from the top of his tankard. 'Youth before beauty. What have you found?'

Münster picked up the bundle of pages and leafed through them.

'Well,' he said. 'There's this Podworsky –'

Van Veeteren nodded.

'Eugen Podworsky, yes. What about him?'

'I know nothing about him,' said Münster. 'But there's a link, in any case. I assume the others, Bausen and the inspectors, can make a better judgment. If he's known in Kaalbringen, that is . . .'

Van Veeteren lit a cigarette.

'I've just spoken to Bausen,' he said. 'He says it's not impossible, at least. Seems to be the right type – a loner who lives out in the boonies, on the way to Linden. About four miles inland in a straight line from the coast. He's been inside for manslaughter as well, although that was an age ago. Yes, this could be an opening; it could be him.'

'Violent?' asked Münster.

'Has a long memory, in any case, according to Bausen. Not quite right in the head either, it seems. He doesn't have much contact with other people. Took early retirement in 1975, I think it was. Anyway, we can look into that tomorrow – it would probably be as well to prepare ourselves a bit before we land on him. He could certainly stir up a lot of trouble if it turns out not to be him, says Bausen.'

Münster nodded. Van Veeteren drank deeply, and smacked his lips in contentment.

'Dammit all, Münster,' said Van Veeteren. 'I only have to set eyes on his type, and I'll be able to tell if he did it or not. It's time we went back home, don't you think?'

Münster shuffled around on his chair.

'What's the matter?' asked Van Veeteren. 'Are you about to lay an egg?'

'Just a little detail, that's all,' said Münster hesitantly. 'No doubt it's not important. I had a message from Inspector Moerk. She'd come across something and asked me to ring her –'

'And?'

'Well, she doesn't answer. She was supposed to be home by eight or so. I've tried several times.'

Van Veeteren checked his watch.

'Five past eleven,' he said. 'Try one more time before you go to bed. It'll just be a man, no doubt.'

Yes, thought Münster. It's just a man, of course.

THREE

24–27 SEPTEMBER

32

Bausen looked unshaven but energetic. He hung his dirt-brown jacket over the back of his chair and rolled up his shirtsleeves to well above the elbow.

'Eugen Podworsky,' he said, pointing at Kropke with a yellow pencil. 'What do we know about him?'

'Quite a lot,' said Kropke enthusiastically. 'Shall we start from the beginning, or—'

'Yes,' said Bausen. 'I don't suppose anybody's managed to miss the fact that he is involved in two of the cases, but it's probably just as well to establish a comprehensive background before we get going.'

'One moment,' said Van Veeteren. 'I think we need to discuss Inspector Moerk first.'

Bausen looked around the table, as if he had only just realized that not everybody was present.

'What's the matter with Moerk? Why isn't she here?'

'Hmm,' said Van Veeteren. 'I think Münster had better explain.'

Münster took a deep breath.

'Well,' he said, 'I received a message at the hotel last night . . . from Inspector Moerk. She asked me to call her. Something had struck her in connection with the Melnik report, the note said, but she doesn't seem to have been home since yesterday evening. I haven't been able to contact her.'

'What the hell?' said Bausen. 'Something had struck her . . . Podworsky, you mean?'

Münster flung his arms out wide.

'I don't know. Presumably, but it's not certain. She was going to check it out, the message said.'

'Check it out?'

'Yes.'

'What?'

'I've no idea,' said Münster.

'Do you still have the note?' asked Bausen.

Münster nodded and produced the envelope from his inside pocket. From the corner of his eye he noticed that Van Veeteren was watching him closely, and he knew he was blushing. There was nothing he could do about it, of course, and naturally, it didn't mean anything in the circumstances. He certainly hadn't slept for more than two hours, and ever since getting up, he'd had this image of the conference room in his mind's eye. Either she would be sitting there in her usual place in front of the bookcase . . .

or she wouldn't. Either it had just been a man, or it had been . . . another sort of man. He hardly dared to admit, even to himself, that he had felt a faint glow of satisfaction on discovering that it was not the first alternative. Just a man! Of course that reaction had immediately been swamped by all the possible implications of the other alternative, but it had certainly been there, and undeniably gave him something to think about.

Bausen read the note. Passed it on.

'I've already seen it,' said Van Veeteren when it came to him. Münster took it back.

'"Home by about eight,"' said Bausen. 'Hell and damnation! You don't think that—?'

'What did it say?' asked Kropke. '"Rather bizarre"?'

'"Pretty bizarre, but I need to check it out,"' said Münster.

Bausen took out his pipe and sat there with it in his hand. The silence in the room was almost tangible. Bang was chewing gum. Van Veeteren was devoting meticulous attention to two toothpicks, comparing them in detail, before dropping one into his breast pocket and sticking the other between his front teeth. Kropke was drumming his fingertips against one another, and Mooser was gazing out the window.

Good Lord! thought Münster. They're all seeing her in their mind's eye! He swallowed, and felt something cold and wet creeping up into his throat. There was a cramplike convulsion in his diaphragm.

'Excuse me,' he managed to blurt out as he stood up and hurried to the toilet.

'Kropke,' said Bausen, 'go to your office and phone her.'

Kropke did as he was bidden. Van Veeteren removed the toothpick.

'Not much point,' he said. 'We've already tried twice from the hotel. You noticed the form of address, I suppose?'

Bausen nodded and went over to the window. He rubbed at his stubble as he contemplated the back court-yard, breathing heavily. Münster and Kropke returned. Kropke shook his head.

'No reply,' he said. 'What does everybody think?'

'Podworsky?' said Bausen, turning around to face the room. 'Do you really think that she'd get it into her head to drive out to Podworsky's place?'

Kropke cleared his throat.

'No,' he said. 'That would be most unlike her, in fact—'

'Sheer lunacy,' said Mooser. 'Nobody in his right mind would go there of their own volition. Not even in normal circumstances. If in addition you suspect he might be the Axeman, I can't understand why—'

But now Münster had had enough.

'Stop!' he yelled, hitting the table with his fist. 'Dammit, it's time we did something instead of sitting here chewing the cud! All we need to do is to get in a car and drive out to this bastard! What are we waiting for?'

Bausen looked at him with eyebrows raised.

'I really believe—' he began.

'Bravo, Münster!' interrupted Van Veeteren. 'I'm inclined to agree with you. A bit of action is called for.'

Münster leaned back in his chair and sighed.

'I'm sorry,' he said.

'That's OK,' said Bausen. 'This is really ugly. If we're going to—'

'Just a minute,' said Van Veeteren, leaning over the table. 'I think we need to clarify a few things before we take any action. In the first place, I don't think it's especially likely that Inspector Moerk did, in fact, drive out to Podworsky's place. In fact, I'd go so far as to say it was out of the question.'

'Why?' asked Kropke.

'The time,' said Van Veeteren. 'She didn't have enough time. She left here when the rest of us went, didn't she? Around about half past four, or thereabouts?'

Kropke and Mooser nodded.

'She had the Melnik report in her briefcase just like we all did. At twenty past six, according to the receptionist, she handed over the message at The See Warf. It said she intended to check something out. Notice that she hadn't yet done so – she wouldn't have had time to do anything but read through the report and change into her tracksuit between half past four and twenty past six.'

'True,' said Bausen.

'Whatever it was she intended to check out, she did it after leaving the hotel – between half past six and a quarter past seven, roughly. Forty-five minutes, in other words.'

'A quarter past seven? How do you know that?' asked Kropke.

'Because I saw her,' said Van Veeteren.

'Saw her?' bellowed Bausen. 'Where?'

Van Veeteren bit off the toothpick.

'I saw her on the beach . . . at a quarter past seven.'

'What was she doing there?' wondered Mooser.

'Running,' said Van Veeteren. 'Westward.'

Silence again.

'Expected to be back home by eight,' said Münster.

'Was she alone?' asked Kropke.

Van Veeteren shrugged and looked at Münster.

'Yes,' he said. 'All by herself – I think it might be a good idea for Münster and me to go and take a look. Maybe we could take Mooser with us?'

Bausen nodded.

'Back in two hours?' he suggested. 'I think Kropke and

I will take a little trip out to Podworsky's place in the meantime – to see how the land lies, if nothing else.'

'Is that it?' asked Van Veeteren.

Mooser nodded.

'Sure?'

'Of course I'm sure,' said Mooser. 'It's hers. Mazda 323 – I've even helped her change the fan belt.'

'It's hers,' muttered Münster.

'Hmm,' said Van Veeteren. 'It was more or less down there that I saw her – two or three hundred yards from here, I should think.'

He pointed towards the beach. It was no longer the deserted stretch of sand it had been the evening before. It was Saturday, and masses of men, women and children were sauntering about down below. A group of long-haired youths were playing football, dogs were romping around, and several kites were bobbing about in the wind – yellow trembling lumps of butter against the practically clear blue sky. The clouds, the mist and showers of the last few days seemed to have blown away during the night; the gulls were soaring high again and the air felt pure. Salty and invigorating.

Münster bit his lip. Van Veeteren was swaying back and

forth, looking for once at a loss. Unless it's just a pose, thought Münster. Wouldn't surprise me.

It was Mooser who broke the spell.

'Do you think—?' he said.

'We don't think anything,' interrupted Van Veeteren. 'What the hell do you mean?'

'But—?'

'Shut up!' said Van Veeteren. 'This is no time to be playing guessing games. Do you know what track she used to follow?'

'Well,' said Mooser, 'Track and track – back and forth along the beach, perhaps. Or maybe she would take the path through the woods on the way back.'

'Hmm,' said Van Veeteren. 'Did she always go jogging on her own?'

'No,' said Mooser. 'I think she and Gertrude Dunckel used to run together sometimes.'

'Who's she?' asked Münster.

'A friend of hers. Works at the library—'

'Did she have a boyfriend?' asked Van Veeteren.

Mooser thought.

'She used to . . . but not at the moment. She was with a guy for a few years, then he left her, I think. And then there was Janos Havel, but I think that's all over as well.'

'Yes, it's all over,' said Münster. 'Do we have to go through her whole life story before we do something?'

Mooser cleared his throat.

'The beach out and the woods back?'

'Just the woods,' said Van Veeteren. 'They'd have already found her if she was on the beach – he doesn't usually bother too much about hiding them.'

'Oh, Christ,' said Münster.

'I assume the car was her starting and finishing point,' said Van Veeteren, ignoring Münster. 'Do you know if there's more than one path? Through the woods, I mean?'

'I don't think so,' said Mooser. 'It's only a narrow stretch of trees, in fact. There's a path that most people use – quite hilly. Shall we try that?'

'Let's get going, then!' said Van Veeteren. 'We haven't got all day.'

33

'Don't drive so damn fast,' said Bausen. 'We must be clear about what we're going to do when we get there.'

Kropke slowed down.

'Have you got your weapon with you?' he asked.

'Of course,' said Bausen. 'I had the feeling something funny was going on. I take it you have yours as well?'

Kropke slapped under his arm.

'Thank God, it isn't dangling against your thigh, at least,' muttered Bausen. 'Stop! This is where we turn off.'

Kropke braked and turned onto the narrow ribbon of asphalt running over the heath. A flock of big black rooks busy with the dead body of some small animal or other took off from the road and landed again the moment they'd passed. Cawing loudly, and self-assured.

Bausen turned to gaze over the desolate wilderness. In the far distance he could make out the skeletons of a row of low buildings, more or less dilapidated – a few walls, roofs destroyed by the rain; once upon a time, half a century or more ago, they had served a purpose. When peat was still being cut from these marshy wastes, he recalled. Odd that the drying sheds were still standing; he recalled how they had fulfilled a different function when he was a kid – love nests for the young people of the district with no homes to go to. It had been quite an undertaking to get out here, of course, but once that detail had been fixed, these isolated buildings provided excellent opportunities for all kinds of intimacies – almost like the *urgas* of the Mongols, it struck him. Holy sites dedicated to love. He had no difficulty in remembering two, no, three occasions when it really did happen . . .

'That's it just ahead of us, isn't it?' said Kropke.

Bausen turned to look ahead and agreed. There it was. Eugen Podworsky's house, scantily protected by a rectangle of spruce firs. He was familiar with its history. Built towards the end of the previous century, it had served for a few decades as the home of the more senior peat-cutter families, before the bottom fell out of the industry and it became uneconomical early in the twentieth century; and eventually, like so much else in Kaalbringen and vicinity, it fell into the hands of Ernst Simmel. And eventually into the none-too-tender care of Eugen Podworsky.

'It looks like hell,' said Kropke as he parked in the shelter of a comparatively bushy double spruce.

'I know,' said Bausen. 'Can you see the truck anywhere?'

Kropke shook his head.

'No point in trying to creep up on him,' said Bausen. 'If he's at home, he'll have been watching us for the last five minutes – plenty of time to load his shotgun and take position in the kitchen window.'

'Ugh,' said Kropke. 'No wonder Simmel didn't succeed in evicting him.'

'Hmm,' said Bausen. 'I don't understand why he even bothered to try. Who do you think would want to buy a place like this?'

Kropke considered that one.

'No idea,' he said. 'Some naïve newcomer, perhaps. What shall we do, then?'

'We'd better get inside and check the place out,' said Bausen. 'Now that we're here. I'll go first. Keep some way behind me, and have your pistol at the ready in case anything happens. You never know—'

'OK,' said Kropke.

'But I don't think he's in.'

Bausen got out of the car and followed the row of straggly fir trees, passing through the gateway, where a rusty, peeling mailbox bore witness to the fact that the post office still made the effort to drive the extra miles over the heath – presumably because Podworsky had threatened to kill the manager if he withdrew the service, Bausen thought. He took the newspaper out of the mailbox.

'Today's,' he confirmed. 'You can put your revolver back in your armpit. He's not at home.'

They walked along the path to the veranda. On either side of the door was a worn-out leather armchair and a hammock. Evidently Eugen Podworsky was in the habit of making the most of warm summer and autumn evenings. About ten crates of empty bottles were stacked up against the wall; piles of newspapers were all over the place, and on a rickety metal table were a transistor radio, a large can full of sand with cigarette butts sticking out of it, and a badly washed beer glass. A yellowish grey cat rubbed itself against the table leg; another one, slightly darker, lay outstretched in front of the door.

'Well,' said Kropke, 'now what?'

'God only knows,' said Bausen. 'Who interrogated Podworsky after the Simmel murder? I take it we've interviewed him?'

Kropke scratched his unoccupied armpit.

'Oh, shit,' he said. 'Moerk . . . yes, it was Moerk, I'm sure of it.'

Bausen lit a cigarette. He walked up the veranda steps and over to the door. The cat hissed and shifted a couple of feet to one side.

'It's open,' said Bausen. 'Shall we go in?'

Kropke nodded.

'Do you think the inside will be any better than the outside?'

'I was here once about twelve or fifteen years ago,' said Bausen, entering the dingy entrance hall. He looked around. 'I don't think he's done much in the way of decorating . . .'

Twenty minutes later they were back in the car.

'A pointless visit,' said Kropke.

'Maybe,' said Bausen. 'He has a hell of a lot of books.'

'What do you think, Chief Inspector?'

'What do you think, as new chief of police?'

'I don't know,' said Kropke, trying to avoid sounding embarrassed. 'Difficult to say. Coming here wasn't much help, though. We need to get hold of the man himself. Give him an aggressive interrogation. I think it would help if we were a bit rougher with him than we usually are.'

'You think so?' said Bausen.

Kropke started the car.

'Where do you think he is?'

'In Fisherman's Square, presumably,' said Bausen. 'I seem to remember he has a stall there on Saturdays – I take it you noticed the greenhouses around the back?'

'Yes . . . of course,' said Kropke. 'Shall we go pick him

up? Or do we have to leave him alone because we didn't find any bloodstained clothing under the bed?'

Bausen said nothing for some time.

'I think we'd better ask the advice of our guests first,' he said. 'We have the little problem of Inspector Moerk as well, or had you forgotten that?'

Kropke drummed at the steering wheel.

'Do you think . . . do you think they've found her?'

'I sincerely hope not,' said Bausen. 'Not in the state that you're hinting at, in any case.'

Kropke swallowed and stepped on the gas. He suddenly saw the previous victims with their almost severed heads in his mind's eye. He glanced down and saw that his knuckles had turned white.

God, he thought, surely she can't be . . .

34

'Nothing?' asked Bausen.

'No,' said Van Veeteren. 'Thank God, I suppose you could say. But I'm afraid it's not much to celebrate – she hasn't come back from jogging.'

'How do you know?'

'Her car. It's still parked next to the smokehouse,' said Mooser.

Bausen nodded.

'What about you?' asked Münster.

'Left the nest,' said Bausen with a shrug.

'The market?' suggested Mooser. 'He usually sells vegetables in the square.'

Kropke shook his head.

'No. We've just come from there. He hasn't shown up today.'

'Ah, well,' said Van Veeteren with a sigh, draping his jacket over the back of his chair. 'We need to get a grip now. This business is becoming as clear as porridge.'

'Bang,' said Bausen. 'Go to Sylvie's and tell her we need something really special today.'

Bang saluted and left the room. The others sat down around the table, apart from Van Veeteren, who opened the window and stood gazing out over the rooftops. The chief of police leaned forward and rested his head in his hands. He sighed deeply and stared at the portraits of three of his predecessors on the wall opposite.

'OK,' he said after a while. 'What the hell do we do now? Please be kind to somebody who's about to become an old-aged pensioner! What the hell do we do now?'

'Hmm,' said Münster. 'That's a good question.'

'I have one more week before I retire,' said Bausen, blowing his nose. 'Fate seems to want me to spend it trying to find one of my inspectors. Find her in some damn ditch with her head cut off – that's what I call a great way to end a career.'

'Oh, shit,' said Münster.

Nobody spoke. Bausen had clasped his hands in front of him now and closed his eyes. For a brief moment it seemed to Münster that he was praying, but then he opened both his eyes and his mouth again.

'Yes, a big heap of shit is what I'm surrounded by,' he said.

'Ah, well,' said Van Veeteren, sitting down. 'That could well be. But perhaps we ought to spend a little less time swearing and a little more trying to get somewhere – that's just a modest suggestion, of course.'

'Excuse me,' said Bausen, sighing deeply. 'You're right, of course, but we might as well wait for the coffee, don't you think? Kropke, you can tell us the Podworsky story, as we intended in the first place.'

Kropke nodded and started sorting out his papers.

'Shall we make this public knowledge?' asked Mooser. 'That she's . . . disappeared, I mean.'

'Let's take that later,' said Van Veeteren. 'It can wait for a second or two, I think.'

'Podworsky,' said Kropke. 'Eugen Pavel. Born 1935. Came to Kaalbringen as an immigrant at the end of the fifties. Got a job at the canning factory, like so many others. To start with, he lived in the workers' hostel down there; but when they pulled it down, he moved out to the house on the heath. It had been empty for a few years, and the reason he was allowed to move in was that he was engaged to Maria Massau, whom he was living with. She's the sister of Grete Simmel—'

'Aha,' said Münster. 'Ernst Simmel's brother-in-law.'

'More or less, yes,' said Bausen. 'Carry on!'

'Podworsky has always been an odd type, you could say. Difficult to deal with, as many people have found to their cost. On the booze from time to time – the very thought of allowing that poor woman to live out there on the heath – well, it can't have been a great time for her . . .'

'Go on,' said Bausen.

'Then there was that killing in 1968. For some unknown reason – and entirely out of character – Podworsky had invited some fellow workers out to his house – men only, if I've understood it correctly?'

Bausen nodded.

'There was some hard drinking, one assumes, and eventually one of them made a pass at Maria – a bit of flirting, probably no more than that, but Podworsky was furious. He started an enormous row that ended with him kicking the whole lot of them out of the house, apart from the one who had made the pass. He kept him inside, and beat him to death with a poker later that night – Klaus Molder, his name was.'

'Found guilty of manslaughter,' said Bausen, taking up the tale. 'Was inside at Klejmershuus for six years. In the meantime, Maria Massau fell ill with leukaemia. She'd had it since she was a child, it seems, but it had been dormant. She got worse and worse, and died the same month that Podworsky was released.'

'Did they let him out on parole to see her?' asked Van Veeteren.

'Yes, but she didn't want to see him,' said Kropke,

taking over once again. 'I don't think she needed to, in fact. She was living with the Simmels for most of the time – more often in the hospital towards the end, of course. When Podworsky got out, he moved straight back into the house, even though it was Simmel who owned it and had only allowed him to live there because of the family connection, as it were. Anyway, Simmel tried to kick him out several times, but he eventually gave up.'

'Why?' asked Van Veeteren.

'Dunno,' said Kropke.

'No,' said Bausen. 'It's unclear if he simply got tired of trying, or if there was some other reason, as rumour had it. Has had it for years.'

'What kind of rumour?' wondered Münster.

'All kinds,' said Bausen. 'That Podworsky had scared the shit out of Simmel, for instance – to put it bluntly – or that he had some kind of hold over him.'

Van Veeteren nodded.

'OK,' he said. 'They weren't especially well liked in Kaalbringen, either of them, if I've understood the situation correctly?'

'Right,' said Kropke.

'Why was Podworsky given early retirement?' asked Van Veeteren. 'Was that immediately after he was released from jail?'

'More or less,' said Bausen. 'He'd managed to pick up

a back injury or something of the sort while in prison – didn't have much chance of getting another job anyway, I suppose.'

'And so he's been living out there on his own ever since,' said Kropke. 'Since 1974 . . . a real prairie wolf, you could say.'

'No more brushes with the law since then?' asked Münster.

'Well . . .' said Bausen. 'It was rumoured that he was distilling and selling moonshine, or buying it from the Eastern bloc duty-free. I was out there at the end of the seventies, but I didn't find anything. Maybe he'd been tipped off.'

Van Veeteren scratched his head with a pencil.

'Yep,' he said. 'And then there's this Aarlach business . . .'

'I must say it's a damn peculiar coincidence,' said the chief of police. 'Don't you think? What the hell was he doing there? It's a hundred and fifty miles from here, and Eugen Podworsky has never been renowned as a great traveller, quite the contrary. What was the date, by the way?'

'March 15, 1983,' said Kropke. 'For some reason or other he gets involved in a violent bar brawl with two young medical students, one of whom is Maurice Rühme. They smash up furniture and fittings to the tune of thousands of guilders, and both Podworsky and Rühme's pal are hospitalized for several weeks. There's talk of prosecution, but eventually a settlement is reached—'

'Jean-Claude Rühme?' said Van Veeteren.

'Presumably,' said Bausen. 'We have to dig deeper into this, I guess. Get more flesh on the bones from Melnik; and track down this other student, Christian Bleuwe, wasn't that his name?'

'Unfortunately—' said Van Veeteren.

'Unfortunately what?'

'He's dead. It doesn't say so in the report, but I phoned Melnik this morning and he told me. Died in connection with an explosion two years ago. I asked Melnik to find out more details of that brawl as well. He says he'll get back to me.'

Kropke was making notes. Bausen frowned.

'An explosion?' he said.

Van Veeteren nodded and dug into his breast pocket.

'No toothpicks left,' he said. 'Do you happen to have a cigarette?'

Bausen handed over a pack.

'What kind of explosion?'

'A terrorist thing, it seems,' said Van Veeteren, clicking away at his lighter. 'Basque separatists, according to Melnik, but he wasn't sure.'

'Where?' asked Münster.

'Where?' said Van Veeteren, managing to light his cigarette at last. 'In Spain, of course. Somewhere on the Costa del Sol. Car bomb. Bleuwe and two Spaniards killed—'

Kropke stood up and seemed to be chewing his words.

'Was it . . . was it in . . . what the hell's the place called?'

'Could it be that you are trying to think of Las Brochas?' wondered Van Veeteren, attempting to produce a smoke ring.

He sometimes almost excels himself, thought Münster.

'Las Brochas, yes, that's it!' almost yelled Kropke.

'Not quite,' said Van Veeteren. 'Fuengirola, but that's only a dozen miles away.'

'But what the hell does all this mean, in fact?' said Kropke. 'Can somebody explain it to me?'

Bausen was filling his pipe, and looked at Van Veeteren.

'Well,' said Van Veeteren. 'Hard to say. In any case, we'll have to wait until we hear more about that bar brawl. It could be just a strange coincidence – there are more of those than we often imagine. But it's possible that it might be of significance, of course.'

Nobody spoke for a few seconds, and suddenly Münster could detect a tremor in the air. The concentration and intense thinking being done by everyone in the room seemed tangible, and a familiar shiver ran up his spine. Was this the moment when things started to fall into place? Were they about to start wrapping it up now?

'I'll contact Melnik,' said Bausen.

'What are we going to do about Moerk?' asked Kropke.

Bausen hesitated.

'Hmm,' he said. 'What do you think?'

'Münster and I will go to her flat,' said Van Veeteren after another pause. 'I think we might try to do a bit of ferreting around as well, without making it obvious—'

'Are we going to keep this hushed up, then?' asked Kropke, looking at everybody in turn.

'For a while, at least,' Bausen decided. 'When the newspapers get hold of this, all hell will let loose.'

'No doubt about that,' said Van Veeteren.

'Kropke and Mooser,' said Bausen. 'Go find Podworsky!'

Kropke nodded.

'Any tips?'

'No.'

'And Bang?' wondered Bang.

Bausen thought for a moment.

'Cycle over to Mrs Simmel's and find out if she knows anything about the car bomb. And about Podworsky, of course.'

'Er . . . ?' said Bang, looking rather worried.

'Kropke will tell you what questions to ask.'

'All right,' sighed Kropke.

'We meet again and report at six o'clock,' said Bausen.

Van Veeteren stood up.

'Have you got any good picklocks?' he asked.

Bausen shook his head.

'OK, we'll have to tell the janitor some fairy stories instead.'

Münster crumpled a paper cup and threw it into the trash can.

'Forgive me for asking,' he said, 'but is it really right not to put all available resources into finding Inspector Moerk?'

'You mean the mass media and search parties and the whole shebang?' said Bausen.

'Yes.'

Bausen scratched the back of his head and looked worried.

'You're wrong, Münster,' said Van Veeteren. 'We mustn't start thinking with our hearts. If she's alive, she's alive. If she's dead, she's dead. That might sound callous, but it's a fact. In no circumstances will she be lying somewhere just now and bleeding to death. We'll give ourselves another forty-eight hours – till Monday lunchtime. If all hell is going to break loose anyway, there's no reason why we should hasten the process.'

'All right,' sighed Münster.

35

It took almost half an hour to walk from the police station to Vrejsbakk and Beate Moerk's apartment, mainly because Van Veeteren didn't seem to be in much of a hurry. He walked all the way with his hands in his trouser pockets and his shoulders hunched, as if he felt cold in the pale autumn sunshine. Münster tried asking a few questions, but soon gave up; it was obvious that Van Veeteren was deep in thought and had no intention of being disturbed. He was evidently also convinced that Münster knew the way, for he stayed a couple of paces behind him the whole time, staring fixedly at Münster's heels.

After some considerable effort Münster succeeded in tracking down the janitor, a grumpy old man surrounded by a distinct aroma of stale sweat. Mentioning vaguely in passing that their visit was important in connection with the ongoing investigation, and that Miss Moerk happened to be away on important police business, Münster also persuaded him to let them into the apartment.

'I hope you can sort something out soon,' said the old man, with a sharp glint in his eye. 'It's not everybody who can afford to live at The See Warf for weeks on end.'

Van Veeteren came to life and fixed the janitor with his steely gaze.

'If I were you, I'd be damn careful what I say,' he growled. 'And I'd also go home and have a good wash. Open that door!'

The janitor said nothing, and unlocked the door.

'Thank you, we'll manage on our own now,' said Van Veeteren.

'I shouldn't think we'll find anything relevant here.'

Münster looked around.

'Why not?'

'Because the murderer has had plenty of time to come here and hide away whatever he wanted to hide away – loads of time.'

Münster saw his point.

'You've been here before, haven't you?'

'Once,' said Münster. 'What are we looking for?'

'The Melnik report, of course,' said Van Veeteren. 'But I'll bet you a hundred guilders that we don't find it.'

'Oh, yes?' said Münster. 'Why not?'

'You can work that out for yourself. Where should it be, do you think?'

Münster thought for a moment.

'In her study,' he said. 'She was working on a few theories of her own about the murder; she has several exercise books full of notes.'

'Is this it, in here?'

'Yes.'

'Stop,' said Van Veeteren. 'Before we start rummaging around, can you see anything unusual? Anything to suggest that he's been here and snooped around?'

Münster eyed the neat and tidy desk with its penholder, notepad, telephone, papers. The bookcases with bamboo curtains, the reproductions by Kandinsky and Schaffner.

'No,' he said.

'An orderly woman, obviously,' said Van Veeteren. 'It ought to be on her desk, don't you think?'

'I would assume so,' said Münster.

After looking around for ten minutes, Van Veeteren had had enough and they gave up. They left the apartment and told the janitor that he could lock the door again. The old man muttered something, but evidently didn't dare come out with any more views about their alleged benefits to society.

'There are two possibilities,' said Van Veeteren as they emerged into Rejders Allé, which led back towards the town centre. 'Either she had them in the car with her, or he was here and took them away last night.'

'Forgive my stupidity,' said Münster, 'but why do you think it's so important?'

'Because she'll have made a note, of course,' snorted Van Veeteren. 'She wrote in the message to you that something had struck her regarding the Melnik report. Whatever it was, it's virtually certain that she'll have made a note in the margin. A question mark, a cross, some underlining – could be anything. That would no doubt be enough for us to nail him if we discovered what it was. Are you with me?'

'If you say so,' said Münster.

They walked on in silence for another fifty yards.

'So it's not Podworsky?' said Münster.

'I don't know. I've started to have my doubts but, the devil only knows, it could be him. It's that word *bizarre* that intrigues me. You can think all kinds of things about that loner on the heath, but why should he be bizarre?'

Münster didn't answer. I'd better read that report again as soon as I get back to the hotel, he thought. Maybe something might strike me—

'If we're really lucky, it might be in the car, of course,' said Van Veeteren. 'But we'd have to be goddamn king-sized lucky. Let's go there now.'

*

'Are you good at breaking into cars?' asked Van Veeteren as they approached the smokehouse.

'Could be worse,' said Münster.

'It would be useful if we didn't attract too much attention. There are a lot of people around here, after all. It would be a pity if they were to start smelling a rat when we've postponed the arrival of hell until Monday.'

He took a piece of steel wire from his pocket.

'Is this good enough?'

Münster examined it.

'I should think so.'

'OK, then. I'll stay here. You go and open up. Thirty seconds – no more.'

Münster walked across the parking lot. He crouched down by the red Mazda and had unlocked it inside ten seconds.

'Good,' said Van Veeteren, joining him. 'Impressive skills. Jump in, for God's sake!'

It didn't take them long to establish that Beate Moerk's car was as devoid of leads as was her apartment. In any case, it was clear that neither she nor her presumed murderer had been careless enough to leave a vital report lying around in the car.

Well, to tell the truth, it was possible that Inspector Moerk had been . . . Van Veeteren sighed and got out of the car.

'Come on,' he said. 'Let's follow the route she took once again. The beach as well this time.'

Münster nodded.

'Make sure you keep your eyes peeled! It was somewhere around here that she disappeared last night, that's definite. There's not much in this case that you can say that about.'

'No,' said Münster. 'I agree with you there.'

Van Veeteren rummaged around in his pockets for cigarettes, and to his delight came up with Bausen's pack.

'Somewhere,' he said, gesturing with his arm, 'somewhere out there he was lying in wait and then pounced yesterday evening. Waited for her to come running, and then—'

'And then?' said Münster.

Van Veeteren lit a cigarette and examined the spent match before flicking it over his shoulder.

'I don't know,' said Van Veeteren. 'I'm damned if I know. But one thing is clear. He didn't attack her with the axe this time – not out here, at least. We can't have missed that much blood.'

'That's some consolation,' said Münster.

'Of course it is,' said Van Veeteren. 'Shall we go, then?'

36

'How's it going?' asked Hiller.

Van Veeteren regarded the telephone with repugnance.

'Well,' he said.

'Well?' said Hiller. 'You'll soon have been at it for a month. There are those who think it's high time the case was solved.'

'They're welcome to come give us a hand,' said Van Veeteren.

'At least you could send us some kind of report. Some people would like to know what you're actually doing—'

'Some people are welcome to disappear up their own asses.'

Hiller muttered something incomprehensible.

'Do you need reinforcements?'

'No,' said Van Veeteren. 'But Münster would no doubt like to go back home for a few days.'

'Why?'

'Wife and children. Have you heard of such creatures?'

Hiller muttered again.

'Would you like Reinhart to relieve him?'

'Possibly,' said Van Veeteren. 'I'll have a word with Münster, but we'll wait until after Monday.'

'Monday? Why after Monday?'

'Read the newspapers, and you'll understand.'

'What the hell—?'

'Or watch the box. Monday's when some new light will
be cast on the case, you might say.'

Various strange noises could be heard in the receiver,
but Van Veeteren could not be certain if they were due to
a bad line or the chief of police gasping for breath.

'Are you saying that your report is going to come via the
mass media? That is the goddamnedest thing,' he eventually managed to articulate, before Van Veeteren interrupted
him.

'I'm afraid,' he said, 'that I have to go out and tail an
ugly crook now. I'll get back to you.'

There was a crackling noise again. Van Veeteren put
down the receiver and pulled out the plug.

With three bottles of brown ale in a bucket of cold water
on the floor, and a dish of fat olives within easy reach, he
slid down into the bath and switched off the light.

He closed his eyes and made his head comfortable

against the edge of the tub, then stretched out a hand, fished up the open bottle and took a couple of deep swigs.

I'm not going to get up until I've solved this business, he thought, but soon realized that it might be prudent to adjust the demands somewhat. What the hell would the others say on Monday if they found themselves with not only a missing inspector to deal with, but a drowned DCI as well?

Enough of setting silly deadlines and similar nonsense, he decided. Back to basics. The Axeman. Concentrate.

There was an old rule that occasionally used to crop up, which he had no doubt inherited from Borkmann, one of the few police officers he'd come across for whom he had nothing but respect and admiration. Probably the only one, now that he came to think of it, which was most likely connected with the time aspect: Borkmann had completed his final years in post as a chief inspector up in Frigge, where Van Veeteren himself was just beginning his career as a probationer. Be that as it may, he still felt confidence and trust in the old guy; of course, he no longer needed to analyze the circumstances in detail. Even a hardened old cop needs the occasional firm foothold or lifeboat to cling to, he used to tell himself. Borkmann's rule was hardly a rule; in fact, it was more of a comment, a landmark for tricky cases.

In every investigation, he maintained, there comes a point beyond which we don't really need any more information. When we reach that point, we already know enough to solve the case by means of nothing more than some decent thinking. A good investigator should try to establish when that point has been reached, or rather, when it has been passed; in his memoirs, Borkmann went so far as to claim that it was precisely this ability, or the lack of it, which distinguishes a good detective from a bad one.

A bad one carries on unnecessarily.

Van Veeteren emptied the first of the bottles and took two olives.

What happened when information continued streaming in once that point had been reached?

In the best-case scenario, it made no difference.

In most cases it didn't cause too much damage.

In the worst-case scenario, it was a big disadvantage. Made smoke screens, splintered resources and caused problems.

Van Veeteren chewed away and sucked the stones clean. Borkmann was right, certainly. And this case was definitely a worst-case scenario. How much easier it was to catch somebody who was content with just one murder than to track down a serial killer, in which case the information –

tips, tracks, leads and suspicions – almost inevitably led to the simple and obvious being engulfed by the mass of material.

How much easier it was to cash in on a one-pawn advantage when there were fewer pieces on the board.

The question was simple: Had the point been passed?

Did he already know enough, sitting here in his hot bath, to pick out the Axeman? Was there any point in continuing to search for tracks and leads?

He groped around the bottom of the bucket for the opener. Already he knew the answer. Or at least, he had made up his mind about it.

Yes.

Yes. The murderer was there. Carefully concealed in the mishmash of interrogations and minutes and discussions. Hidden and tucked away in the even more confused convolutions inside his own brain. The Axeman was there. It was just a matter of fishing him out.

He found the opener. That was something, at least.

Pro primo, he thought.

Three men have been murdered in Kaalbringen. Heinz Eggers on June 28. Ernst Simmel on August 31. Maurice Rühme on September 8. Same weapon, same method. Same killer.

No doubt about that.

Pro secundo.

Despite comprehensive and assiduous work, we haven't succeeded in finding the slightest link between the three victims (apart from the fact that they had moved to Kaalbringen this year) until a report concerning the third victim's time in Aarlach comes into the investigators' hands. Everybody notices immediately that a certain Eugen Podworsky occurs in the background (but only in the background, nota bene) of two of the cases. Inspector Moerk reads the report and is struck by something 'bizarre'. She announces that she is going to check out the matter, does so, and –

Pro tertio.

– is exposed, no, discovered or observed while carrying out this check (whatever it might have been) by the murderer. (He might possibly have seen her purely by chance.) The murderer follows her and strikes (?) when Moerk appropriately enough is in the woods, in the back of beyond . . .

Something like that, yes. That was it, really. Was there any possibility of different scenarios? Yes, of course. But he didn't want to think so. This is how it must have happened. He took another drink and started wondering if he ought to get out of the bath and fetch a cigarette.

Smoke in the bath? What decadence!

But why not? Dripping and shivering, he padded into his room. He collected an ashtray, his lighter and Bausen's old, crumpled pack of HB cigarettes, then flopped back into the warm water, lit up and inhaled deeply.

Pro . . . what the devil's the Latin for *four*? Who the hell cares?

Fourth: What had Moerk discovered? What was it?

What the hell was it that nobody else, not even he, had noticed? Unless it was just Podworsky, that is; and the more he thought about it, the more sure he was that it wasn't. He had scrutinized the report once again earlier in the evening, and hadn't found a thing – neither had Bausen nor Münster nor Kropke. It was incomprehensible. Bizarre.

Bizarre?

And where had she gone to?

To check?

Check what?

He slammed his fist down into the water and was surprised for a second by the lack of resistance. Was she so damn stupid that she'd walked straight into the murderer's web? Straight into his arms, like some half-witted girl in any crime movie you cared to name?

He couldn't believe that. Surely that wasn't possible? If there was anybody based in this station whom he had confidence in, it was Inspector Moerk . . . well, Bausen as well,

of course, he had to admit that. But would Beate Moerk
have –

No, he refused to believe it.

What other possibility was there?

That the murderer had got lucky?

Very possible.

That she'd been on his trail earlier and he'd realized
that? Kept an eye on her?

Possible, also. Münster had spoken about her ambitions
as a private detective.

He dropped the cigarette into the bucket. No need to
dirty the ashtray, he thought.

But where had she gone?

That was the key. He took a few olives. Between half
past six, approximately, and five or ten minutes past seven
yesterday evening, Beate Moerk had driven her red Mazda
from The See Warf to the parking lot close to the smokehouse off the Esplanade. Somewhere along the way she
had checked up on something bizarre and attracted the
attention of the murderer.

Let's hope to God, thought Van Veeteren, that the red
car attracted the attention of somebody else as well . . . that
would be enough.

But all hell would have to be let loose first, he reminded
himself.

Then Laurids Reisin came into his head – and Mrs

Reisin in her shabby coat, and Miss Marnier, one of Simmel's lady friends he'd interviewed one afternoon a hundred years ago; and he realized that he was being subjected to yet another unnecessary information attack. He put the light on and decided to go through the Melnik report one more time. As an antidote, if nothing else.

Then he would have a chat with Münster in the bar.

He needed to find out for sure if Münster really did want to get back to his family and garden.

'It's not necessary,' said Münster.

'What do you mean, not necessary? And what the hell are you sitting there smiling at?'

Münster turned his head away and coughed into his hand.

'Excuse me,' he said. 'But Synn and the kids are coming up here tomorrow. She phoned half an hour ago.'

'Coming up here?' exclaimed Van Veeteren, looking confused.

'Yes, she's borrowed a holiday cottage from a friend of hers out at Geelnackt. That's only about six miles from here. I'm moving out there tomorrow afternoon.'

Van Veeteren thought for a moment.

'Münster,' he said, 'I think that's a fantastic woman you've got hold of.'

'I know,' said Münster, looking embarrassed.

They drank each other's health, and Van Veeteren gestured to the waiter.

'Just a small beer,' he explained. 'How many times have you read the Melnik report?'

'Twice,' said Münster.

'Found anything?'

Münster shook his head.

'What do you think about that bomb business?' he asked.

Van Veeteren hesitated briefly.

'Hard to say,' he said. 'I don't really understand what somebody like Heinz Eggers could have to do with Basque separatists, or the others, come to that. We'll hear tomorrow morning if Bausen has found out any more about it, I expect. What do you think?'

'Nothing,' said Münster. 'I hope I don't have to go to the Costa del Sol, in any case, now that I've got my family up here and so on.'

'You can take my word for that,' said Van Veeteren. 'Where's Cruickshank, by the way? I thought he was a permanent resident in the bar.'

'He went up to bed about a quarter of an hour ago,' said Münster. 'I think he was sulking because you cancelled that insider interview.'

'Oh, yeah. Poor bastard,' said Van Veeteren. 'Still, if he can keep calm until Monday, he'll have all the more to report.'

He certainly will, thought Münster.

37

The Sunday before the infernal Monday served up a clear morning with warm winds from the southwest. Without needing to exchange any words on the subject, Van Veeteren and Münster chose to walk to the police station.

It was quite simply one of those mornings, and Münster could feel the sluggishness and reluctance in both his own and Van Veeteren's footsteps. The very moment they emerged from Weivers Gränd, the Bungeskirke bells started ringing for the first service of the day. Van Veeteren paused for a moment to gaze at its dark portals and muttered something incomprehensible. Münster contemplated the canvas spread out before him. The splendid Hanseatic gables. The mythological bronze sculptures with the gently trickling water. The lopsided square resting peacefully under the tinkling chimes, completely deserted apart from an occasional pigeon strutting around, pecking food from between the cobbles. And a dark-skinned road sweeper standing by the bookshop, whistling Verdi.

Münster plunged his hands into his pockets and gripped his thin briefcase under his arm, and as they crossed over the uneven cobbles, a perception of the absurdity of his surroundings slowly took possession of him. The inherent and indisputable lunacy. Their task and activities seemed preposterous in this sleepy little coastal town on a Sunday morning like this. How pale a murderer looks in daylight, as somebody once said. And how impossible it was to grasp that they were on their way yet again, for the nth time, to assemble around the oval table in the bilious-yellow conference room at the police station, to sit down and roll up their shirtsleeves for yet another discussion of who this madman might be.

The man wandering around this idyllic little town chopping the heads off his fellow men.

The man because of whom a whole community was living in fear and trembling, and whose doings had been on everybody's lips as practically the only topic of conversation for week after week now.

The man, in fact, whose identity it was his own, DCI Van Veeteren's, and all the others' duty to discover and establish so that these goings-on could be banished from this world at last.

And what the hell were people going to say tomorrow?

Yes, preposterous is the only word for it, thought Münster, squinting up at the sun above the copper roof of the police station. Or perhaps bizarre, to use Beate Moerk's word.

And the most difficult thing to understand, the most impossible thing to comprehend, was, of course, what could have happened to her.

Could it really be that at this very moment she was lying with her head cut off somewhere in the town or its vicinity? A slowly decomposing corpse just waiting to be discovered. Was that possible to imagine? She, the woman he had so nearly . . .

He swallowed and kicked at an empty cigarette pack that had evidently avoided the attention of the road sweeper.

And this afternoon he would be reunited with Synn and the children.

He had to ask himself how she could have made the decision to come here without the slightest warning – a sudden impulse, she had explained over the telephone – and just right now?

A quarter to eight last Friday evening.

It must have been more or less exactly the moment when . . .

During the long time they had been working together, on two or three occasions Van Veeteren had started talking to him about the patterns in life. About hidden connections, orchestrated incidents and similar phenomena –

determinants, whatever they are; but this one must surely surpass most others.

He shuddered, and held open the door for the oracle.

'We've got him,' said Bausen.

'Got who?' said Van Veeteren, with a yawn.

'Podworsky, of course,' said Kropke. 'He's in one of the cells down below. We picked him up half an hour ago, in the harbour.'

'In the harbour?'

'Yes. He's been out fishing since yesterday morning – or so he says, at least. Hired a boat from Saulinen, it seems, evidently does now and then.'

Van Veeteren flopped down on a chair.

'Have you confronted him?' he asked.

'No,' said Bausen. 'He has no idea what it's all about.'

'Good,' said Van Veeteren. 'Let him stew a bit longer, I'd say.'

'I agree entirely,' said Bausen. 'I don't want us to get ahead of ourselves this time.'

Miss deWitt came in with a coffee tray.

'As Sylvie's is closed on Sundays,' she explained, revealing two aromatic Rillen cakes.

'Bramble?' asked Bausen.

Miss deWitt nodded and tried to suppress a smile.

'Irmgaard, you're a star,' said Bausen, and the others mumbled polite agreement.

'What's new since yesterday?' asked Van Veeteren, wiping his mouth clean.

'I've spoken to Melnik,' said Bausen. 'He's busy looking into that bar brawl, of course, but he doubted if he'd be able to find out very much. It never became a police matter, after all. He's only dug up one witness, a woman who was present, but she has no idea what started it. Perhaps it was just a drunken brawl, a quarrel over something completely insignificant that got out of hand for some reason. In any case, it's no doubt best if we try to press Podworsky on the matter ourselves.'

Van Veeteren nodded.

'And the Spain thing?' asked Münster.

Bausen shrugged and looked doubtful.

'As we said yesterday, it seems to be pure coincidence. Bleuwe wasn't one of Rühme's inner circle in Aarlach. Neither of them had any known links with Spain, and the bombing seems to have been purely a terrorist outrage. ETA claimed responsibility, and they normally do that only when they were, in fact, behind it.'

'And Grete Simmel had no idea what Bang was talking about,' said Kropke.

'That doesn't necessarily mean much,' said Bausen.

'Pure chance, then,' said Van Veeteren, contemplating his empty plate. 'There seems to be a lot of that around.'

Bausen lit his pipe.

'Anything else before we confront Podworsky?'

Kropke cleared his throat.

'Well, nothing important,' he said. 'But I've also retraced Moerk's steps. I jogged the same route this morning.'

'And?' said Bausen.

'I didn't find anything either,' said Kropke.

'Really?' said Van Veeteren.

'Podworsky, then,' said Bausen. 'How shall we approach this?'

Münster looked around the table – Kropke, Mooser and Bausen. Van Veeteren and himself. Constable Bang had evidently overslept, or perhaps the chief of police had granted him the day off – nothing very startling about that, when you think about it.

Van Veeteren spoke up.

'If you've nothing against it,' he said, 'I'd like to take the first round, along with Münster.'

It's possible that Kropke looked slightly put out, but Bausen merely nodded and went to fetch the tape recorder.

38

Eugen Podworsky certainly looked as if he was in a very bad mood. When Kropke and Mooser brought him to the interview room, his furrowed face was red with indignation; and to make his attitude crystal clear, he thumped his enormous fists on the table.

'Get these fucking things off my wrists!' he bellowed.

Van Veeteren gave the signal. Kropke unlocked the handcuffs and left the room, together with Mooser.

'Please sit down,' said Van Veeteren. 'My name is Detective Chief Inspector Van Veeteren.'

'I couldn't give a shit what your name is,' said Podworsky, sitting down on the chair. 'What the hell is all this?'

'I'm going to ask you some questions in connection with the murders of Heinz Eggers, Ernst Simmel and Maurice Rühme.'

'What the fuck?' said Podworsky. 'Again?'

Van Veeteren indicated that Münster should start the

tape recorder. Münster pressed the appropriate button, and his superior went through the formalities. Podworsky answered mainly by snorting or swearing, but once he'd been allowed to light a cigarette, he started – at least as far as Münster could see – to be a little more cooperative.

'OK,' he said. 'Let's move it, and get this out of the way; I have half a ton of fish starting to go bad.'

'What were you doing last Friday evening?' asked Van Veeteren to set the ball rolling.

'Last Friday?' said Podworsky. 'What the hell do you want to know what I was doing last Friday for? It's ages since the last of them died, surely—?'

'If you answer my questions instead of repeating them, it will go more quickly,' said Van Veeteren. 'I thought you said you were in a hurry.'

Podworsky opened his mouth, then shut it again.

'All right,' he said, and seemed to be thinking back.

Van Veeteren didn't move a muscle.

'Nothing special in the evening,' Podworsky eventually decided. 'I went around to chat with Saulinen about the boat in the afternoon – got the keys and so on. Then I drove home. Next question, please!'

'What were you doing the night Simmel was murdered?'

'I've already explained that to the skirt who's supposed to be a cop. I was at home asleep. That's what I usually do at night.'

'Can anybody confirm that?' asked Münster.

'My cats,' said Podworsky.

'And when Rühme died?' asked Van Veeteren.

'When was that?'

'The night between the eighth and ninth of this month.'

'God only knows. The same, I suppose.'

'Did you know Heinz Eggers?'

'No.'

'Any alibi for the Eggers murder?'

'I was in Chadów. Stop pissing around and asking me things I've already told you guys!'

'All right,' said Van Veeteren. 'What were you doing in Aarlach in March 1983?'

'What?'

'You heard.'

'Aarlach in 1983?'

'Stop messing me around,' snorted Van Veeteren. 'You were in the hospital for a week, for God's sake.'

'Ah,' grunted Podworsky. 'You mean that damn business. What the hell has that got to do with this?'

'Is it you or me who's asking the questions?'

Podworsky groaned.

'You're a real ugly bastard!'

'I think we'll take a pause there,' said Van Veeteren. He pushed back his chair and stood up. 'I gather they eat rotten fish in some countries – Sweden, unless I'm much mistaken.'

'Hang on, for fuck's sake!' said Podworsky. 'Aarlach – of course I can tell you about that, if you damn well insist. Sit down!'

Van Veeteren sat down. Podworsky lit another cigarette and scratched his head.

'Well?' said Van Veeteren.

'What's the time limit on proceedings for illegal distilling?' asked Podworsky.

'You'll be all right,' said Van Veeteren.

'Sure?'

Van Veeteren nodded.

'Never trust the fucking cops,' said Podworsky. 'Switch that fucking machine off!'

Van Veeteren nodded, and Münster switched off the tape recorder. Podworsky gave a hoarse laugh.

'All right. Here you have it. I'd hit upon a consignment of spirits that needed selling on—'

'Hit upon?' said Van Veeteren.

'Let's call it that,' said Podworsky.

'How much?'

'Quite a lot.'

Van Veeteren nodded.

'And you see, I had this pal, a Dane, in Aarlach who had a buyer, a fucking medic, as it turned out, who wasn't too fond of paying what he owed.'

'What was his name?' interrupted Münster.

'His name? Fuck knows. I can't remember. Well, something beginning with B. Bloe-something—'

'Bleuwe?' suggested Van Veeteren.

'Yeah, that's probably it – one of those academic assholes who thought he could make some easy cash by selling booze to his snotty pals. We'd reached agreement on everything, the delivery was arranged, everything fixed up, all that remained now was payment—'

'And?' said Van Veeteren.

'That was what we were going to sort out at that pub . . . and this little prick sits there with his pal and thinks he can pull a fast one on me! What do you reckon the odds are on that, Constable?'

'How much are we talking about?' asked Münster.

'Quite a bit,' said Podworsky. 'We'd sunk a fair amount, and I got a bit annoyed, of course. I only regret one thing—'

'What?' said Van Veeteren.

'That I didn't wait for the Dane before I went for them,' said Podworsky, succumbing to a sudden coughing fit. He had to turn away and double up with his hands over his mouth, and it lasted for nearly half a minute. Münster looked at Van Veeteren. Tried to work out what he was thinking, but that was impossible, as usual. As for himself, he thought Podworsky's story sounded pretty plausible; at least he didn't give the impression of making it up as he went along.

Although you could never be sure, of course. He'd seen this kind of thing before. And got it wrong before, as well.

'What was the name of his pal?' asked Van Veeteren when Podworsky had finished coughing.

'Eh?'

'Bleuwe's mate. What was he called?'

'No idea,' said Podworsky.

'Did he ever introduce himself?' asked Münster.

'He might have, but I'm fucked if I can remember the name of somebody I punched on the nose twelve years ago.'

'Ten,' said Van Veeteren. 'What was his name?'

'What the fuck?' said Podworsky. 'Are you not all there, and what's going on?'

Van Veeteren waited for a few seconds while Podworsky stared at them, shifting his gaze from one to the other as if he were asking himself how on earth he could have landed in front of two idiots instead of two police officers.

Mind you, in his world the difference probably wasn't all that great, Münster conceded.

'His name was Maurice Rühme,' said Van Veeteren.

Podworsky gaped at him.

'Oh, fuck,' he said.

He leaned back in his chair and thought things over for a while.

'OK,' he said eventually. 'Let's be clear about one thing – I didn't manage to kill the bastard in that goddamn bar, and I haven't succeeded in doing it since then either. Any more questions?'

'Not right now,' said Van Veeteren, standing up again. 'But you can sit here and think this over, and maybe we'll get back to you.' He knocked on the door and Kropke and Mooser returned with the cuffs.

'You fucking bastards,' said Podworsky, and there's no doubt that it sounded as if he meant it.

39

The decision to release Eugen Podworsky, and as soon as possible inform the media of the disappearance of Inspector Moerk, was taken at about nine p.m. on Sunday evening, by a majority vote of three to one. Bausen, Münster and Van Veeteren were in favour, Kropke against. Mooser abstained, possibly because he was somewhat overwhelmed by the sudden and very definitely onetime adoption of democratic procedures.

'I'll speak to Cruickshank now, tonight,' said Van Veeteren. 'I've promised him a bit of advance information. Press conference tomorrow afternoon?'

Bausen agreed.

'Three o'clock,' he decided. 'And we can expect the whole parade, as I said before – television, radio, the lot. It's not all that common for a murderer to put the cuffs on the police, you have to say.'

'The general public reckon it ought to be the other way

around,' said Van Veeteren. 'One can see their point, it has to be admitted.'

'What shall we say about Podworsky?' wondered Kropke.

'Not a goddamn word,' said Bausen. 'Mouths shut is the order of the day.' He looked around the table. 'DCI Van Veeteren and I will talk to the press, nobody else.'

'Typical,' muttered Kropke.

'That's an order,' said Bausen. 'Go home and get some sleep now. Tomorrow is another day, and we're certain to be on TV. It might help if we looked like normal human beings. I'll release Podworsky.'

'I'll come with you,' said Van Veeteren. 'It might be useful for there to be more than one of us.'

It was past eleven before the kids finally went to bed. They opened a bottle of wine and put on a Mostakis tape, and after several failed attempts, they finally managed to get a fire going. They spread the mattresses out on the floor and undressed each other.

'We'll wake them up,' said Münster.

'No, we won't,' said Synn. She stroked his back and crept down under the blankets. 'I put a bit of a sleeping pill into their hot chocolate.'

'Sleeping pill?' he thundered, trying to sound outraged.

'Only a little bit. Won't do them any lasting harm. Come here!'

'OK,' said Münster, and restored relations with his wife.

Monday announced its arrival with a stubborn and persistent downpour that threatened to go on forever. Van Veeteren woke up at about seven, contemplated the rain for a while and decided to go back to bed. This place changes its weather more often than I change my shirt, he thought.

By a quarter past nine he was sharing a breakfast table in the dining room with Cruickshank, who seemed to be remarkably invigorated and in a strikingly good mood, despite the early hour and the fact that he must have been up working for most of the night.

'Phoned it through at three this morning,' he said enthusiastically. 'I'll be damned if the night desk didn't want to stop the presses, but they eventually settled for the afternoon edition. Talk about Jack the Ripper hysteria!'

Van Veeteren looked decidedly miserable.

'Cheer up!' said Cruickshank. 'You'll soon have cracked it. He's gone too far this time. Did she really have some idea who he was?'

'Presumably,' said Van Veeteren. 'That's what he must have thought, at least.'

Cruickshank nodded.

'Have you sent out the press release yet?' he asked, looking around the empty dining room. 'I don't notice any of my colleagues rushing in for the kill.'

Van Veeteren checked his watch.

'Another quarter of an hour, I think. Must finish breakfast and then go into hiding. It's pissing out there.'

'Hmm,' said Cruickshank, chewing away at a croissant. 'It'll be shit over the ankles down there.'

'Down where?'

'On the beach and in the woods, of course. With all the photographers and private dicks.'

'You're probably right,' said Van Veeteren, sighing again. 'Anyway, I think it's time I went to the police station and locked myself in.'

'Good luck,' said Cruickshank. 'I'll see you this afternoon. I expect I'll still be here, waiting for my fellow union members.'

'Well, that was that,' said the chief of police, flopping back onto the leather sofa. 'I have to say that I prefer the newspaper boys.'

Van Veeteren agreed.

'Those well-oiled talking heads on TV make me vomit; they really do. Do you have a lot to do with that crowd?'

He kicked off his shoes and wiggled his toes rather

cautiously, as if he were uncertain whether or not they were still there.

'I can't say that I have much of an interest in encouraging them,' said Van Veeteren. 'Let's be honest; it's reasonable that they should start forming their own ideas. But you handled them pretty well, I thought.'

'Thank you,' said Bausen. 'But we're definitely in trouble, no matter how you look at it. Has Hiller been onto you?'

Van Veeteren sat back in his chair behind the chief of police's desk.

'Of course,' he said. 'He wanted to send ten men from Selstadt and another ten from Oostwerdingen – plus a team of forensic officers to run a fine-tooth comb over the jogging track.'

Bausen linked his hands behind the back of his head and gazed out of the window.

'A brilliant idea, in weather like this,' he said. 'Does he want you to take charge completely? I mean, damn it to hell, I've only got five days left. I'm quitting on Friday, no matter what. Made up my mind last night – I'm starting to feel like a football coach with a two-year losing streak.'

'The leadership question never came up,' said Van Veeteren. 'In any case, I've promised to clear up the whole thing by Friday.'

Bausen was distinctly sceptical.

'Glad to hear it,' he said, filling his pipe. 'Let's leave it at that. Have you spoken to her parents?'

'Mrs Moerk, yes,' said Van Veeteren.

'Did it go well?'

'Not especially. Why should it?'

'No, it's a long time since anything went well,' said Bausen.

'I've been watching TV,' said Synn. 'They don't give you very good marks.'

'That's odd,' said Münster. 'Something smells good; what are we eating?'

'Creole chicken,' said his wife, giving him a kiss. 'Do you think she's dead?' she whispered in his ear; there's a limit to what the children of a police officer can be expected to put up with, after all.

'I don't know,' he said, and just for a moment he once again felt the cold despair well up inside him.

'I saw Dad on TV,' said his daughter, interrupting their conversation and hugging his thigh. 'I've been swimming in the rain.'

'You've been swimming in the sea, you idiot,' said his son.

'Have we any more sleeping pills?' wondered Münster.

*

Van Veeteren leaned back against the pillows and picked up the Melnik report yet again. He weighed it in his hand for a while, his eyes closed.

Horrific, he thought. Absolutely horrific.

Or perhaps painful might be a better word to describe it. Hidden away somewhere in these damn documents was the answer, but he couldn't find it. Thirty-four pages, a total of seventy-five names. He'd underlined them and re-counted twice – women, lovers and possible lovers, good friends, fellow students, colleagues, neighbours, members of the same golf club – right down to the most casual acquaintances, marginal figures who had happened to cross the path of Maurice Rühme at one time or another. And then occasions – journeys, exams, final exams, appointments, parties, new addresses, congresses, cocaine withdrawal clinics – it was all there, noted down in those densely packed pages, neatly and comprehensively recorded in the dry prose of DCI Melnik. It was a masterpiece of detective work, no doubt about it; but even so, he couldn't draw any conclusions from it. Not a damn thing!

What was it?

What the hell had Beate Moerk noticed?

Or did she know something that the others didn't know? Could that be it? Could it be that he hadn't passed Borkmann's point yet, despite everything?

He had her notebooks on his bedside table. Three of them, which he hadn't got around to looking at yet.

It went against the grain. If they really did contain something of significance, why had the murderer left them there? He'd had plenty of time, and didn't seem to be a person who left anything to chance.

And if in fact she was still alive, despite everything, would he be intruding upon the holy territory of her private life? Trampling all over her most sacred ground? Before he opened them, he couldn't have the slightest idea about what she had confided to these notebooks. They hadn't been meant for him to read, that was for sure.

Did the same reservations apply if she was still alive, come to that?

Yes, of course. Maybe even more so.

He shut his eyes and listened to the rain pattering down. It must have been raining for more than twenty-four hours, heavy and relentless, from an unremitting sky. Leaden and impenetrable. Did the weather never change in this god-forsaken hole? he thought.

Whatever; it wasn't a bad way of presenting what they were up against. Nonstop nudging at the same point. Marking time and never moving on. Waves in a dead sea . . .

The clock in St. Anna's church struck twelve. He sighed, opened his eyes, then concentrated for the fourth time on the report from Aarlach.

40

'Well, what the hell was I supposed to do?' said Wilmotsen with a sigh, contemplating the layouts.

'All right,' said the editor. 'If we've printed a double run, we might as well make everything double.'

The news of Inspector Moerk's disappearance and the circumstances in which it took place had clearly proved to be a trial of manhood for Wilmotsen, the headline setter on *de Journaal*. The opposing concepts Important Information and Big Letters were simply not possible to reconcile within the space available, and for the first time in the newspaper's eighty-year-old history, they had been forced to prepare two separate placards.

In order not to abandon the duty to provide full information, that is. In order not to undervalue the dignity of this hair-raising drama that was now entering its fourth (or was it the fifth?) act in their peaceful hometown of Kaalbringen.

NEXT VICTIM?

it said on the first placard, over a slightly blurred picture of a smiling Beate Moerk.

HAVE YOU SEEN THE RED MAZDA?

the public was asked on the second one, where it was also stated that

BAFFLED POLICE APPEAL FOR HELP.

Inside the newspaper, more than half the space was devoted to the latest development in the Axeman case. There was a mass of pictures: aerial photographs of the parking lot at the smokehouse (with a white cross marking the spot where Moerk had left her car; since Sunday evening it had been securely garaged in the police station basement after being searched for eight hours by forensic officers from Selstadt) and another of the beach and the woods, and more photos of Moerk and of Bausen and Van Veeteren taken at the press conference. Van Veeteren was leaning back with his eyes closed, a position that was mainly reminiscent of a state of deep peace – a mummy or a yogi sunk deep inside himself was the first thing that came to mind. Far removed from the exertions and idiocies of this life, and perhaps one had to ask oneself if these people were really the ones best equipped to track down and put away criminals of the calibre of the killer they were seeking in this case.

Indeed, had there ever been anything like this? A police inspector abducted, probably murdered! In the middle of an ongoing investigation! The question was justified.

The text was also variable in character, from the cool assessment in the leading article that the only honourable thing for the local council to do in the current circumstances was to accept responsibility for the Axeman scandal and announce new elections, to the eloquent if divergent speculations about the lunatic, the madman (the ice-cold psychopath) or the terrorist (the hired hit man from an obscure murderous sect) – and, of course, the still very popular theory featuring the perfectly normal, honest citizen, the respectable head of the family, the man in the same apartment block with a murky past.

Among the more reliable items, and hopefully also the most productive ones from the point of view of the investigation, was Bausen's renewed and urgent appeal to the general public to come forward with any information they might have.

In particular, the critical period between six-fifteen and seven-fifteen on the Friday evening needed to be pinned down in detail – Inspector Moerk's movements from the moment she left The See Warf until she set off jogging and was observed by Detective Chief Inspector Van Veeteren.

If it was possible to establish the route taken by Beate Moerk during those sixty minutes, with and without her red Mazda, well, 'it would be a damn scandal if we couldn't nail the bastard,' wrote Herman Schalke, quoting the exact words used by the chief of police.

As early as four in this infernal afternoon, Bausen and Kropke withdrew to the latter's office in order to go through and collate the tip-offs and information that had been received so far – a total of no fewer than sixty-two firsthand sightings, as well as another twenty or so pieces of secondhand information of various kinds. Münster and Mooser were delegated to receive and conduct preliminary interviews with the nonstop stream of witnesses, who were held in check by Bang and Miss deWitt in the office downstairs, all names and personal data duly recorded.

Nobody was quite clear about what Detective Chief Inspector Van Veeteren was up to. He had left the police station after lunch to 'make a few inquiries', but he had not confided their nature to anybody. On the other hand, he had promised to be back by five p.m. for the compulsory run-through. A small press conference was then scheduled for seven-thirty; the time was a concession to the local television company, whose regular news programme took place then. Anything other than a live broadcast would be regarded by viewers as a failure and a crime against all press ethics, the company had argued peremptorily, and even if Bausen could have taught the young media guru a thing or two about the law and justice, he had swallowed his objections and acceded to his request.

'Damn Jesuits!' he had nevertheless exclaimed after replacing the receiver. 'Inquisitors in silver ties, huh, no thank you!'

But given the circumstances, of course, it was a question of making the most of a bad job.

41

'What the hell is that?' asked Van Veeteren, leaning forward over the table.

'It's a map,' explained Kropke. 'The drawing pins represent sightings of Inspector Moerk and her Mazda – or rather, of red Mazdas in general.'

'There are several in Kaalbringen,' said Bausen. 'Presumably at least two of them were on the streets on Friday evening – in addition to hers, that is.'

'Pins with red and yellow heads stand for sightings of the car,' said Kropke, keen to take over and assert his ownership of the patent. 'Red for the period six-fifteen to six-forty-five, yellow for six-forty-five to seven-fifteen.'

Van Veeteren leaned farther over the table.

'The blue and white pins are witnesses who claim to have seen her in person – blue for the first half hour, white for the second. That one is DCI Van Veeteren, for instance.'

He pointed to a white pin on the beach.

'I'm honoured,' said Van Veeteren. 'How many are there?'

'Twenty-five red and twenty yellow,' said Kropke. 'That's the car – and then twelve blue and five white.'

Münster moved up alongside his boss and studied the pattern of the drawing pins. Not a bad idea, he had to admit – provided you knew how to interpret it properly, that is. They seemed to be quite widespread; evidently sightings had been made in all parts of town, but in most cases there was just one isolated pin.

'The point,' said Kropke, 'is that we don't need to worry about whether a single witness is sufficient or not. Places where there are several pins ought to be a sufficiently clear pointer.'

He paused to allow the others to count the pins, and recognize the stroke of genius behind the method.

'Quite clear,' muttered Münster. 'The white ones as well.'

'Indubitably,' said Van Veeteren. 'No doubt about it.'

'Exactly,' said Kropke, looking pleased. 'As you can see, there are only three conglomerations – in Fisherman's Square outside The See Warf, in Grande Place, and the smokehouse. Twenty-four pins outside The See Warf, eleven out here, eight by the smokehouse – forty-three out of sixty-two. The rest are scattered all over the place, as you will have noticed. And it seems that nobody saw her after

DCI Van Veeteren's sighting. Apart from the murderer, that is. The beach must have been pretty deserted.'

'True,' said Van Veeteren.

'Hmm,' said Bausen. 'I still don't think we should get carried away – a third of the sightings must be wrong, if I understand things.'

'Well,' said Kropke. 'I think you realize—'

'And both The See Warf and the smokehouse have been written about in the newspapers.'

'True enough,' said Kropke. 'But I think it's fair to say that doesn't matter. The most interesting thing is, of course, Grande Place – there are eleven witnesses who claim to have seen either Moerk or her car outside the police station here between half past six and seven, roughly. Two saw her getting out of the car . . . those two white drawing pins over there.'

He pointed, and Bausen nodded. Van Veeteren snapped off a toothpick and dropped it in St. Pieter's churchyard.

'Which direction was she going?' he asked.

Kropke looked at Bausen.

'Towards here,' he said.

Bausen nodded again.

'OK,' he said. 'So there are indications that she came here. Back to the station.'

★

'Well?' said Münster, feeling as if he'd just missed the point of a long and complicated joke. Van Veeteren said nothing. He dug his hands deeper into his pockets, stood erect again and emitted a slight hissing noise through his teeth. Münster recalled his boss's back trouble, which occasionally manifested itself.

They sat down around the table again. Kropke was still looking pleased with himself, but also slightly bewildered, as if he couldn't quite work out the implications of what his efforts had produced. Once again Münster could feel those butterfly-like vibrations in his temples – the ones that usually suggested something was afoot, that a critical point was being approached. That the breakthrough could come at any moment. He looked around the untidy room. Bang was sitting opposite him, sweating. Van Veeteren appeared to be half asleep. Bausen was still studying the map and the drawing pins, sucking in his cheeks and looking almost as if he was dreaming.

Eventually it was Constable Mooser who put into words the general bewilderment that seemed to be filling the room.

'Here?' he exclaimed. 'Why on earth did she come here?'

Three seconds passed. Then both Kropke and Mooser groaned and said more or less simultaneously:

'Her office!'

'Holy shit!' gasped Bausen, and dropped his as yet unlit cigarette on the floor. 'Has anybody checked her office?'

Mooser and Kropke were already on their way. Münster had stood up, and Bausen looked as if he'd just failed the first exam testing the basics of police work. Only Van Veeteren seemed unperturbed, and was digging around in his breast pocket.

'Of course,' he muttered. 'There'll be nothing there. But take a look by all means; six eyes will see more than two, or so one hopes.'

FOUR

27 SEPTEMBER TO 1 OCTOBER

42

'I take it you know where you are?' he said, and his voice sounded weary in the extreme.

'I think so,' she said into the darkness.

He coughed.

'You realize that you have no chance of getting out of here without assistance?'

'Yes.'

'You're in my hands. Can we agree on that?'

She didn't answer. She suddenly wondered how such resolute determination could be combined with the deep sorrow that was obvious in his voice. Wondered and yet understood at the same time that this was the key to the whole business.

Sorrow and determination.

'Can we agree on that?'

'Yes.'

He paused and adjusted his chair. Probably crossed his

legs, but she was only guessing. The darkness was extremely dense.

'I . . .' she began.

'No,' he said flatly. 'I don't want you to speak unless it's necessary. If I want you to say something, I'll tell you. This is not going to be a conversation; my intention is simply to tell you a story. All I ask is that you listen.

'A story,' he repeated.

He lit a cigarette, and for a moment his face was illuminated by a faint red glow.

'I'm going to tell you a story,' he said for the third time. 'Not because I'm asking for understanding or forgiveness – I'm way past such things – but simply because I want to remind myself of it one more time, before it's all over.'

'What are you going to do with me?' she asked.

'Don't interrupt me,' he said. 'I beg you not to spoil this. Perhaps I haven't yet made up my mind . . .'

She could hear his breathing through the dense silence and darkness. Nine or ten feet away from her, no more. She closed her eyes, but that didn't make any difference.

The darkness was there. The smells – stale soil, fresh tobacco smoke. And the murderer.

43

Bausen produced two beers from his briefcase, and opened them.

'We mustn't forget the other sightings,' he said. 'There are seven or eight other people who are convinced they saw her in quite different places. She might have had time to do something else as well. The witnesses who saw her here at the station said it was between half past and a quarter to, isn't that right?'

Van Veeteren didn't answer. He lit a cigarette and adjusted the pieces.

'Kropke had stuck in more than a hundred drawing pins by the time he went home,' said Bausen. 'He's almost run out of red ones. That seems to be giving him a bit of a headache, in fact. Anyway, what do you think?'

Van Veeteren shrugged.

'Let's say she did in fact come here,' he said. 'For simplicity's sake, if nothing else. OK, Mr Chief of Police, your turn to start. The Sicilian, I assume?'

'Of course,' said Bausen with a smile, moving his e-pawn. 'All right, she came here. But what the hell did she do?'

'I don't know,' said Van Veeteren, 'but I intend to find out.'

'Really?' said Bausen. 'How? Her office didn't produce much in the way of leads.'

Van Veeteren shrugged.

'I'll grant you that,' he said. 'Your move. If I win, I'll take the lead. I hope you're aware of that.'

'Of course,' said Bausen. 'Have you invented some homemade defence against the Sicilian as well? It could be useful to know.'

'You'll soon find out,' said Van Veeteren, and allowed himself what might have been meant as a smile, but which in fact made Bausen wonder if he had a toothache.

Ah, well, life isn't a game of chess after all, he thought, gazing out of the window. A game of chess involves so very many more possibilities.

It was dark and deserted out there in the square. A few minutes past eleven; they had agreed to play a sixty-minute game, but you never knew ... The chess clock was at home in the bookcase, and if they got themselves into a fascinating position, neither of them was likely to want to have to ruin it because of time pressure. On the contrary. There were some positions that should never be taken any further. They had discussed this before and reached agreement on the matter: Games should be deep-frozen after the thirty-fifth or fiftieth move and never completed. (Such as Linkowski versus Queller in Paris, 1907. After the forty-second. Or Mikoyan versus Andersson, 1980 – in Brest, if he remembered rightly? After the thirty-fifth, or the thirty-seventh, at any rate.) Games in which the beauty of the situation was so great that any further move was bound to ruin it.

It was like life, when you wished that time would call a halt, at least for a while, he thought. Although there was nothing to suggest that this game would turn out to be one of those special ones. Nothing at all.

Three days? In three days he would leave this office, and never set foot in it again . . .

It felt odd, to say the least, and he wondered how those three days would turn out. When he observed Van Veeteren on the other side of his desk, one hand hovering over the board, there were voices inside him that told him this detective chief inspector would in fact fulfill his promise and put the Axeman behind bars before Friday. How he would go about it was not easy to judge, but his colleague was showing signs that he couldn't fail to notice: increasing introversion, a tendency to irritation that had not been present earlier, a certain secretiveness – or whatever you call it – all of which must surely indicate that he was onto something. Getting him to talk about it seemed to be an impossibility; Münster had also started to notice the signs, and had explained that they were not unusual. Familiar indications, rather, for anybody who had seen them before – clear pointers that something was brewing and that DCI Van Veeteren was in top gear mentally. That the situation was precisely as Bausen had suspected, in other words. It could well be that the thaw was imminent, and this sombre police officer was on the brink of assembling all the pieces of this complicated jigsaw puzzle.

Ah, well, thought Bausen. But three days? Would that really be enough?

When it came to the crunch, of course, it wasn't just a matter of these three days; he was the piece who'd be removed from the board on Friday. Nevertheless, over this last week he had steadily formed an impression that the whole business was a race against time. The murderer would have to be caught before October 1. That's what they'd said, and the first was on Friday.

On Friday he would retire. Exit Bausen. A free man with every right to fill his time with whatever he fancied. Who didn't need to give a damn who the Axeman was, and could do whatever he liked.

Or might he not be too happy about that freedom? Would this case cast a shadow over his hard-earned future?

That was not impossible. He thought about his wine cellar and its valuable contents.

Three days?

He eyed Van Veeteren's weighty figure on the other side of his desk, and concluded that he had no idea where he would have placed his bet if he'd needed to do so.

'Your move,' said Van Veeteren again, raising his bottle to his lips.

'What's your name?' said Kropke, starting the tape recorder.

The well-built man opposite sighed.

'You know perfectly well what my damn name is. We were in the same class at school for eight years, for God's sake.'

'This is an official interview,' said Kropke. 'We have to stick to the formalities. So?'

'Erwin Lange,' said the well-built man. 'Born 1951. Owner of the photographer's shop Blitz in Hoistraat. I'm due to open twenty minutes from now, so I'd be obliged if you could get a move on. Married with five children – is that enough?'

'Yes,' said Kropke. 'Would you mind telling me what you saw last Friday evening?'

Erwin Lange cleared his throat.

'I saw Inspector Moerk leave this police station at ten minutes to seven.'

'Six-fifty, in other words. Are you sure about the time?'

'One hundred per cent certain.'

'How can you be so sure?'

'I was due to meet my daughter in the square at a quarter to. I checked my watch and saw that I was five minutes late.'

'And you're sure that the person you saw was Inspector Moerk?'

'Certain.'

'You had met her before?'

'Yes.'

'How close to her were you?'

'Six feet.'

'I see,' said Kropke. 'Did you notice anything else?'

'Such as?'

'Er, her clothes, for instance.'

'Tracksuit . . . red. Gym shoes.'

'Was she carrying anything?'

'No.'

'OK. Many thanks,' said Kropke, switching off the tape recorder. 'I hope you're not intending to leave Kaalbringen during the next few days?'

'Why on earth do you want to know that?'

Kropke shrugged.

'We might need to ask you some more questions . . . you never know.'

'No,' said Erwin Lange, rising to his feet. 'That's the problem with you guys. You never know.'

'Ten to seven?' muttered Bausen. 'Shit, that means she could well have fitted in something else as well. Or what do you think?'

Kropke nodded.

'It takes fifteen minutes max from here to the smoke-house,' he said. 'So there's a gap of at least fifteen minutes.'

'What's the situation on the drawing pin front?' asked Münster.

'A hundred and twelve,' said Kropke. 'But there are no more conglomerations. No pattern, if you like – and nothing more from the beach.'

'She might have sat in her car for a while before driving off,' said Bausen. 'Down by the sea, perhaps. Or outside the station. That seems the most likely.'

'Not necessarily,' said Van Veeteren. 'She must have attracted his attention somehow. Or do you think he already knew about her jogging plans?'

Nobody spoke for a few seconds. Mooser suppressed a yawn. Where's the coffee? thought Münster.

'Ah well,' said Bausen. 'I'm damned if I know, but it's important, obviously.'

'Extremely important,' said Van Veeteren. 'When was the earliest sighting at the smokehouse?'

'Ten or eleven minutes past, or thereabouts,' said Kropke.

Van Veeteren nodded, and contemplated his thumbnail.

'Ah, well,' he muttered. 'I suppose every move has to be considered in its context. There's always another island.'

'Excuse me?' said Kropke.

He's going senile, thought Münster. No doubt about it.

44

'What did you say?' asked Münster.

'Eh?' said Bang.

'Will you repeat what you just said about Inspector Moerk and that fruit shop?'

Bang looked up from the lists and looked slightly shifty.

'I don't understand . . . I just said that I met her there last Friday – at Kuipers, the place that sells fruit out at Immelsport.'

'What time?'

'A quarter past five, roughly. It was before she went to The See Warf. Obviously, I'd have mentioned it if it had been afterward.'

'What did she do there?'

'At Kuipers? Bought some fruit, of course. They have really cheap fruit there . . . and vegetables as well. But I don't see why this matters.'

'Just a minute,' said Münster. 'She left the police station

shortly after half past four . . . around twenty to five, perhaps. How long does it take to get to Immelsport?'

'By car?'

'Yes, by car.'

'I don't know . . . about twenty minutes, I suppose.'

'And you saw her there at quarter past five. That means she can't have had time to go home first, doesn't it?'

'I suppose so, yes,' said Bang, trying to frown.

'How long would it take her to drive home from Kuipers – to Vrejsbakk, that is?'

Bang shrugged.

'Er, about a quarter of an hour, I'd say. Depends on the traffic. But I don't see why you're going on about this.'

Münster contemplated his colleague's rosy-cheeked face with an almost pitying smile.

'I'll explain why,' he said slowly, emphasizing every word. 'If Inspector Moerk was out at Immelsport at a quarter past five, she can hardly have got home until about . . . let's say twenty to six. She was at The See Warf in a tracksuit at quarter past six. Can you tell me when the hell she could have found time to read the Melnik report?'

Bang thought that over for a while.

'You're right, of course,' he said eventually. 'So she didn't read it, is that it?'

'Exactly,' said Münster. 'She didn't read it.'

★

He knocked and went in.

Van Veeteren had moved from the room's only arm-chair to the balcony. He sat there smoking and gazing out in the direction of Fisherman's Square, at the spiky outlines of the buildings as twilight began to descend over the bay. The chair was placed diagonally; all Münster could see of him were his legs, his right shoulder and right arm. Even so, it was enough for him to understand.

Something had happened. And it wasn't a question of his being struck down by senility. On the contrary. I must learn to be humble in thought, Münster decided. Not just in deed.

'Sit down,' said Van Veeteren wearily, gesturing with his hand.

Münster moved the desk chair and sat down next to the detective chief inspector at an angle he hoped would at least give him the opportunity of some eye contact if necessary.

'Let's hear it again!' said Van Veeteren.

Münster cleared his throat.

'Bang met Moerk out at Immelsport at quarter past five last Friday afternoon.'

'Is he sure?'

'Yes. They exchanged a few words. Not even Bang could get that wrong.'

Van Veeteren nodded.

'I'm not sure where that is. Do the times fit?'

'I've checked,' said Münster. 'There's no possibility of her having read the report. She left the police station at exactly four-thirty-five, together with Miss deWitt. They were the last to leave. She went to her car; drove out to that greengrocer's and bought various items; drove home; got changed; tried to phone me, presumably, but received no answer. Instead, she wrote a message and drove here with it, and then—'

Van Veeteren grunted and sat up in the armchair.

'That's enough. Well, what conclusions do you draw from this?'

Münster spread out his arms.

'That she must have discovered something without having read it, of course, something right at the beginning. On the first page, perhaps . . . I don't know.'

He paused and observed his boss, who was gazing up at the evening sky and slowly wagging his head from side to side.

'Bang?' he said, with a deep sigh. 'What the devil are we going to do with Bang?'

'Excuse me?' said Münster, but it was clear that Van Veeteren was talking to himself now. He continued muttering for a while, holding his spent cigarette vertically between his thumb and his index finger and staring at the column of ash as long as his thumb. Only when a puff of wind blew it away did he give a start and seem to become conscious of the fact that he wasn't alone in the room.

'OK, this is what we'll do,' he said, dropping the cigarette end into his glass of water on the balcony floor. 'If it works, it works . . . Münster!'

'Er, yes,' said Münster.

'You take the day off tomorrow and spend your time with Synn and the kids.'

'What?' said Münster. 'Why the . . . ?'

'That's an order,' said Van Veeteren. 'Make sure you're reachable in the evening, though. I think I'll need to talk to you then.'

'What are you going to do?'

'I'm going to make a little trip,' said Van Veeteren.

'Where to?'

'We'll see.'

Here we go again, thought Münster. He gritted his teeth and pushed the humility principle to one side. He's sitting there playing the asshole and being mysterious again, as if he were a gumshoe in some book or film or other! It's disgusting, really. I don't understand why I should be expected to put up with such goddamn—

'I have my reasons,' said Van Veeteren, as if he'd been able to read Münster's thoughts. 'It's just that I have an idea, and it's not one to shout from the rooftops. In fact, if I'm wrong, it's better for nobody to know about it.'

Münster stood up.

'OK,' he said. 'A day off with the family tomorrow. Make sure I'm at home in the evening – anything else?'

'I don't think so,' said Van Veeteren. 'Well, I suppose you could wish me luck. I might need it.'

'Good hunting,' said Münster, leaving Van Veeteren to his fate.

He remained in the armchair for a while, gazing out over the town. He smoked another cigarette and wished he had something to wash away the unpleasant taste in his mouth.

Once this case is over, he thought, I won't want to be reminded of it. Not ever.

Then he sat down at the desk and made two phone calls.

He asked two questions, and received more or less the replies he'd been looking for.

'I'll be there at around noon,' he said. 'No, I can't tell you what it's about. It would be such a goddamn disaster if I'm wrong.'

Then he took a shower and went to bed. It was only eleven o'clock, but the earlier he could set off the next day, the better.

I'll know tomorrow, he thought.

We'll have him behind bars the day after tomorrow, and I can go home on Saturday.

But before he could go to sleep, thoughts about Beate Moerk came flooding into his mind, and it was well into the early hours before he finally dozed off.

45

'Evil,' he began, and his voice was deeper now, barely audible in the densely packed air, 'is the concept we cannot avoid, the only certainty. A young person might find that hard to grasp, but for those of us who have understood, it becomes steadily clearer. What we can be sure of, what we can rely on absolutely, is evil. It never lets us down. Good . . . goodness is only a stage set, a backdrop against which the satanic performs. Nothing else . . . nothing.'

He coughed. He lit another cigarette, a glowing point trembling in the darkness.

'When you eventually acquire that insight, it brings with it a certain degree of comfort despite everything. The difficult thing is simply to rid oneself of all the old hopes, all the illusions and castles in the air that one builds at the beginning. In our case her name was Brigitte, and when she was ten she promised never to hurt me. That was the time she came running over the sands; it was a very windy day at the end of May. Out at Gimsvejr. She flung herself into my arms and hugged me so tightly that I remember having a pain in the back of my neck afterward. We'll love each other all our lives and never do anything silly to each other – those were her very words. Anything silly . . . never do anything silly to each other . . . ten years old, blonde braids. She was the only child we had, and some people said they had never seen such a happy child. Nobody laughed like she did – she sometimes even woke herself up, laughing in her sleep – who can blame us for having hopes?'

He coughed again.

'She took her final exams in 1981, then went to England and worked there for a year. Was accepted by the university in Aarlach the following year. Met a boy called Maurice – Maurice Rühme – yes, we're there already. I think she knew him slightly from before; he came from Kaalbringen. He was reading medicine. Came from an upper-class family, very attractive, and he taught her how to use cocaine . . . he was the first, but I kept him until last.'

The cigarette glowed again.

'They moved in together. Lived together for about a year until he threw her out. By then he had taught her other things . . . LSD, pure morphine, which he never used himself, and how a young woman can earn money most easily and most effectively. Perhaps she provided for him, perhaps he was her pimp . . . I don't know, we never talked about that. Perhaps it hadn't gone quite as far as that, not then.

'She stayed in Aarlach on her own for another eighteen months. She had no place of her own, but moved around from man to man. And she was going in and out of hospitals and treatment centres. Detoxified, ran away, moved on . . .'

He swallowed, and she could hear him holding his breathing in check.

'She lived at home for a short period as well, but then went back. Kept clean for a while, but before long it was the same old story. Eventually she was ensnared by some kind of sect, kept away from drugs but was brought down by other things instead. It was as if she didn't have the strength, or as if she shied away from any normal sort of life . . . or perhaps it was no longer enough for her, the everyday, I don't know. Nevertheless, after two years she agreed to leave Aarlach and live with us again, but now all that happiness had vanished . . . Brigitte . . . Bitte. She was twenty-four. She was only twenty-four, but in fact she was much older than me and my wife. She knew, I think she knew even then that she had burned up her life . . . she could still do her hair in blonde braids, but she had burned up her life. She realized that, but we didn't. I don't know, in fact . . . perhaps there was a faint glimmer of hope left, a possibility of sorting everything out. That's what we told ourselves, at least, what we had to tell ourselves . . . the desperate illusion of vain hope. We believe what we have to believe. Until we've taught ourselves to see reality, that is what we do. That's what this damn life looks like. We cling on to whatever is at hand. Anything at all . . .'

He fell silent. She opened her eyes and saw the cigarette glow illuminate his face, and pulled the blankets more tightly around her. She felt and sensed the extreme hope-lessness that came flowing out of him uninterruptedly. Coming in waves, and for a moment it seemed to compress the darkness, making it solid and impermeable even for words and thoughts.

I understand, she tried to say, but the words wouldn't come out. They stayed deep inside her. Frozen and mean-ingless.

'I went to see Maurice Rühme that same autumn,' he said, breaking the silence. 'One day during the few months she was at home with us again I went to see him. Visited him in that same well-kept apartment she had shared with him, and where he now lived with another woman . . . a young and beautiful woman who still retained all her happiness and never discovered the reason for my visit. He kept her out of the way, and when I wanted to talk to him about Brigitte, we went out and sat in a bar. Sat on a peculiar plush velvet sofa and he waved his arms around and wondered what the devil I wanted; he paid for the wine and asked me if I wanted money . . . I think that's when he sowed the seeds of his own destruction, but it wasn't until he came back here, and the others as well, that I realized the time was ripe. When I killed him, the pleasure was all the greater. Somehow deeper and more intense than with Eggers and Simmel, and that doesn't surprise me. He was the one who had started it all off, it was the image of a living Maurice Rühme who caused the greatest torture during all those sleepless nights before I made up my mind . . . a living, smiling Maurice Rühme sitting on that sofa, flailing his arms about and regretting that Brigitte wasn't made of sterner stuff. That she would fall so badly and hurt herself so much . . . he had never imagined that, the little rich boy with the strong safety net.'

He fell silent once again and shifted his position on the chair.

'I have to leave you now,' he said. 'I'll tell you about the others another time. If nothing unexpected happens . . .'

He remained sitting there for another minute, then she heard him stand up and open the door. Heard the squeaking hinges as he closed it again, locked and bolted it, and it was only after his footsteps had long since faded away that her tongue loosened again.

'And what about me?' she whispered, and for a moment

she thought her words remained hanging like symbols in the darkness.

Small, rapidly fading sparks in a black, black night.

Then she wrapped the blankets around her and tried to close the eyes of her soul.

46

When he drove out of the parking lot behind The See Warf, it was no later than half past seven, and the sun had barely risen over the high coast to the east. A clear day seemed to be in store, and he was rather looking forward to sitting behind the wheel for a few hours.

Sitting there and travelling through an autumnal land-scape with glowing colours and the sharp contours of a drypoint engraving. Perhaps he could pretend that he was an ordinary person on some mundane errand – on the way to Bochhuisen to give a lecture on modern management techniques. Checking the sulphur dioxide emissions from some obscure chemical factory. Meeting a relative at the airport.

Or whatever ordinary folk did.

Sometime in March he had hemmed and hawed and wondered if he ought to change his car, or be satisfied with buying a better auto stereo system. He'd gradually come around to the latter option, and as he now crawled along

Kaalbringen's narrow alleys he was grateful that he had made such a sensible decision. He would never have been able to afford the extra few thousand he'd invested in some very exclusive loudspeakers if he'd had to buy a new car as well.

As things were now, the value of his stereo system was far more than anybody could be expected to give for the rest of his old Opel, and he preferred it that way.

The car was a means of transport. The music was a luxury. No doubt about which ought to be given priority.

He selected something Nordic for this morning. Cold, clear and serene. Sibelius and Grieg. He inserted the CD, and as the first notes of *Tuonela* enveloped him, he could feel how the hairs on his arms bristled.

It was dazzlingly beautiful. Like being in Lämminkäinens cave and the whole mountain echoing with this inspiring music. For the first time in weeks – indeed, ever since he had come to Kaalbringen – he managed to exclude the Axeman from his thoughts. Forget him. Just sat there, lost in the music . . . inside a dome of crystal-clear sound, as the mists lifted and disappeared over the extensive, rolling countryside.

After a stop at a mundane and gloomy roadside café on a level with Urdingen, however, there was a sea change. He realized that instead of travelling farther away, it was now a question of coming closer. His starting point was dropping farther and farther behind, his destination looming . . . rising, falling . . . as ever. He had passed the crown of the hill. He would soon be there. The time was out of joint, and everything would click into place.

Or fall apart. This damn case!

And although he tried once again to distance himself from it, to banish it from his mind, it kept popping up in his consciousness, not in the form of thoughts, speculations or conclusions, but as images.

All the way through the 'Hall of the Mountain King' and 'Anitra's Dance' flowed a constant stream of sharp, unretouched photographs. They throbbed their way forward with a regular and persistent but quite slow rhythm. Like one of those old film strips from a history lesson at school, it struck him. There was plenty of time to evaluate each individual image, although the content was rather different, of course.

Ernst Simmel's head at an unnatural angle on the pathologist's marble table, and the latter's ballpoint pen poking around inside the open gullet.

The lawyer Klingfort's trembling double chin when he gaped in surprise.

The hall carpet soaked in blood in Maurice Rühme's

apartment. And the butcher's axe, the origin of which they had never managed to establish.

Louise Meyer, Eggers's heavily made-up whore, whom he had spent a whole afternoon trying to interview, but she was so high that it was totally impossible to get through to her.

The ice-cold eyes of Jean-Claude Rühme, and Inspector Moerk's beautiful hair when she entered the room with the Melnik report in her hand . . .

Dr. Mandrijn and his wife carting that deformed creature around the grounds at the Seldon Hospice.

And Laurids Reisin. An imagined and persistent image of the man who didn't dare to set foot outside his home.

And the Axeman.

The image of the Axeman himself. Still blurred in outline and unidentifiable, but if Van Veeteren really was on the right track now, it was only a matter of an hour or so before the image emerged with all the clarity that could be wished for.

A few little checks. Confirmation of a nasty suspicion, and it would all be over.

Perhaps.

He was sitting behind his desk, twiddling his mustache. Slim, in a black suit and with thin hair combed back, he was more reminiscent of a funeral director than anything else. That was precisely how Van Veeteren remembered him; in fifteen years he seemed to have aged by one, or at most two months. There was no sign of his having been operated on only a week ago.

With a slight, somewhat acid smile he welcomed his visitor and indicated the visitor's chair, which was directly in front of the immaculately tidy desk.

'What the devil's all this about, then?'

Van Veeteren recalled that the man was reputed to be incapable of opening his mouth without swearing. He turned the palms of his hands in the direction of the ceiling and tried to look apologetic.

'I'm sorry,' he said. 'Just let me have a look at the material I came here to see . . . it's a rather delicate matter.'

'Like hell it is!' He opened a desk drawer and took out a brown folder.

'Here you are. You're welcome to the damn thing!'

Van Veeteren took the folder and wondered for a moment if he ought to read it there and then, on the visitor's chair, but when he looked at the man in black he knew that the matter was over and done with. Finished! He remembered also that his host had never been one to indulge in superfluous details – conversation and that sort of thing. He stood up, shook hands and left the office.

The whole visit had taken less than two minutes.

People who claim I'm bad-tempered ought to meet this happy guy, thought Van Veeteren as he hurried down the stairs.

He crossed the street and opened his car, then took the briefcase from the back seat and put the folder inside it. He looked around. Some fifty yards away, on the corner of the street, was what appeared to be a café sign.

Just the thing, he thought, and set off for it.

He waited until the waitress had left before opening the folder on the table in front of him. He leafed through a few pages and nodded. Leafed some pages backward and nodded again.

Lit a cigarette and started reading from page one.

He didn't need to keep going for long. Confirmation came as early as page five; maybe it wasn't quite what he'd expected, but dammit, it was confirmation even so. He put the papers back in the folder and closed it.

Well, I'll be damned, he thought.

But the motive was far from being clear, of course. What the hell did the other two have to do with all this? How the hell . . . ?

Ah, well, it would become clear eventually, no doubt.

He checked his watch. Just turned one.

Thursday, September 30. Chief of Police Bausen's last

day but one in office. And all of a sudden, the case was on its way to being solved.

Just as he'd suspected from the start, it was hardly the result of laborious routine investigations. Just as he'd thought, the solution had come to him more or less out of the blue. It felt a little odd, he had to concede; unfair almost, although there again, it was hardly the first time this kind of thing had happened. He'd seen it all before, and had realized long ago that if there was any profession in which virtue never got its due reward, it was that of police officer.

Justice has a certain preference for cops who lounge around and think, instead of working their butts off, as Reinhart had once put it.

But what struck him above all else was how reluctantly he would want to look back on this case in the future. His own contribution was certainly nothing to be proud of. Quite the opposite. Something to draw a line under and then forget immediately, for Christ's sake.

Not quite as usual, in other words.

47

Something gnawing away from inside? Or a creeping numbness? A movement going nowhere?

Something like that. That's roughly what it felt like. Insofar as she could feel anything at all.

The time that still existed was for the fading rhythms and needs in her own body. In this deadening darkness day and night no longer existed; time was split into fragments: She slept and woke up, stayed awake and fell asleep. It wasn't possible to judge how long anything took; it might be day outside, or it might be night . . . perhaps she had slept for eight hours, or was it only twenty minutes? Hunger and thirst cropped up merely as faint signals from something that didn't concern her, but she ate nevertheless from the bowl of bread and fruit that he replenished now and again. Drank from the bottle of water.

With her hands chained together, her feet too, her mobility was greatly restricted, and not just by the room; she lay curled up under the blankets, almost in the foetal position. The only times she stood up were when she needed to use the bucket . . . crouching down and groping her way forward. The smell from the bucket had troubled her at first, but soon she no longer noticed it. The overwhelming smell of soil was the only thing she was constantly aware of, the thing that struck her the moment she woke up, that stayed in her consciousness all the time . . . soil.

Interrupted only by the pleasant smell of tobacco when he sat in the chair and told her his story.

The enormous fear she had felt at first had also ebbed away. It had vanished and been replaced by something else: a heavy feeling of lethargy and tedium; not hopelessness, perhaps, but an increasingly strong impression that she was some kind of vegetable, a being that was gradually fading away and becoming an apathetic, numb body . . . a body that was increasingly indifferent to all inner pressures, thoughts and memories. The all-enveloping darkness was eating its way into her, it seemed, slowly and relentlessly penetrating her skin . . . and yet she realized that this might be her only chance of surviving, her only chance of not going mad. Simply lying there under the blankets, maintaining her bodily warmth as much as possible. Letting the dreams and fantasies come and go as they wished, without paying too much attention to them . . . both when awake and when asleep.

And not hoping for anything. Not trying to imagine or think about what might be the final outcome. Just lying there. Just waiting for him to come back and continue his story.

About Heinz Eggers and Ernst Simmel.

'No,' he said, and she could hear him tearing the cellophane off his new pack of cigarettes. 'I don't know if it was already over when she came back from Aarlach. Or if there was still a chance. Of course, it doesn't make any difference now, afterward, there's no point in speculating . . . things turned out the way they did, and that's that.'

He lit his cigarette, and the flame from his lighter almost blinded her.

'She came back, and we didn't know whether to hope or have doubts. We did both, of course; you can't carry on living in a state of constant despair, not until you've achieved that final insight; but it's probably still not possible, not even then. In any case, she refused to live at home with us. We found an apartment for her in Dünningen. She moved in at the beginning of March; it was only one room and a kitchen, but quite big, even so. Light and clean, on the fifth floor with a view over the sea from the balcony. She was still on the sick list and could only work part-time. Detoxified and attending therapy, so it should have been OK . . . she worked afternoons at Henkers. We discovered later that she couldn't handle it, but we knew nothing at the time. We didn't interfere; didn't want to give the impression that we were checking up on her. It had to be on her terms, not ours, some bloody self-important, know-it-all social worker had insisted. So we kept in the background, stayed out of the way . . . damn pointless, all that. Anyway, she lived there that spring, and she managed, we thought, but her income, the money she had to have for the things we thought she didn't need any more, well, that came from guys like Ernst Simmel. Ernst Simmel . . .'

He paused and took a deep drag on his cigarette. She watched the glowing point moving around and suddenly felt an urge to smoke herself. Perhaps he would have given her one if she'd asked, but she didn't dare.

'One evening at the end of April, I drove out to visit her for some reason or other. I'd hardly been there at all since she'd moved in. I can't remember why I went; it can't have been anything especially important, in any case, and it disappeared from my head the moment I got there . . .'

Another pause, and the cigarette glowed again. He coughed a few times. She leaned her head against the wall and waited. Waited, and knew.

'I rang the doorbell. It was evidently broken, so I tried the handle . . . it wasn't locked, and I went in. Entered the hall and looked around. The bedroom door was half open . . . I heard noises and couldn't help looking in. Well, I was able to see him getting full value for his money . . .'

'Simmel?' she whispered.

'Yes.'

More silence. He cleared his throat and inhaled again. Stabbed out the cigarette on the ground, and stamped on the glowing ash with his foot.

'As I stood in the doorway, our eyes met. She looked straight at me over the shoulder of that shit . . . they were standing pressed up against the wall. I think that if I'd had a weapon with me at that moment, an axe or a knife or whatever, I'd have killed him there and then. Or maybe I'd have been too paralyzed . . . those eyes of hers, Brigitte's eyes as she allowed that man to have his way with her, it was the same look I'd seen once before. I recognized it immediately; she was seven or eight then, and it must have been the first time she'd seen starving, dying children and understood what was involved . . . some television report from Africa. It was the same eyes that had looked at me all those years ago. The same desperation. The same feeling of helplessness when confronted with the evil of the world . . . I went back home and don't think I slept a wink for a whole month.'

He paused and lit another cigarette.

'Was it the same year that Simmel moved to Spain?' she asked, and was surprised to discover how strong her curiosity was despite everything. To find that she was listening carefully to his story and that she was affected by it as if the wounds were her own . . . that her own predicament and despair were perhaps no more than a reflection and an example of something far, far greater.

The totality of suffering in the world down the ages?

The overall power of evil?

Or it might just be that damn obstinacy everybody talks about. My obstinacy and peculiar strength . . . and the fact that I always keep putting off having that baby . . .

Or maybe a bit of both? The same thing?

If that was the case, what the hell did it matter? Her thoughts wandered off and she could no longer find the thread. She clenched her fists, but after a few seconds could no longer feel them. They turned numb and evaporated; in the same inevitable way as her vain efforts to follow a line of thought.

'Yes,' he said eventually. 'It was that same year. He vanished that same summer . . . came back last spring, as did the other two. Surely it has to be a sign when all three suddenly turn up in Kaalbringen within a few weeks of each other. Don't try to tell me that it's just a coincidence. It was a sign from Bitte. From Bitte and from Helena, it's so damn obvious that you can't possibly ignore it . . . Will anybody be able to understand that?'

There was a sudden sharp edge to his voice. Indignation

at having been wronged. As if it wasn't in fact he himself who was behind it all. As if he was not responsible for these murders. As if . . .

Merely an instrument.

Something that Wundermaas had said came back to her – possibly not word for word, but the gist – something about there being a necessity behind most murders, a compulsion that was stronger than anything behind other actions; if that was not the case, they would never take place, never need to be carried out.

If there was an alternative.

Necessity. Sorrow, determination and necessity . . . yes, she understood that this was the way it was.

Sorrow. Determination. Necessity.

She waited for the continuation, but there was none. Only his heavy breathing that cut through the darkness, and it struck her that it was this very moment, at this second, when time had stood still, that he was making up his mind about her own fate.

'What are you going to do with me?' she whispered.

Maybe it was too early. Maybe she didn't want to give him time to think it through.

He didn't answer. He stood up and backed out through the door.

Closed it and locked it. Shot the bolts.

Once again she was alone. She listened to his footsteps

fading away and huddled up against the wall. Pulled the blankets over her.

One left, she thought. He has one more to tell me about. And then?

And then?

48

If he'd had the ability to see into the future, if only for a few hours, it is possible that he'd have given lunch a miss without more ado. And set off for Kaalbringen as quickly as possible.

As it was – with the solution of this long drawn-out case clearly within reach – he decided instead to indulge himself with a Canaille aux Prunes at Arno's Cellar, a little seafood restaurant he remembered from the occasion more than twenty years earlier when he'd spent a week here on a course.

In any case, he probably needed a few hours to think things over in peace and quiet; how he directed the final act of this drama was of some significance – of considerable significance, in fact. The Axeman needed to be arrested as painlessly as possible, and also as far as possible, the question of motives investigated and clarified. And then there was the problem concerning Inspector Moerk, of course. There were probably plenty of opportunities to put a foot wrong and, to quote Bausen, it was a long time since anything had gone well with this case.

However, he could think of no better companion than a good meal.

After the pear in brandy and the coffee, he had made up his mind about the various problems – a strategy that seemed to him to have good odds of working and involved as good a chance of avoiding injury to Inspector Moerk as could be hoped.

Assuming she was still alive, that is. He wanted to believe it, of course, but probabilities didn't seem to play much of a role in this case.

Probabilities? he thought. I ought to have known by now.

It was half past three. He paid his bill, left his corner table and occupied the phone booth in the vestibule.

Three calls. First to Bausen at home in his nest; then Münster – no answer at the cottage – no doubt he was still on the beach with Synn and the kids. Then Kropke at the police station. This call cost Van Veeteren half an hour; the inspector evidently found it a little difficult to catch on to what was happening, but when they eventually finished the conversation, Van Veeteren had the feeling that everything would work out well, notwithstanding.

★

He set off shortly after four o'clock, and he had barely reached Ulming, after a mere seven or eight miles, when he noticed his generator warning light blinking. Before long it was emitting a constant and ominous glow, and matters were not helped by the driver cursing and beating the dashboard with both fists. On the contrary, the bastard of a car started coughing and losing speed, and when he came to a service station, he was forced to admit that he had no choice.

He uttered a few more choice oaths, put on his right-hand blinker and left the highway.

'A new generator,' said the young mechanic after a cursory look under the hood. 'Probably not possible to do anything about it today.' He put his hands in his pockets and looked apologetic. Van Veeteren cursed.

'Well, okay, if it's so urgent and if you're prepared for what it'll cost.'

Hmm. It might well take four or five hours . . . he'd have to drive to town, of course, to buy a new one, but if the customer was in a hurry, he could hire a car, naturally. There were one or two available.

'And leave my stereo system here?' roared the detective chief inspector, with a broad gesture encompassing the depressing sight of the workshop interior. 'What the hell do you take me for?'

'All right,' said the mechanic. 'Might I suggest that you wait in the café? You can buy books and magazines at the news-stand.'

Damnation! thought Van Veeteren. Bloody car! I won't be back in Kaalbringen until one or two in the morning.

'Phone!' yelled Bart.

Münster and his family had stayed on the beach until the sun had started to sink behind the line of trees in the west. They had only just walked through the door after a day filled with games, relaxation and reunion. Münster carefully placed the sleeping four-year-old in bed while Synn went to answer the phone.

'It's DCI Van Veeteren,' she whispered, with her hand over the earpiece. 'He sounds like a barrel of gunpowder about to go off. Something to do with the car.'

Münster took the receiver.

'Hello?' he said.

That was more or less the only word he spoke for the next ten minutes or more. He just stood there in the window recess, listening and nodding while his wife and his son prowled around and around him in ever-decreasing circles. A single look was enough for Synn to understand,

and she passed on her knowledge to her six-year-old, who had been through this many times before.

No doubt about it. The car was not what this call was really about. She could hear that in the voice of her husband's boss at the other end of the line: a muffled but unstoppable tornado. She saw it in her husband's face as well – in his body language, the profile of his jaw. Tense, resolute. A slight touch of white under his ears . . .

It was time.

And slowly that feeling of worry surged towards and over her. The feeling she couldn't speak about, not even to him, but which she knew she shared with every other policeman's wife all over the world.

The possibility that . . . The possibility of something happening that . . .

She grasped her son's hand firmly, and refused to let go. Grateful despite everything that she'd had the opportunity of coming here.

'About two o'clock?' asked Münster in the end. 'Yep, I'm with you. We'll assemble here, yes . . . OK, I can fix that.'

Then he replaced the receiver and stared fixedly ahead, looking at nothing.

'That was the damnedest . . .' he said. 'But he's right, of course . . .'

He shook his head, then became aware of his wife and

son, staring at him with the same unspoken question on their faces.

'We're going to arrest the Axeman tomorrow morning,' he explained. 'The others are coming here tonight to sort out tactics.'

'Coming here?' said Synn.

'Wicked,' said the six-year-old boy. 'I'll go with you.'

Plans were laid by half past four. It had taken a bit longer than Van Veeteren had imagined; the question of motive had been kicked around, and nobody was quite sure how it all hung together. But they had sorted it out as far as possible. They couldn't get any further now, and even if a few pieces of the puzzle were still missing, everybody was clear about the overall picture.

'No point in waiting any longer,' said Van Veeteren. 'Everybody knows what they have to do . . . I don't think we're exposing ourselves to much of a risk, but it's just as well to take precautions. Mooser?'

Mooser tapped his bulging hip.

'Münster?'

Münster nodded.

'Chief of Police?'

Another nod, and Van Veeteren closed his notebook. 'All right. Let's go!'

49

The thought of death came like a considerate guest, but once she had let it in, it decided to stay.

All at once it was living with her. Uninvited and inexorable. Like a hand squeezing her midriff. Like a slowly swelling tumour. A grey cloud spreading throughout her body, smothering her thoughts under still more hopeless darkness.

Death. Suddenly it had become the only reality she possessed. This is the end, she told herself, and it was nothing especially traumatic or upsetting. She was going to die . . . either by his hand or of her own accord. Lying curled up here on the floor under all these blankets, with this aching body of hers and with this writhing soul, which was the most fragile part of her . . . that was what would give way first, she knew now; once she had opened the door to death, the spark of life inside her was slowly dimming. Perhaps it would be only a hundred or seventy or even twenty intakes of breath before it would be extinguished. She had started counting now; people always did when they were in prison, she knew that. She'd read about prisoners who had kept themselves sane thanks to this constant counting, the only snag being that she had nothing to count. No events. No noises. No time.

Only her own breathing and pulse.

She was waiting for him now. Longing for him as if he were her lover . . . her warder, her executioner, her murderer? Whatever. Every change, every incident, every imaginable interruption . . . anything but this constant intercourse with death.

Her considerate and demanding guest.

The dish of food was half full, but she could no longer get anything down. She would occasionally moisten her tongue with water, but she was not in the least thirsty either. She struggled as far as the bucket, but could produce nothing . . . all her bodily functions had left her, one after another, it was as simple as that.

Why didn't he come?

Even if time no longer existed, she had the feeling that something must have delayed him. She made up her mind to count up to four thousand heartbeats, and if he hadn't arrived by then, she would . . .

. . . she would count another four thousand heartbeats.

Was it possible to distinguish between a thousand heart-beats and another thousand heartbeats? Could it be done? And if so, what was the point?

And as she counted, that hand squeezed tighter and tighter.

The cloud grew.

Death filled her.

'I'm late,' he said, and she could barely hear his voice.

'Yes,' she whispered.

He sat there in silence, and she noticed that she was now counting his breaths. Rasping in the darkness as usual, but even so his, not hers . . . something that didn't emanate from herself.

'Tell me your story,' she begged.

He lit a cigarette and suddenly she felt the faint glow growing and forcing its way inside her . . . all at once the whole of her body was filled with light and the next moment she lost consciousness. She woke up in a glittering white world, where a pulsating and vibrant gleam was so strong and powerful that it was rumbling inside her. Vertiginous spirals spun around inside her head, and she plunged into them, was sucked up and carried by this infernally rotating whiteness, this flood of raging light . . .

Then it began to recede. The torrent slowed down and

found a slowly swaying rhythm; waves and breakers, and the smell of earth returned. Of earth and smoke. Once again she saw only darkness and a trembling red point, and she realized that something had happened. She didn't know what, but she had been elsewhere and was now back. And the cloud was no longer spreading.

Something had happened.

'Tell me your story,' she said, and now her voice was steady, like before. 'Tell me about Heinz Eggers.'

'Heinz Eggers,' he said, and hesitated as he usually did at the start. 'Yes, I'll tell you about Heinz Eggers as well. It's just that I am so tired, so very tired . . . but I'll keep going to the end, of course.'

She had no time to reflect on what his words might imply. He cleared his throat and started.

'It was in Selstadt . . . she moved there. Or was moved there. Was taken in hand by the social services and placed in Trieckberg; do you know Trieckberg?'

'No.'

'One of those community homes that manages to help the odd patient . . . doesn't just allow them to drift out then back in, out and back in, until they finally die of an overdose or a dirty needle. It manages to help the odd patient. Then . . . we had contact, good contact; we went to visit her, and she wasn't too bad. There was a spark of light again, but after a few months we heard that she had run away . . . it was a long, long time before we were tipped off that she might be in Selstadt. Trieckberg isn't far from there. I drove to Selstadt and searched . . . after a few days I dug up an address and went there. It was a drug den, of course. I've seen a fair amount, but I've never seen anybody in a worse state than Brigitte and the other woman in Heinz Eggers's stable . . . that's what he called it. His stable. He obviously thought I'd come for a quick session with one or both of his whores. He might have had more, come to that . . .'

He paused.

'What did you do?' she asked after a while.

'I hit him. Punched him on the nose. Hadn't the strength to do any more than that. He disappeared. I phoned for an ambulance and got both of them into hospital . . . she died three weeks later. Bitte died at the hospital in Selstadt. Forgive me, I'm too tired to go into the details.'

'How?'

He waited again and inhaled deeply on his cigarette. Dropped it on the floor and stamped out the glow with his foot.

'Slit her own throat as she threw herself out of a

sixth-floor window . . . wanted to make sure. That was September 30, 1988. She was twenty-seven years old.'

He remained sitting there for longer than usual this time. Sat the usual three or four yards away from her in the darkness, breathing heavily. Neither of them spoke; she gathered there was nothing else to add. He had finished now.

He had achieved his vengeance.

The story was told.

It was all over.

They sat there in the darkness, and it seemed to her that they were simply two actors who happened to be still onstage, even though the curtain had long since come down.

What now? she wondered. What comes next?

What will Horatio do after the death of Hamlet?

Live and tell the story one more time, as he had been requested to do?

Die by his own hand, which is his wish?

In the end she dared to put the question:

'What do you intend to do?'

She could hear him give a start. Perhaps he had actually fallen asleep. He seemed to be enveloped by infinite weariness, in any case, and she immediately felt that she would have liked to give him advice.

Some kind of comfort. But there was none, of course.

'I don't know,' he said. 'I've played my part. I must receive a sign. Must go there and wait for a sign . . .'

He stood up.

'What day is it?' she asked suddenly, without knowing why.

'It's not day,' he said. 'It's night.'

Then he left her again.

Well, I'm still alive, she thought in surprise. And night is the mother of day . . .

50

Van Veeteren took the lead.

Led the way through the darkness that was starting to become less intense. A narrow strip of grey dawn had forced its way in under the trees, but it was still too early to make out anything but vague outlines, flickerings and shadows. Sound still held sway over light, the ear over the eye. A jumble of faint rustling and squeals from small animals scuttling away from their feet as they moved forward. A strange place, thought Münster.

'Take it easy now,' Van Veeteren had urged them. 'It's a helluva lot better to arrive a quarter of an hour later without being discovered.'

They eventually turned the corner and emerged onto the stone paving. Van Veeteren opened the door. It squeaked faintly, and Münster could sense that he was concerned; but they were all inside within half a minute.

They split up. Two up the stairs. He and Münster downstairs.

It was pitch-dark, and he switched on his flashlight.

'It's only a guess,' he whispered over his shoulder, 'but I'm pretty damn sure that I'm right, even so!'

Münster nodded and followed hard on his heels.

'Look!' exclaimed Van Veeteren, stopping. He pointed the beam at an old doll's house crammed full of toys: dolls, teddy bears and everything else you could think of. 'I ought to have realized even then . . . but that would have been asking a bit much, I suppose.'

They continued downward, Münster half a step behind him. The smell of soil grew stronger – soil and the slight remains of stale cigarette smoke. The passage grew narrower and the ceiling lower, making them crouch slightly, leaning forward – groping their way forward, despite the flickering beam from the flashlight.

'Here,' said Van Veeteren suddenly. He stopped and shone the flashlight on a solid wooden door with double bolts and a bulky padlock. 'Here it is!'

He knocked cautiously.

No sound.

He tried again, a little harder, and Münster could hear a faint noise from the other side.

'Inspector Moerk?' said Van Veeteren, his cheek pressed against the damp door.

Now they could hear a clear and definite 'Yes,' and simultaneously Münster felt something burst inside him.

Tears poured down his face and nothing on earth could have stopped them. I'm a forty-two-year-old cop standing here weeping like a little kid. Godammit!

But he couldn't care less. He stood behind Van Veeteren's back and wept under the cover of darkness. Thank you, he thought, without having any idea whom he was addressing.

Van Veeteren took out the crowbar, and after a couple of failed attempts managed to make the padlock give way. He drew back the bolts and opened the door . . .

'Take the light away,' whispered Beate Moerk, and all Münster could see of her were the chains, her mass of tousled hair and the hands she was holding over her eyes.

Before doing as she'd asked, Van Veeteren shone the beam around the walls for a few seconds.

Then he muttered something unintelligible and switched off.

Münster fumbled his way over to her. Raised her to her feet . . . she leaned heavily on him, and it was clear that he would have to carry her. He carefully lifted her up, and noticed that he was still crying.

'How are you?' he managed to blurt out as she laid her head on his shoulder, and his voice sounded surprisingly steady.

'Not too good,' she whispered. 'Thank you for coming.'

'No problem,' said Van Veeteren. 'I ought to have realized sooner, though . . . I'm afraid you'll have to keep the chains on for a bit longer. We don't have the right equipment with us.'

'Doesn't matter,' said Beate Moerk. 'But when you've got them off, I want a bathroom for three hours.'

'Of course,' said Van Veeteren. 'You've built up plenty of overtime.'

Then he started to lead them back.

Kropke and Mooser were already waiting for them on the patio.

'He's not at home,' said Kropke.

'Oh, shit,' said Van Veeteren.

'You can put me down if you like,' said Beate Moerk. 'I might be able to walk . . .'

'Out of the question,' said Münster.

'Where the hell is he?' grunted Van Veeteren. 'It's half past five in the morning . . . shouldn't he be in his goddamn bed?'

Beate Moerk had opened her eyes, but was shading them with her hand from the faint light of dawn.

'He was with me not long ago,' she said.

'Not long ago?' said Kropke.

'I have a bit of a problem with judging time,' she explained. 'An hour . . . maybe two.'

'He didn't say where he was going?' asked Van Veeteren.

Beate Moerk searched her mind.

'No,' she said. 'But he wanted a sign, he said—'

'A sign?' said Mooser.

'Yes.'

Van Veeteren thought that over for a while. He lit a cigarette and started pacing up and down over the paving stones.

'Hmm,' he said eventually and came to a halt. 'Yes, that's possible, of course . . . why not? Münster!'

'Yes.'

'See to it that the chains are removed and get Inspector Moerk to the hospital.'

'Home,' said Beate Moerk.

Van Veeteren muttered.

'All right,' he said. 'We'll send a doctor instead.'

She nodded.

'Kropke and Mooser, come with me!'

'Where do you think he is?' asked Kropke when Münster and Moerk had left.

'With his family,' said Van Veeteren. 'Where he belongs.'

51

'I'll be all right,' said Beate Moerk.

'Sure?'

'Of course. A spell in the bath and I'll be a rose again.'

'The doctor will be here in half an hour. I'd prefer to stay until then.'

'No, thank you,' she said with a faint smile. 'Get back to your family now.'

He paused, his hand on the door handle.

'That report . . . ' he said. 'How much of it did you read, in fact?'

She laughed.

'All right, I'll come clean. Nothing. It was the pagination that intrigued me. When I handed over the original, I looked at the last page and saw that it numbered thirty-five, at the bottom . . . I think I said something about it at the time.'

'True,' said Münster, remembering the moment.

'There were no numbers on the copy . . . that's all. I

didn't know a thing about his daughter when I drove to the station. I've only been working here for four years; she was dead when I started. I just wanted to check if I could find anything in the copying room. I suppose he must have seen me when I arrived, or as I was leaving . . . that's all. Maybe it was pure coincidence; I don't know if he thought I knew something. Anything else you're wondering about?'

Münster shook his head.

'Well, quite a bit in fact,' he said. 'But it can wait.'

'Go now,' she said. 'But give me a hug first, if you can stand the stink.'

'Come on, I've been carrying you around all morning,' said Münster, throwing his arms around her.

'Ouch,' said Beate Moerk.

'So long, then,' said Münster. 'Look after yourself.'

'You too.'

He saw him from some considerable distance away.

In the faint light of dawn, he was standing in the same place as he'd been that evening, right at the beginning.

Back then, when he'd chosen not to approach him. Not to disturb his sorrow.

Like then, he had his hands thrust deep into his pockets. Head bowed. He was standing perfectly still, legs wide apart, as if he'd been waiting for a long time and wanted to make sure that he didn't lose his balance.

Concentrating hard. Deep in what might have been prayer, Van Veeteren thought, but perhaps he was simply waiting. Waiting for something to happen.

Or perhaps it was just sorrow. His back made it so clear he didn't want to be disturbed that Van Veeteren hesitated to approach. He gestured to Kropke and Mooser to keep their distance . . . so that he would have him to himself for at least a short while.

'Good morning,' he said when there were only a couple of yards left, and Bausen must have heard his footsteps in the gravel. 'I'm coming now.'

'Good morning,' said Bausen, without moving.

Van Veeteren put his hand on Bausen's shoulder. Stood still for a while, reading what it said on the headstone.

BRIGITTE BAUSEN

6/18/1961 – 9/30/1988

HELENA BAUSEN

2/3/1932 – 9/27/1991

'Yesterday?' said Van Veeteren.

Bausen nodded.

'Five years ago. As you can see, her mother didn't quite make it in the end . . . but she was only three days short.'

They stood in silence for a while. Van Veeteren could

hear Kropke coughing in the background, and held up a
warning hand without looking around.

'I ought to have realized sooner,' he said. 'You've given
me a few signs.'

Bausen didn't answer at first. Shrugged his shoulders,
and shook his head.

'Signs,' he said eventually. 'I don't receive any signs . . .
I've been standing here, waiting, for quite a long time, not
just right now . . .'

'I know,' said Van Veeteren. 'Perhaps . . . perhaps the
absence of any is a sign in itself.'

Bausen raised his eyes.

'God's silence?' He shuddered, and looked Van Veeteren
in the eye. 'I'm sorry about Moerk . . . have you released
her?'

'Yes.'

'I needed somebody to explain everything to. Didn't
realize that before I took her, but that's how it was. I never
thought of killing her.'

'Of course not,' said Van Veeteren. 'When did you
gather that I'd caught on?'

Bausen hesitated.

'That last game of chess, perhaps. But I wasn't sure—'

'Nor was I,' said Van Veeteren. 'I had trouble finding a
motive.'

'But you know now?'

'I think so. Kropke did a bit of research yesterday . . . what a disgusting mess.'

'Moerk knows all about it. You can ask her. I haven't the strength to go through it all again. I'm so tired.'

Van Veeteren nodded.

'That telephone call yesterday . . .' said Bausen. 'I wasn't fooled; it was more a question of being polite, if you'll excuse me?'

'No problem,' said Van Veeteren. 'It was an opening gambit I'd made up myself.'

'More of an endgame,' said Bausen. 'I thought it took you a bit long, even so . . .'

'My car broke down,' said Van Veeteren. 'Shall we go?'

'Yes,' said Bausen. 'Let's.'

FIVE

2 OCTOBER

52

The beach was endless.

Van Veeteren paused and gazed out to sea. There were big waves, for once. A fresh wind was gathering strength, and on the horizon a dark cloud bank was growing more ominous. No doubt it would be raining by evening.

'I think we should go back now,' he said.

Münster nodded. They'd been walking for more than half an hour. Synn had promised a meal by three o'clock, and the children would no doubt need some cleaning up before they would be allowed at the table.

'Bart!' yelled Münster, waving. 'We're going back now!'

'All right!' shouted the six-year-old, completing his final attack on the enemy buried in the sand.

'I'm tired,' said Münster's daughter. 'Carry me!'

He lifted her onto his shoulders, and they started walking slowly back along the beach.

'How is he?' asked Münster when he felt that Marieke had fallen asleep and Bart was sufficiently far ahead.

'Not too bad,' said Van Veeteren. 'He's not that concerned about the future. The main thing is that he's done what he had to do.'

'Did he want to be caught?'

'No, but it didn't matter very much either. He was in an impossible position once Moerk started on his trail, of course.'

Münster thought for a moment.

'How many lines were there about Brigitte Bausen in the Melnik report, in fact?' he said. 'There can't have been all that much—'

'Exactly one page. About that year they were living together, that is. Her name was mentioned twice. Melnik had no idea, of course; not even he can know the names of every chief of police in the country. If he'd had a bit more time – Bausen, that is – he could have substituted another name instead of removing a whole page. If he had, he might have got away with it. But we were standing waiting for him, more or less, and for Christ's sake, we were bound to have noticed that something funny was going on.'

Münster nodded.

'I find it hard to see that what he did was so dreadful,' he said. 'Morally speaking, I mean—'

'Yes,' said Van Veeteren. 'You might say that he had every right – maybe not to cut the heads off three people – but to do something about his enormous sorrow.'

He fumbled around in his pockets and produced a pack of cigarettes. Was forced to stop and cup his hand around the lighter before he could produce a flame.

'Enormous sorrow and enormous determination,' he said, 'those are the main ingredients in this dish. Those are Moerk's words, not mine, but they're pretty good as a summary. Sorrow and determination – and necessity. The world we live in is not a nice place – but we've been aware of that for quite some time, haven't we?'

They walked in silence for a while. Münster remembered something else Beate Moerk had said about her conversations with Bausen in the cellar.

Life imposes certain conditions upon us, she reported that he said. If we don't accept the challenge, we become petrified. We don't have any real choice.

Petrified? Was that right? Was that really what it looked like – this vain battle against evil? Where the result, no matter how puny and unsuccessful it might turn out to be, was nevertheless the important thing; where only the deed itself, the principle, had any significance?

And the only reward was to avoid petrification. Only?

Perhaps that was enough.

But the lives of three people—?

'What do you think?' Van Veeteren interrupted his train of thought. 'What punishment would you give him if it were up to you?'

'In the best of all worlds?'

'In the best of all worlds.'

'I don't know,' said Münster. 'What do you think?'

Van Veeteren considered for a while.

'Not easy,' he said. 'Lock him up in the cellar, perhaps, like he did with Moerk. But in rather more humane conditions, of course – a lamp, some books . . . and a corkscrew.'

They fell silent again. Walked side by side down to the water's edge and let their summaries sink in. The wind was growing stronger. It came in gusts, which you could almost lean into at times, Münster felt. Bart came running up with some new finds for his collection of stones. He off-loaded them into his father's pockets and raced ahead again. When the low whitewashed cottage came into view once more, Van Veeteren cleared his throat.

'In any case,' he said, 'he's the most likable murderer I've ever come across. It's not often you have an opportunity of mixing so much with them either – before you put them behind bars, that is.'

Münster looked up. There was a new tone in Van Veeteren's voice, a totally surprising hint of self-irony. Something he'd never detected before, and could barely imagine. It was suddenly hard to hold back a smile.

'How did the chess go?' he asked.

'I won, of course,' said Van Veeteren. 'What the hell do you think? It took some time, that's all.'

A few hours later he went to the water's edge one last time. He lit his last cigarette as well, and stood there all alone until it was finished, contemplating the agitated breakers rolling in towards the shore.

Things were breathing again. Both sky and sea – the same threatening grey-violet combination, the same irresistible force; and when he felt the first drop of rain in his hand, he turned his back on it all and made his way up towards his car.

Time to get away from here, he thought.

The curtain has fallen. The tragedy is over.

Exit Oedipus. Exit Van Veeteren.

He started the car. Switched on the headlights as darkness fell rapidly, and set off inland.

And yet, it might not be for good. Perhaps Kaalbringen would have the pleasure of entertaining his presence again . . .

For even retired Axemen must eventually be allowed

time out on parole. And even the narrowest of leads at chess must allow a challenge.

What wouldn't one do for a decent glass of wine?

Thought Detective Chief Inspector Van Veeteren as he started groping in the glove compartment for Penderecki.

If you enjoyed Borkmann's Point *you'll love*

THE RETURN

the next Inspector Van Veeteren mystery

An unmissable hospital appointment is looming for Inspector Van Veeteren, when a corpse is found rolled in a rotting carpet by a young child playing in a local beauty spot. Missing head and limbs, the torso is too badly decomposed for forensic identification – bar one crucial detail . . .

Circumstantial evidence soon points to a local man, a double murderer who disappeared nine months before, shortly after being released on parole; a local hero, who turned monster after being convicted of killing two women over a span of three decades.

Recuperating after an operation, Van Veeteren is nevertheless directing investigations from his hospital bed, for he is convinced that only the innocence of this new victim can be the motive for his murder. But is he on the wrong track completely?

The first chapter follows here . . .

1

It was the first and the last day.

The steel door was locked behind him and the metallic click hovered for a while in the cool morning air. He took four paces, paused and put down his suitcase. Closed his eyes, then opened them again.

A thin morning mist hung over the deserted car park, the sun was just rising over the nearby town and the only sign of life was the flocks of birds swooping over the fields that surrounded the cluster of buildings. He stood there for a few seconds and indulged his senses. The scent of newly harvested corn wafted into his nostrils. The dazzling light quivered over the asphalt. In the distance, a mile or so to the west, he could hear the persistent hum of traffic on the motorway that carved a path through the open country-side. The sudden realization of the world's true dimensions gave him a moment of vertigo. He had not set foot outside these walls for twelve years; his cell had been seven feet by ten, and it dawned on him that it was a long way to the town and the railway station. An incredibly long way, perhaps impossibly far on a day like this.

He had been offered a taxi, that was normal practice, but he declined. Didn't want to take a shortcut into the world at this early stage. Wanted to feel the burden and the pain and the freedom in every step he took this morning. If he were to have a chance of succeeding in the task he had set himself, he understood what he needed to overcome. Overcome and get the better of.

He picked up his suitcase and started walking. It didn't weigh much. A few changes of underwear. A pair of shoes, a shirt, pants and a toiletry bag. Four or five books and a letter. He had tried on the clothes he was wearing and signed for them at the equipment store the previous day. Typical prison clothing. Black synthetic-leather shoes. Blue trousers. Pale grey cotton shirt and a thin windcheater. As far as the locals were concerned he would be as easily identifiable as a Roman Catholic priest or a chimney sweep. One of the many who wandered into the railway station carrying a cardboard suitcase, eager to leave. Having spent time out here in the Big Grey between the municipal forest and the motorway. Having been so near and yet so far away. One of them. The easily identifiable.

The Big Grey. That's what they called it around here. For him it was nameless – just a brief stretch of time and hardly any space. And it was a long time since he'd been worried about other people staring at him; a long time since he'd been forced to turn his back on that kind of superficial and pointless contact. He had left his former life without hesitation; there was no alternative, and he'd never longed to return. Never.

You could say he had never really been a part of it.

The sun rose. He had to stop again after a hundred yards. Wriggled out of his jacket and slung it over his shoulder. Two cars overtook him. A couple of warders, presumably, or some other staff. Prison people in any case. Nobody else ventured out here. There was only the Big Grey here.

He set off once more. Tried to whistle but couldn't hit upon a tune. It occurred to him that he ought to have sunglasses: Maybe he could buy a pair when he got to town. He shaded his eyes with his hand, squinted and scrutinized the townscape through the dazzling haze. At that very moment church bells started ringing.

He glanced at his wristwatch. Eight. He wouldn't be able to catch the first train. There again, he hadn't really wanted to: better to sit in the station café over a decent breakfast and today's paper. No rush. Not this first day, at least. He would carry out the task he'd set himself, but the precise timing depended on factors he knew nothing about as yet, naturally enough.

Tomorrow, perhaps. Or the day after. If all these years had taught him anything, anything at all, it was precisely this. To be patient.

Patience.

He continued walking purposefully towards town. Took possession of the deserted, sun-drenched streets. The shady alleys leading from the square. The worn cobbles. Strolled slowly along the path by the brown, muddy river where listless ducks drifted in a state of timeless inertia. This was in itself something remarkable – walking and walking without coming up against a wall or a fence. He paused on one of the bridges and watched a family of swans huddled together on a muddy islet, in the shade cast by chestnut trees on the riverbank. Observed the trees as well, their branches that seemed to stretch down as much as upwards. Towards the water as well as the sky.

The world, he thought. Life.

A spotty youth stamped his ticket with obvious distaste. Single ticket, yes, of course. He gave him a look, then headed for the news-stand. Bought two newspapers and some men's magazine or other featuring large, naked breasts, without displaying the slightest embarrassment.

Next, a pot of coffee in the café, freshly made sandwiches with jam and cheese. A cigarette or two. Another hour to go before the train, and it was still morning.

The first morning of his second return, and the whole world was full of time. Innocence and time.

Hours later he was nearly there. He'd been alone in the carriage for the last few miles. Looked out through the scratched, dirty window; watched fields, forests, towns and people marching past – and suddenly everything fell into place. Took on their own specific significance. Buildings, roads, the subtle interplay of the countryside. The old water tower. The soccer fields. The factory chimneys and people's back gardens. Gahn's Furniture Manufacturers. The square. The high school. The viaduct and the houses along Main Street. The train ground to a halt.

As he disembarked he noticed that the platform had a new roof of pale yellow plastic. The station building had been renovated. New signs as well.

Apart from that it was just as before.

He took a cab. Left the town behind. A quarter of an hour's drive with nothing said, following the shore of the lake that sometimes vanished, sometimes glittered beyond cornfields and copses of deciduous trees, and then he was there.

'You can stop after the church. I'll walk the last bit.'

He paid and got out. There was something vaguely familiar about the driver's wave as he drove off. He waited until the car had made a U-turn and disappeared behind the dairy. Then he picked up his suitcase and the plastic carrier bag of groceries and set out on the last lap.

The sun was high in the sky now. Sweat was running down his face and between his shoulder blades. It was farther than he remembered, and more uphill.

But then, it was twelve years since the last time.

The house was also twelve years older, but it was still there. She had cleared a path as far as the steps, as promised, but no more. The borderline between garden and forest seemed to be blurred, birch saplings had invaded, grass and undergrowth were three or four feet high along the house walls. The roof of the barn was sagging, the roof tiles seemed to be rotting away, an upstairs windowpane was broken, but it didn't bother him. Insofar as he had expected anything, it all came more or less up to expectations.

The key was hanging under the gutter, as it should have

been. He unlocked the door. Had to give it a heave with his shoulder in order to open it. It seemed to have swelled a bit.

It smelled stuffy, but not excessively so. No rot, no mice, apparently. There was a note on the kitchen table.

She wished him all the best, it said. That was all.

He put his suitcase and the plastic carrier on the sofa under the clock and looked around. Started to walk round the house and open windows. He paused in front of the mirror in the bedroom and examined his own image.

He had aged. His face was grey and hollow. His lips thinner and more severe. His neck looked puffy and wrinkled. His shoulders lopsided and somehow dejected.

Fifty-seven years old, he thought. Twenty-four behind bars. No wonder.

He turned his back on himself and started looking for a gun. He had to have a gun, no matter what, so he'd better find one right away. Before he started having second thoughts.

As evening approached he sat in the kitchen with the letter. Read it through one more time, his cup of coffee standing on the flowery tablecloth.

It wasn't long. One and a half pages, almost. He closed his eyes and tried to see her in his mind's eye.

Her dark eyes, marked already by death, on the other side of the grille. Her hands wringing.

And her story.

No, there was no other way.

www.panmacmillan.com